Acclaim for Mel

T0031449

Famous for a Living

"Calling all fans of slow-burn, opposites-attract romance! Melissa Ferguson brings another fresh, delightful romcom in *Famous for a Living*. Cat and Zaiah are an imperfectly perfect match with swoony chemistry and plenty of back-and-forth banter. The gorgeous national park setting provides a lush backdrop for this fish-out-of-water story as influencer Cat hopes to escape a media fallout and finds much, much more. Readers who loved *The Cul-de-Sac Wars* and *Meet Me in the Margins* won't be disappointed in Ferguson's latest read!"

—*USA TODAY* BESTSELLING AUTHOR EMMA ST. CLAIR

Meet Me in the Margins

"Ferguson (*The Cul-de-Sac War*) enchants with this whimsical tale set against the evergreen culture war between literary and commercial fiction . . . An idealistic, competent heroine, a swoon-worthy hero, and delightfully quirky supporting characters bolster this often hilarious send up of the publishing industry, which doubles as a love letter to the power of stories. This is sure to win Ferguson some new fans."

—*PUBLISHERS WEEKLY*

"A marvelous book on the power of positive feedback, the various struggles of being an emerging writer, and how to find a balance between work and life, this book is a very entertaining read."

—*BOOK RIOT*

"*Meet Me in the Margins* is a delightfully charming jewel of a book that fans of romantic comedy won't be able to put down—and will want to share with all their friends. Readers will lose themselves in Melissa Ferguson's witty, warm tale of Savannah Cade and the perfectly drawn cast of characters that inhabits her world. This literary treat full of missed opportunities, second chances, and maybe even true love, should be at the top of your reading list!"

—KRISTY WOODSON HARVEY, *NEW YORK TIMES* BESTSELLING AUTHOR OF *UNDER THE SOUTHERN SKY*

"Ferguson has penned a lively romance for every bookworm who once longed to step through the wardrobe or sleep under the stairs. *Meet Me in the Margins* brims with crisp prose and crinkling pages as Savannah Cade, lowly editor at a highbrow publisher, secretly reworks her commercial fiction manuscript with the help of a mystery reader—and revises her entire life. You'll want to find your own hideaway to get lost in this delightful, whip-smart love story."

—ASHER FOGLE PAUL, AUTHOR OF *WITHOUT A HITCH*

The Cul-de-Sac War

"Melissa delivered a book that is filled with both humor and heart!"

—DEBBIE MACOMBER, #1 *NEW YORK TIMES* BESTSELLING AUTHOR

"Melissa Ferguson delights with a grand sense of humor and a captivating story to boot! With vivid detail that brings the story roaring to life, *The Cul-de-Sac War* brings us closer to the truth of love, family, and home. Bree's and Chip's pranks and adventures turn into something they never expected, as Melissa Ferguson delivers another heartwarming, hilarious, and deeply felt story."

—PATTI CALLAHAN, *NEW YORK TIMES* BESTSELLING AUTHOR OF *BECOMING MRS. LEWIS*

"Melissa Ferguson's *The Cul-de-Sac War* is sweet, zany, and surprisingly tender. Bree and Chip will have you laughing and rooting for them until the very end."

—DENISE HUNTER, BESTSELLING AUTHOR OF *CAROLINA BREEZE*

"With her sophomore novel, Melissa Ferguson delivers hilarity and heart in equal measure. *The Cul-de-Sac War*'s Bree Leake and Chip McBride prove that sometimes it isn't the first impression you have to worry about—it's the second one that gets you. What follows is a delightful deluge of pranks, sabotage, and witty repartee tied together by heartstrings that connect to turn a house into a home worth fighting for. I was thoroughly charmed from beginning to end."

—BETHANY TURNER, AWARD-WINNING AUTHOR
OF *THE SECRET LIFE OF SARAH HOLLENBECK*

"Witty, wise, and with just the right amount of wacky, Melissa's second novel is as charming as her debut. Competition and chemistry battle to win the day in this hilarious rom-com about two people who can't stand to be near each other—or too far apart."

—BETSY ST. AMANT, AUTHOR OF *THE KEY TO LOVE*

The Dating Charade

"Ferguson's delightful debut follows a first date that turns quickly into a childcare quagmire . . . Ferguson's humorous and chaotic tale will please rom-com fans."

—*PUBLISHERS WEEKLY*

"*The Dating Charade* will keep you smiling the entire read. Ferguson not only delights us with new love, with all its attendant mishaps and misunderstandings, but she takes us deeper in the hearts and minds of vulnerable children as Cassie and Jett work out their families—then their dating lives. An absolute treat!"

—KATHERINE REAY, BESTSELLING AUTHOR
OF *THE PRINTED LETTER BOOKSHOP*

"*The Dating Charade* is hilarious and heartwarming with characters you truly care about, super fun plot twists and turns, snappy prose, and a sweet romance you're rooting for. Anyone who has children in their lives will particularly relate to Ferguson's laugh-out-loud take on the wild ride that is parenting. I thoroughly enjoyed this story!"

—RACHEL LINDEN, BESTSELLING AUTHOR
OF *THE ENLIGHTENMENT OF BEES*

"A heartwarming charmer."

—SHEILA ROBERTS, *USA TODAY* BESTSELLING
AUTHOR OF THE MOONLIGHT HARBOR SERIES

"Melissa Ferguson is a sparkling new voice in contemporary rom-com. Though her novel tackles meaningful struggles—social work, child abandonment, adoption—it's also fresh, flirty, and laugh-out-loud funny. Ferguson is going to win fans with this one!"

—LAUREN DENTON, BESTSELLING AUTHOR
OF *THE HIDEAWAY* AND *GLORY ROAD*

"A jolt of energy featuring one of the most unique romantic hooks I have ever read. Personality and zest shine through Ferguson's evident enjoyment at crafting high jinks and misadventures as two people slowly make way for love in the midst of major life upheaval. A marvelous treatise on unexpected grace and its life-changing chaos, Cassie and Jett find beautiful vulnerability in redefining what it means to live happily ever after."

—RACHEL MCMILLAN, AUTHOR OF *THE LONDON RESTORATION*

"Ferguson delivers a stellar debut. *The Dating Charade* is a fun, romantic albeit challenging look at just what it takes to fall in love and be a family. You'll think of these characters long after the final page."

—RACHEL HAUCK, *NEW YORK TIMES* BESTSELLING
AUTHOR OF *THE WEDDING DRESS*

FAMOUS for a LIVING

a novel

ALSO BY MELISSA FERGUSON

NOVELS

The Dating Charade

The Cul-de-Sac War

Meet Me in the Margins

How to Plot a Payback (available April 2024)

STORIES

Dashing Through the Snow included in *On the Way to Christmas*

Pining for You included in *This Time Around*

FAMOUS
for a
LIVING

a novel

MELISSA FERGUSON

THOMAS NELSON
Since 1798

Famous for a Living

Published in Nashville, Tennessee, by Thomas Nelson. Thomas Nelson is a registered trademark of HarperCollins Christian Publishing, Inc.

Thomas Nelson titles may be purchased in bulk for educational, business, fundraising, or sales promotional use. For information, please email SpecialMarkets@ThomasNelson.com.

Publisher's Note: This novel is a work of fiction. Names, characters, places, and incidents are either products of the author's imagination or used fictitiously. All characters are fictional, and any similarity to people living or dead is purely coincidental.

Library of Congress Cataloging-in-Publication Data

Names: Ferguson, Melissa (Assistant professor), author.
Title: Famous for a living : a novel / Melissa Ferguson.
Description: Nashville, Tennessee : Thomas Nelson, [2023] | Summary: "The world's most beloved social media star is about to get a rude awakening . . . she's going from Park Avenue to the Parks Department"--Provided by publisher.
Identifiers: LCCN 2022049889 (print) | LCCN 2022049890 (ebook) | ISBN 9780840702487 (paperback) | ISBN 9780840702494 (epub) | ISBN 9780840702906
Subjects: LCGFT: Christian fiction. | Novels.
Classification: LCC PS3606.E7263 F36 2023 (print) | LCC PS3606.E7263 (ebook) | DDC 813/.6--dc23/eng/20221019
LC record available at https://lccn.loc.gov/2022049889
LC ebook record available at https://lccn.loc.gov/2022049890

Printed in the United States of America

23 24 25 26 27 LBC 5 4 3 2 1

To Laura Wheeler, my editor. Your kindness, wit, wisdom, and presence throughout this book have been more of a blessing than you know.

CHAPTER 1

The Launch

*O*ne doesn't intentionally wear itchy, viridian-green jumpsuits to match the elaborate wainscoting on the walls around oneself.

Did I know it would match?

Of course.

Was I aware it would look fantastic in pictures?

Naturally.

But to actually pick out my birthday-party-turned-surprise-launch-party ensemble for the sake of matching the walls? That'd be ridiculous.

I did it to match Bobby.

More specifically, I did it because viridian green is Bobby Braswell's personal color of choice for the year.

And when your birthday-party-turned-surprise-launch-party partner is *the* Bobby Braswell, designer *and* partner of Club, the social media app forecasted to, as Bobby liked to say, "make Instagram and Facebook a distant and unsettling memory," you dress accordingly.

"Cat's turning thirty. She doesn't need to broadcast it with a thousand candles." Serena hip checks Kiel, one of the most renowned caterers in the city (who also happens to be a foot taller and a solid hundred pounds heavier than Serena), out of the way.

"The icing!" Kiel protests, as Serena begins plucking the glittering golden candles out one by one as though defeathering a dead chicken.

She doesn't budge.

And, just as this scenario has gone between them the past three catering events, he throws his hands in the air.

As Kiel shuffles down the spiral staircase of the loft overlooking my living room, muttering the same murderous phrases he always does in his thick German accent, Serena works.

Her auburn hair curls around her shoulders, pushed back just enough from her face to highlight a delicate jawline leading to lips that, instead of being artificially plumped to one degree shy of clown-sized proportions—as was the way of 99 percent of the forgettable faces walking the streets of Manhattan these days—are magnificently thin. On her head is perched a silky cream top hat, matching a cream pantsuit and four-inch heels, and on her ears twinkle Daddy's latest little trinket: a six-thousand-dollar pair of earrings he spotted in a shop window on the way to a business lunch, dropped in, and purchased, all because he thought they would look nice on his little princess.

And they do.

Simply put, Serena Whitman is my best friend. Has been since that very first day we met at a fundraising event for childhood diabetes when, upon hearing my name, she lost that vague my-manager-said-I-should-be-here expression in favor of an enthusiastic handshake.

I couldn't shake her that evening.

Or the next.

And eventually, I gave up trying.

And while her interest in becoming an influencer has long passed, our friendship—nearer to sisterhood level at this point—stuck.

Serena blows a strand of hair from her eyes as she plucks the three-tier cake with surgical-level intensity. "Bobby's still missing."

"He'll be here." While my words come in a breezy haze, I'm well aware my heart is pounding twice as fast as the seconds ticking on the countdown clock on the wall opposite. And that my business partner—the one who thought of this whole plan to reveal the release of Club at the most extravagant birthday party I've ever thrown—is still nowhere to be seen. And that the guests are flowing into the living room below, the room now bobbing in a sea of ruched bodices and dark satin.

Gold and viridian-green balloons hover overhead in their net, ready with a pull of a string to be dispensed on the many guests below. The new long, white sectionals quickly fill with glossy legs exposed by the deep slits of cocktail dresses.

Everywhere there are cameras.

Cameras aimed at oneself as guests grin, chins raised for the best angle.

Cameras panning the room, taking in the scene.

Cameras aimed at others—even a few, I notice as I pull my shoulders back and give my public smile, trying to capture me.

My penthouse, the one I got the keys to just four weeks ago after two years of anticipation and waiting during the Montana's construction, is ready, is perfect.

A projector screen covers the two-storied wall above the glowing white crystal coals in the gas fireplace. On the screen the digits blink as the clock counts down to showtime.

Even the twinkling skyline seems somehow twice as bright tonight—all evidence that in just a few minutes, my life will change forever.

My fingers tingle. As they do a hundred times per day. I rise and slip the phone out of my jumpsuit pocket.

How will I do it now?

With one glossy nail my finger slides and taps so quickly across various screens the phone struggles to keep up. I capture two still-frame photos of the banquet spread covering the long table splattered with brilliant hesperidium-orange roses and golden cutlery. One close-up of my fingers—polish a gentle gold matching perfectly with my glass of bubbling prosecco—the backdrop of the skyline blurred behind.

Brighten the exposure just a touch.

Duplicate the prosecco shot and flip to black-and-white. A simple caption, and yet it does the trick:

To thirty, still a little flirty, and fun. Big news coming in 10 minutes!

Tap.

Tag.

Post.

I take in a small breath as I watch the replies immediately flood in. The hearts. The likes. The overflow of comments—people particularly zealous to compliment me on such a special occasion.

Feel my heart filling up as I see it. Feel my energy rise.

Drinking in the words, the love, as it feeds my soul.

Even if just for a few blissful moments.

Then I'm aware of a sharp jab, and I pull away from my phone to scratch the spot on my wrist where the hem of my jumpsuit is gaily stabbing with a thousand tiny daggers. As it has all evening.

The thread of this suit must be made of razor wire. It must.

"I told you not to partner with Hemms," Serena says, her eyes on the cake as she plucks off a candle.

I slip my phone in my pocket and sniff. "I don't recall."

"I said every time you work with them you end up with some hideous outfit made of something ridiculous like duct tape or entirely of zippers. But do you ever listen?"

"This is a delightful jumpsuit." I lift my chin. "It's positively"—I hunt mentally for the phrases in the campaign brief—"*luxurious*. The pure silk shantung is not only timeless but downright *snuggly*."

I say the last word just as the hem drags simultaneously along collarbone, ankle, and the length of my left leg, and my entire body shudders.

"Cozy as a bug in a rug . . . one might say." Serena rolls her eyes.

I don't respond.

Serena's eyes shoot to mine, and for about thirty seconds we're locked in her challenge. I dare not move. I dare not breathe.

Just as I'm about to give up and inhale, accepting whatever viper bites the suit lashes out with as my rib cage expands and dares touch it, she relents and returns her attention to the cake. "Fine. For your birthday I'll pretend I don't see you rubbing your skin raw for the sake of a crap company that makes crap clothes." She raises her hand, stopping me before I can protest. "And no, I don't care if they fitted half the people at the Met Gala. Just"—she waves a shooing hand at me—"get it all out now, before you're covered up in cameras."

And as I move beyond the railing into the shadows and begin scratching to my heart's content, icing-covered candles fall like bombs onto the terra-cotta tile all around me. After a near hit, I step to the left.

My new heels are a golden suede, shimmering from toe to heel in Swarovski crystals, topped with the most beautiful bouquet of iridescent gemstones on both toes that make each heavy step worth it.

A gift from Jacquie—my new manager, and one who's been nothing short of amazing the past six months. On birthdays my old manager sent me a celebratory text. When, of course, he remembered at all.

Jacquie, however? When I pulled back the tissue paper this morning to see next season's not-even-released-yet Jimmy Choos, I was floored.

I carefully lower myself in my heels and begin collecting the candles from the floor. In my periphery, the countdown clock turns. Less than twenty minutes to go. "Anyway, you know how Bobby is." I turn back to the subject to comfort myself more than anything. "He lives by his own schedule."

"Manipulates everyone into thinking he's an eccentric genius with all his talk of 'protecting one's mind castle from the manufactured construct of time,' when in reality he's just a man-child who doesn't have the brain cells to work an alarm. Yes. I'm aware."

Serena and Bobby went to the same elitist school growing up.

As best as I have been able to gather, Serena's disdain was birthed around a certain swing set on a rubber-mulch playground where, during recess, the children took on the habits of their stockbroker parents, using mulch as currency while those with the fullest pockets ran the playground. Evidently one dark day Bobby and his gang of fellow five-year-olds refused her access to a certain tire swing despite her healthy stash of rubber mulch.

The act was unforgivable.

All the candles mercilessly tossed aside, Serena picks up a butter knife. As she considers the pothole-covered cake, she tilts her head, the butt of the golden knife glinting as she taps her chin.

In this moment Kiel, carrying in a charcuterie board on a silver platter, steps up the top step, takes one look at Serena with the knife standing over his prized cake, and spins back around.

I hear the platter drop loudly at the bottom of the stairs and bite my lip. And there goes my favorite caterer.

And just then, the hum of commotion below alters.

It's nothing that a typical person would notice, but like a dog aware of the high-pitched tune inaudible to the human ear, and with this many years in my line of work, I recognize a shift in atmosphere. I know how to read a room blindfolded.

I move back to the railing and search the gatherers below.

People milling around.

Pointing to my artwork on the walls.

Snapping up shrimp cocktails from passing waiters.

A girl inching toward the end of the hall where my bedroom door stands closed, clearly nosing around.

None of this raises any suspicions.

None of this is the cause.

But there.

Ah. Yes.

Her.

A girl has slipped through the doorway, her slim fingers loosely wrapped around the elbow of Travis Demurabi—a younger, handsomer version of YouTube success Finance Pete, who helps people open their one-participant 401(k), all while talking between bites of drunken noodle filmed by the dim light of his computer screen.

But people aren't watching him.

It's her.

The slender face of the girl making her way beside him through the crowded foyer.

From a single glance I can list the shops she called upon to make her ensemble. The simple black turtleneck curled loosely around the porcelain skin of her neck from Alexander McQueen. The leggings of equal nondescript simplicity from the same, giving her the air of Audrey Hepburn. The Gianvito Rossi suede and plexi pumps, of which Serena herself is wearing a sister pair. Then, of course, the bold red wing wool scarf from Ji Cheng that envelopes her, matching the dramatic Cassiopeia-red lipstick on her perfect, heart-shaped lips.

She owns the room.

She can't be more than eighteen, and yet for a moment, she owns the room.

"Do you have any clementines downstairs? I want to add them around this corner," Serena says, her brows knitted as she peers at the cake.

I move for the lotion in my purse, looking at the rapidly transforming cake as I do. Most of the icing potholes are smoothed over now; on one side she seems to be building a garland of fruit running all the way down to the cake stand.

"I don't think so." I rub lotion methodically over my fingers, forcing myself not to think about the concerning bluish vein that popped up along my outer thigh three weeks shy of my thirtieth birthday. Or the way the skin on my knuckles carries more and more cracks lately.

Just a little varicose vein.

Just dry hands that have seen a bit more wear and tear than the polished skin of the teenagers I seem to be perpetually surrounded by.

All things I just have to carefully blur to keep unnoticed by the world around me. All normal with age and the passing of time.

And yet.

"*You*, my dear, are forever and always going to be the face of Club. No question. Don't even let any other thought linger in your pretty head."

These were Bobby's first words when we met at a party six months ago and he pitched me the idea for Club. That I would not only be partner, but my face would be the logo itself for the exclusive, audio-focused platform.

I'll never forget his eagerness as he clenched my hands with that dramatic and yet compelling way of his and said with all the conviction in the world, "From the moment people crack open their eyelids and reach for their Advil and phones to the second it's lights-out at each day's end, you and your *gorgeous* smile will be right on the screen, beckoning them to click on that button and hold off on their to-do lists a little longer. You. Cat Cranwell. Our *icon*."

Not only would I be the face, but with a bit of algorithm fine-tuning, the app was going to quietly and consistently boost me to the top of everyone's page.

Over and over, day in and day out.

Until the thing that crossed everyone's minds every single day, like a whisper in a breeze, was the question: *What is Cat Cranwell up to today?*

It was the win I needed.

I took a week to discuss with my finance team and another week to gather the strength to ignore their cautionary tales and plunge anyway.

And then, as if materializing from my thoughts, he's here.

"Of course, they still haven't gotten my headshot right," Bobby says, the heels of his boots clicking against the last of the spiral glass steps as he winds up to the top, then snaps a magazine on the banquet table. It's one of the magazines featuring our faces on the newsstand outside the Montana this morning. "You would think after *three hundred* articles someone could have used the correct headshot . . ."

"*Hey.*" Serena swiftly picks up the magazine that had been tossed over a plate of fine cheeses. "No *ink* on the table."

He briefly surveys her with a pinched frown, and I can instantly picture the two of them as five-year-olds going nose to nose on the playground. His eyes flicker toward the butter knife and the cake beyond.

"Overstepping your duties as always, I see," he says.

"Late as always, I see," she retorts sardonically.

I rub more lotion on my hands and wait while they embark on a string of insults, which, given past experience, tend to go on several minutes.

At last, with a triumphant smile and a can-we-be-done-now air, he shifts his attention toward me. Opens his arms. "My birthday girl."

The square brass buttons the size of little doorknobs down his shirt quake at his movement, and several of his gold rings dig into my back as we hug.

It's long. He's a long hugger.

"*This is cashmere,*" he growls and pulls back as Serena pokes his side with the butter knife. He looks on the verge of jumping into another fight, but with visible self-control trains his eyes on me. "I come with news. Tremendous news."

"Oh?"

And somewhere between Bobby's blazer and silk button-down, like a magician, he produces a stack of papers. Takes away my lotion to set them in my hands.

As I turn the stapled pages, I see the writing is, quite literally, in another language.

"What's this?" I look up.

"That"—he clicks a pen—"is yet another major marketing firm confirming they want in. And not just in, but saying they will expend everything they can to push it to the top in their regions." Bobby smiles. "No other app has had this level of support out the gate."

Serena frowns as she steps closer, looking over my shoulder.

"Really? Another one?" I flip through the indistinguishable pages and lines of small-text paragraphs. "What is this? The fifth?"

"Sixth." Bobby's eyes gleam as clear and bright as the tower of Perrier bottles on the table beside us. "Six major companies wanting a piece of the pie. I nearly had a heart attack seeing this last one." He leans forward and taps at a line. "You only need to sign once for this one and we'll be set."

I hesitate. Flip through more pages.

I hate when he does this. Hate looking like I don't trust him. "That's great, Bobby," I say as calmly as possible. "I'll drop these by my lawyers' tomorrow—"

Bobby's expression immediately changes. "There isn't time. They always make things more complicated than they are and waste two months making us go back and forth over things like the exact meaning of the word *advertisement*. I hate them, if you must know the truth."

I already knew the truth.

Bobby "confesses" his hatred for my lawyers every single time their names pop up.

Down below I hear the unmistakable and unexpected entrance of a woman crying out in a singsong tone to both everyone and no one in particular, "Look what I *broooought!*"

My eyes widen and shoot over to Serena.

Who invited Gabby Zegna?

Gabby is a sweetheart; she really is. But after she stumbled into fame a few months ago when a humorous little clip of hers went viral, the bewildered dietician found herself suddenly shoved offers from brands everywhere. It didn't take a genius to see one ten-second post showing off dish soap would equal a month's pay, and to commit to five such posts in a month would bring in five times her salary.

So she made a grave mistake. She quit her job.

And with each ensuing post that crashed and burned, Gabby discovered with sinking suspicion that she was a one-off.

A shooting star. Here one second, gone the next.

Which explains her new and desperate habit of trying to do anything, and *everything*, that works for other influencers, including bizarrely timed high kicks and unpredictable pranks, and doing both in an attempt to trademark herself in thigh-high boots and a red apron like some kind of 1950s veggie-loving pinup model.

The poor girl was desperate.

And there were far too many reporters and journalists with far too many waiting cameras for her to resist the temptation to do something drastic for the irresistible opportunity to snag the spotlight.

Not to mention, again, my new couches were white.

White.

"Serena, could you—" I start to say, but Serena is already moving for the spiral staircase.

"On it," she says, winding down the stairs.

Bobby exhales loudly, and I turn my attention back to him. "Here's the thing, sweetheart." He rakes a hand through his black hair. "This is an incredible win for us. We need this."

"And I'm excited." I stare at the stack of papers I'll have no means of understanding tonight. "It sounds thrilling."

"No. Thrilling was three months ago when we opened up applications and fifty thousand people knocked one another sideways trying to get a golden ticket for release. *This* is extraordinary. Absolutely life changing. And we need it signed and sent tonight."

My eyes tick to the countdown clock, the digits at 15:37 and dropping. "Bobby," I say, leveling my voice. "We're right about to do launch."

"Precisely," he retorts. "Which is why you need to sign it *now*."

"Or what?" I say with deliberate calm, trying to get him to see perspective. "What could they possibly—?"

"Or we stall the launch."

My jaw drops slightly.

No.

He can't be serious.

But his eyes are steely grave.

A laugh bubbles in my throat. "Everybody's here, though. The reporters. The papers. We have a two-week press *tour* starting tomorrow. Nothing is so important we'd stall."

He taps the papers. "That's the thing, sweetheart. *This* is so important we'd stall."

"Surely they wouldn't mind partnering a month or two after launch—"

"*Of course* they would." His voice is so startlingly loud a few guests below pop their heads up. "*Of course* they feel it's imperative they are anchored from the beginning."

My cheeks warm as I become aware of the eyes on us. There's a pause, and momentarily, I feel myself teetering.

Bobby frowns, disappointment in his eyes that I'm even questioning him. After a moment he shifts his posture, clearly trying for another angle.

"Trust me, Cat. It's just like all the others. I've had my lawyers pore over it themselves. I've signed it," he says energetically as he taps on his name beside where mine will go. "Now you sign and we can move on with the celebration."

And it's true. From what I can tell, it looks exactly like the others. The same graphs. The same heavy paragraphs and bullet points.

"And if we really want to launch in ten minutes—"

"I do," I jump in.

"Then there isn't time."

We lapse into silence as a staring contest ensues.

Surely there must be another way. Surely we don't have to have this tremendous setback. All the interviews. The anticipation. The depths and lengths gone to and *dollars* spent for this party . . .

I would never do it this way. I would never spring this on someone. But . . . that's just it, isn't it?

It's not just about my way.

I have a partner, and as such, we have to work collaboratively. Regardless of our differences.

For better and worse, we have to work together.

And yet . . . to sign anything without my lawyers . . . This is like the first episode of Travis's *Finances for Dummies 101.*

The phone in my pocket begins ringing and I break eye contact, eager to escape the decision at least a few moments longer. I read the name *Terry Cranwell* on-screen. "I have to take this."

Frankly, had it been a spam call from Indonesia trying to tell me my nonexistent car warranty was about to expire, I would've taken it. I press the Answer button and lift it to my ear. "Hi, Uncle Terry. How are you?" I twist around to face the wall, shielding myself from Bobby's penetrating gaze.

"Your doorman says I can't come up and surprise you without your permission. *Apparently,*" he continues gruffly, "New York City people don't understand the concept of *surprise.*"

"Wait. You're here?" I swivel my eyes past the loft railing to the crowd of guests gathered in the living room below. All waiting for my entrance. The heels of several crossed legs bouncing impatiently from sofa seats for the party to begin.

His voice booms over the speaker. "What do you mean it's for her protection?"

"Terry?" My eyes tick over to the countdown clock: 8 minutes, 37 seconds.

Pause.

"What do you *mean* there have been *recent attempts?*"

Oookay.

Time to go.

"Uncle." I find my feet and start to move down the spiral staircase, heels clicking on each glassy step. "It's fine. Really. I'm coming down."

"Where are you going?" Serena calls from the doorway of the kitchen, all the while holding on to Gabby's elbow with one hand, the butter knife dripping with icing in the other. "*What are you doing?*"

"I have a situation downstairs," I say, and break for the door.

Uncle Terry's voice is still in my ear. "Catherine, you carry that revolver I got you for Christmas, don't you? I don't like the idea of you having to rely on some random doorman— What do you mean you have a *no-gun policy* in the building? Not even for her? Then how do you expect her to protect herself if she doesn't have one of these when— Well, *of course* I do. I'm a United States citizen, aren't I? UNHAND ME, SIR—"

Several hands are touching me in greeting as I reach the main landing, compliments about my ensemble are flying, but the best I can do is nod and smile overenthusiastically while clutching the phone to my ear and all but elbowing people out of the way for the door.

"Thank you for coming!" I whisper on repeat until I'm finally at the elevator and jam my finger on the button.

The situation must've worsened, because as soon as I get into the elevator, the call ends, leaving me staring with one tapping heel at my own impatient reflection on the closed elevator doors.

And while I may have a launch party starting in a matter of minutes, paperwork in another language regarding millions of dollars I have to decide whether to sign, and a best friend trying to shuffle out a party risk carrying a suspicious amount of blood-red cupcakes into a room full of white couches and paparazzi, my chief concern at this moment is Uncle Terry, who with all his cantankerous ways, is about to get himself Tased.

Uncle Terry is my closest kin. Nobody has ever heard me speak a word of my parents, even Serena. But Uncle Terry?

For all his gruffness, he is the one who calls on every one of my birthdays. Checks in at least once a month like clockwork. The conversations rarely go much longer than ten minutes—as though he doesn't want to intrude too much into my life but wants to make sure I am emotionally, physically, and even financially in check. (He never could wrap his head around my career in content creation and, as such, is convinced I am always one sleep away from complete destitution and in need of the occasional twenty-dollar bill in the mail.)

As though he wants to pick up the torch where my own father, his brother, failed.

"Bernie, it's okay. This is my uncle." I raise my hands as I stride across the marble hall to where poor Bernie has one hand hovering over his hip, clearly struggling to decide which is worse: accidentally letting in a criminal or accidentally Tasing a resident's relative.

Unfortunately, he's stopped the real thing more than once from trying to enter the building. I can't blame him for his lack of trust.

"Oooookay." I take Uncle Terry by the arm, guiding him away. "Thank you so much, Bernie. I'll take him from here."

I don't stop until we are back at the elevators, at which point I swivel him around by the shoulders, grin widely, and take him in. "Well, well, well. And I thought I was the only one pulling birthday surprises today."

Residue of the unhappy incident still lingers in his expression, but I move in for a hug anyway.

His coat smells of tobacco and pine, and after a moment, he gives my back an awkward pat. I smile at the pat of his grizzly-sized palm—the same calloused, sausage-fingered hands that have always been there.

I didn't even realize how much I missed him.

"How long has it been?" I step back and cock my head, trying to remember.

"Two years. September fourth," he replies without hesitation, as though the date is seared in his memory.

"Too long," I say, quietly pleased he cared so much to remember. "So." I tug on his forest ranger jacket. "The truth now. What really dragged you here?"

"I already told you. My favorite niece's birthday." He stuffs his hands into his pockets, but a rueful smile plays at his lips.

"Liar. You don't love me enough for that."

His mustache twitches. A unibrow forms from his bushy brows as he creases his forehead. "'Course I do. I'd take a bullet for you."

"I *know* you'd take a bullet for me," I reply, as though that much was obvious. "But voluntarily entering the city? Come now. Let's be realistic. Plus"—I look down at his olive jacket and pants—"you're in uniform."

He frowns, peering down at his uniform as though it gave him away.

"Fine. I'm here for my niece's—"

"Favorite niece's," I interject.

"—birthday," he continues, then with an agitated undertone adds, "and a conference."

"Really?" My brow hitches up. Last time he had a conference he had to attend was . . . well . . . never.

"New head of the department," he says, giving a revolted sniff. "Two rangers from each park had to go. 'Parently interns don't count, so Zaiah and I made the trek." His face hardens deeper. "Had I known that, I wouldn't have hired the lot."

I raise a brow, having heard my share over the past few months about his interns. "Your *unpaid* lot?"

"They were. But *apparently* that's not the way we do it anymore. *Apparently*, kids have to get paid for knowing nothing and doing nothing. You know—"

Here we go.

"—back in my day, you had to hike three days over Mount Whitney with nothing but a pocketknife. If you survived, you got the *opportunity* to work for free. At the bottom of the ladder, where you belonged. Now all these gov heads tell me I have to judge the content of someone's character by how well they can tap a few buttons on an online application. Calling my methods *hazing*. Telling me I'm setting the US government up for a *lawsuit*."

"But I got a confirmation email," says a figure coming through a revolving door. He pushes his phone from one ear to the other. "No, I don't see it right now, but—"

Ah. So this is Zaiah. He's much taller than Uncle Terry, probably by a good six inches or so. Half his age.

And while I expected as much out of the man I've heard of in conversation over the past three years since Terry took this job, what I didn't expect was his face. Why, it's the kind of accidental, unself-aware face that makes boyfriends do all kinds of stupid things out of jealousy and women's necks ache from craning. The kind of rugged, natural charm that stops modeling scouts on the streets of New York and has them say, "Here. Here is my card. Just take it. Please."

"Exhausting, I'm sure," I absently chime in, vaguely hearing Uncle Terry shift from grumbling about the conference speakers to the conference food, as my eyes follow Zaiah pacing down the wall of windows.

So many symmetrical, no-nonsense features. Ruddy tan skin, not the kind of skin of boys sunbathing on rooftop decks, but that of a man used to bearing the elements. Shoulders straight. And those eyes, dark and deep green as the oval-cut Montana sapphire Aunt Claire gave me on my twenty-first birthday.

The only thing that isn't perfectly clean-cut about his features is the beard. But somehow—I tilt my chin despite myself—it seems to suit him even better.

Fascinating.

The first man I've ever met to pull off a beard.

On that fair face, however, is the same scowl Terry bestowed on the guard just moments ago. His eyes follow the trail of passing cars on the busy street as he stands before the floor-to-ceiling windows. His phone is pressed to his ear, and from the snippet of conversation I catch, it sounds like he's talking with someone from a hotel about missing reservations.

It sounds like he's not making much headway in correcting the accommodation mishap.

His gaze falls on me as he shifts on his heels. Turns.

Our eyes meet.

And then I see it.

A look I'd recognize a mile away.

It's just for a millisecond, but there's no question. Him taking me in, from the bob of my auburn hair slanting down toward my chin, to the *Take Me Out Tonight* red lipstick, to the shimmering crystal heels.

I can practically hear his thoughts.

But of course I can.

I see those words on-screen every day.

What a waste.

What a pathetic, plastic waste.

Me.

My ensemble.

This city.

The phoniness of it all.

He's not playing any games here. He's not looking at me that way because of some kind of fantasy playing out in his head. Him, playing it off coolly. Me, attracted to his disinterest. Us, heading off on some jaunt to Paris, where in the process of our whirlwind romance, *of course*, he gains millions of followers and a record label for his mediocre, never-before-appreciated acoustic skills. Perhaps we marry. More preferable, though, we don't so he can spread his wings with top models and favorite sitcom actresses who have discovered him through his newfound fortune and fame.

No.

There's no ploy in his look.

It's the real thing. Bona fide, shallowly disguised aversion to all that I stand for, all that, to him, I am.

I blink and turn back to my uncle, all the while scratching at my wrist. "Come on up. I'll get us some coffee."

Zaiah trails several feet behind with the phone pressed to his ear, still clearly getting nowhere.

"Because we were told that it was part of the conference fee," he says, irritation simmering on the surface of his voice. "I've already talked to the conference director. He said I should talk to *you*."

The doors shut and I hit the lowest button. The number sixteen glows as I turn to my uncle. "Which hotel are you staying at?"

Local travel is one of my niches—if you can call where to stay and eat in a city of more than eight million niche. I know and have been paid to visit just about every hotel in town, and frankly, at this point, if I haven't been there, it's because one shouldn't.

"Regalia Inn. A half mile from the convention center."

I haven't been there.

"They have a continental breakfast," he adds. "All you can eat."

"Well . . ." I give a polite nod at the idea of traveling thousands of miles to the city with arguably the most vibrant food culture in America . . . to have batches of overcooked bacon and powdered eggs. I rack my brain for a compliment on this decision.

"*You*"—I release a broad smile—"are going to love that." I gauge for a moment which way I should play the fact that I have a party going on, and whether telling him now or waiting until he's securely inside will be my best bet at keeping him from running away.

Better rip the Band-Aid off now.

"So I should give you a heads-up. I have a few people over."

He grimaces, just like I knew he would. What few years Uncle Terry had before marrying Aunt Claire and working with the National Park Service were spent as an all but hermit in Alaska.

Covered in furs.

Fishing for dinner.

To put it in perspective, Uncle Terry considered his promotion three years ago to head ranger at Kannery National Park and the ensuing responsibilities of overseeing the handful of staff and dozens of visitors per day an overwhelming amount of social interaction.

"You don't have to talk to any of them," I add lightheartedly. "I'll set you up right next to the coffee machine in the kitchen while I do a few things"—like entertain the biggest event of my life—"and be back the second I can."

His silence is stone cold, and I throw out, "Plus, there's a charcuterie fountain."

At this, even Zaiah shifts his gaze to me.

"A . . . what?" Uncle Terry says.

"A charcuterie fountain," I repeat, waving my hands around. "Something Serena dreamed up. Mustard spills out the top. A volcano really. The mustard follows a winding little path between the soppressata and Genoa salami and 'nduja."

Uncle Terry and Zaiah both look at me like I'm mad.

I drop my hands to my sides. "Meat. It's a volcano of meat."

I see Uncle Terry, and his reflection in the elevator mirror for that matter, frown. "I didn't know you were having company—"

Of course he didn't. Because to *him*, total isolation is part of the dream package when it comes to birthdays. He probably thought I spent my birthdays watching the fire crackle in my fireplace with a good glass of wine. He'll probably go ballistic seeing my fireplace is electric.

"It's *fine*." I grip his hand as reassuringly as I can. "I am *so thrilled* that you are here."

He turns the khaki-colored, stiff-brim hat in his hands, eyeing my hand on his. "Maybe just a quick cup, and we'll get out of your hair after that. We ought to be hitting the hay soon anyway. Have another early morning."

I smile and release his hand. "Deal. And tomorrow, lunch."

After a few moments he puts one hand in his pocket. Pulls out a box. "Here. I should probably give you this before your party."

The bushy salt-and-pepper mustache overpowering Uncle Terry's face twitches as he holds out a small box. He looks as uncomfortable in this moment as that one time when I was twelve and he visited and asked where I wanted to go, and thirty minutes later found himself inside a Limited Too with a bunch of preteens around him, picking out bras.

The square box is small and unassuming. Cardboard colored, no label. But as my fingers lift off the lid, my breath catches in my throat.

I raise the thin golden chain in my fingertips. The rose-embossed locket is so small you wouldn't think you could fit a picture in there, and yet—

I unlatch it and sure enough, there she is. Aunt Claire on one side, hair tangled and swept up in the wind as she stands on a hillside, grinning. And Uncle Terry, much leaner in both build and facial hair, in the same park uniform he's wearing now.

"No use keeping it locked away," Uncle Terry says gruffly. He stands with his hands at his sides, his posture identical to his stance in the employment photo in the locket from thirty years ago.

I have a hard time finding my voice, so instead I just smile and turn to let him put it on. Aunt Claire passed away four years ago, quite suddenly and unexpectedly. It was a shock, particularly as she was one of the healthiest women I knew. And while they had never had children, I find it hard to accept that she—or he—could really mean for me to have this treasure. I'm well aware of the dozen nieces and nephews they have on her side of the family.

When I feel the clasp lock, I turn. And while my words are "How does it look?" he knows what I'm really saying.

This means so much.

I will take such care of it.

I miss her too.

"Very nice." His mustache twitches as he looks at the necklace resting above the V-neck of my jumpsuit.

"But I *just* spoke with the concierge and she said there was room for two people *tonight*. Then she transferred me to someone else, who—no I don't want to be transferred again—"

My eyes tick over to Zaiah. He really is the spitting image, in personality at least, of Uncle Terry. Down to the bulging vein in his neck while dealing with fellow human beings.

The elevator glides us up as I listen to a few more impatient run-on sentences. They are getting shorter and shorter as we go up, his tension rising at his obvious inability to get anywhere in the matter.

And is that . . . ?

I squint, finding it so hard to believe I think I must be seeing it wrong.

Is this man really using a flip phone? In this era?

Ding. The elevator stops. As the doors begin to glide open, there is Serena standing on the other side, her toes *tap-tap-tapping* as madly as a mouse in heels racing across the marble tile. Before the doors have fully opened, she throws out her arms.

"Are you crazy?" She completely ignores the two men inside.

"The clock is down to *two minutes. TWO.* Jacquie looks like she's about to have a panic attack. I already heard that reporter Adam Adams starting to work up an alternative piece called 'Cat Cranwell Overcome with Rage Abandons Own Birthday Party.' He's telling people about the time his cat got run over by a taxi and then snapping photos of their facial reactions for the piece. The guy will do anything for a story—"

"Excuse me."

It's her. The girl with the Ji Cheng scarf wrapped around her delicate shoulders. She's stepping up to the elevator, her flawlessly long legs tremoring slightly. In her hands, she clutches a phone.

Her voice is barely above a squeak, the memory of her smooth entrance into the apartment shattering with each timid, adolescent word as she raises her long lashes to meet my eyes. "I have to leave but I'm just . . . I'm such a fan. Could you possibly . . . perhaps . . . take a picture with me?"

And while Serena looks like she's about to explode at this interruption, I find myself stricken by her up close.

Even younger.

Even more beautiful.

Eyes full of life.

Nothing but clear eagerness for the world and all it has to offer.

It's an addicting look. A captivating look that will draw people toward her wherever she goes, once she realizes the power she has and loses her fears.

I see her, the bright reflection of what I once was. That effortless vivacity and youth I have to work harder and harder these days to conjure up.

And I know what I need to do.

"Of course. Just. One moment—" I take the pen from the stack of paper and flourish the name I've written a million times across the contract.

Then I do stand in front of the elevator in my viridian-green jumpsuit, giving a deep and warm smile at the camera as I feel the girl's trembling fingers drape oh-so-gently around my side. I know as Serena dispenses a dozen swift clicks through her grumbling that one of these shots will become the profile picture the girl ends up displaying across her social media platforms, the picture of the next dozen texts she'll spend the rest of her evening sending, the story she'll share at parties for years to come.

"Terrific terrific terrific. All beautiful people making beautiful pictures that make people feel terrible about themselves. Congratulations. Let's go," Serena says swiftly, all but tossing the phone to the girl and grabbing me by the wrist.

As I put my hand on the knob of the door, I pause.

Taking in the moment. The anticipation.

This is it.

I suck in a breath and begin to turn the knob.

"Ma'am, I've already *told you*—" Zaiah's voice is like nails down a chalkboard, and something snaps inside me.

Even with the chanting that has begun ahead, I swivel on my heel. "Give me that."

Zaiah looks at my outstretched hand as if it were alien.

After several stalemate seconds, Serena practically shouts. "For goodness' sakes, *do it!*"

Awkwardly, he places the phone in my hand.

The second my palm feels the warm metal, I snap it to my ear and stride down the hall. "Hi, this is Cat Cranwell . . ."

Forty-two seconds later, I'm striding back to the group. I flip the phone shut, which, I have to admit, has a nice snap to it. Really drives that dramatic ending in a satisfying way. "You're in 401A. Two kings. The receptionist will have your keys ready when you get there. Mention my name."

I can't help but feel myself warming slightly as he seems to look at me properly for the first time. His eyes are more of an evergreen with flecks of brown, I see now. A little crease forms between his brows, as though trying to make me out. "How did you—?" Confusion marks his expression, which comes as no surprise, but as I hear the countdown of "ten, nine, eight" through the door, I press the phone back into his hand.

"Welcome to New York."

He doesn't get it.

This. This is what I do.

I'm Cat Cranwell.

Half owner of the platform about to take the world by storm.

And famous for a living.

CHAPTER 2

The Umbrella

3.5 MONTHS LATER

Raindrops pelt against my black umbrella as I stand motionless in front of the newsstand. Frozen for so long people have started to drop quarters at my feet like I'm a living statue and it's all part of a show.

Even the metallic man street performing across the crosswalk is shooting daggers at me with his eyes. Yes, I would be grumpy, too, if I were dressed head-to-toe in copper coating. Yes, he's "frozen in time" as a disgruntled old man. But his eyes have swiveled and stuck my way on purpose. I know it.

Still, I don't move.

Can't.

The sliver of sky above is a streak of gray, cold and lifeless as the towering buildings on either side. People pass, hugging their coats as they sidestep puddles and slower traffic.

Slower traffic like me.

Either the street performer or the deranged girl with the black umbrella.

I stare at the rows and rows of magazines and newspapers. The covers stare back. Sports and presidential activities. Stocks and fashionable women. Hunting and fishing and motor sports and, again, women.

And then there.

Six covers.

Two different glossy magazines. Four black-and-white newspapers.

All of Bobby.

And me.

Some shots of us taken separately, a jagged, angry black line down the middle separating us.

Some together.

And, of course, as seen in so many tabloids and countless posts, a candid shot of Bobby and me at that launch party. Balloons spilling down around us like glittering green and gold snowflakes. Euphoric glee as we joined hands to celebrate our future together.

For better or worse.

The headlines grow more urgent and aggressive as my eyes scan down the row.

CLUB APP OWNERS INDICTED
ON SUSPICION OF FRAUD

CLUB LAWSUIT: ALLEGEDLY SELLING
DATA TO FOREIGN COUNTRIES

CLUB APP'S MASSIVE DATA HARVESTING
PROMPTS US SECURITY CONCERNS

CLUB APP ANTICIPATED TO PAY $46 MILLION
TO SETTLE CLASS-ACTION SUIT

CAT CRANWELL: THE STARLET'S SECRET TOXIC LIFE

CAT CRANWELL: INSIDERS DISH ABOUT THE
INTERNET PRINCESS WHO FOOLED EVERYONE

It's still impossible to believe this could happen.

Could really *be* in the process of happening.

How I could've lost absolutely . . . *everything*.

It takes three rings for me to realize the phone in my pocket is going off.

Raindrops roll off my fingertips as I pull it out and press it to my ear.

Several seconds tick by.

"Where are you?" Serena spouts impatiently. "Bernie called and said you're doing that funereal thing again."

I frown.

Well. Frown deeper.

Like all good but pliable human beings, Bernie was roped by Serena into doing her will: in this case, calling her whenever I left the building looking "anything besides adorable and lottery-winning happy." I now live with a security guard scrutinizing my face and ensemble every time I walk by to see whether the best friend needs to be called in.

She got the call once over a two-minute walk outside in a pair of house slippers.

"I'm going to call management on him if you keep this up, Serena." But it's the same threadbare threat on my lips as last week, and the week before, and we both know it.

"Are you reading the news again?" she says, ignoring me.

I can't speak the words for several seconds. It just . . . it feels as though once I do, I'll be speaking them into existence. Confirming that everything before my eyes is not some horrible hallucination but reality.

I'd like very much to keep that sliver of hope that I'm really just mad for a few minutes more.

I'm clinging to that hope, I realize.

Desperately wishing I've just lost my grip on reality.

"Are you?" Serena presses.

I force hot breath up my throat.

Force words to form. "I wasn't aware it was up to $46 million now."

"Go back inside, Cat. You hear me? *Back. Inside.* I'm on my way, and I'm coming with news."

Her final word snags my attention. Still, though, my feet don't move. "What kind of news?" I ask suspiciously.

Across the street the light turns, and I note a young girl grabbing the arm of her friend midstride. Gaping at me. Pointing.

"Are you moving?" Serena says, just as a taxi horn blows.

The young girl's hand slips out of her pocket and begins snapping pictures faster than paparazzi in training. I tilt the umbrella over my face as a shield.

"What are you wearing right now?" Serena snaps.

What am I wearing today? The days all string together now.

I look down.

Seval black boots—a brand that broke contract to disown me three months ago, at the first rumble. A Degas Regalis trench coat cinched tight around my waist—one of the five who dropped me when the rumbles grew louder. Gold stud earrings by Story Luxe. Disowned three weeks ago. Necklace. Given by Uncle Terry that fateful night.

Umbrella.

"Nothing. Just black."

"So you are standing under an umbrella in all black, staring morosely at some newspapers like you're at a funeral? Perfect, Cat. Just *perfect*. You're really nailing this Keep It Positive motto we *just* discussed."

I catch my reflection through a dripping shop window. She's not wrong.

"Are you at least wearing lipstick? If you're going to walk around like that, can you *at least* pull an Audrey Hepburn and wear some good red lipstick?"

I feel in my pocket for a forgotten tube of lipstick. "What's the news?" My fingers brush against one and I pop the cap off, forcing my feet to move back along the sidewalk as I return to my apartment. Intrinsically my head is already beginning to duck at the sight of people inside.

I itch to reach in my pocket for my sunglasses, but it's too gray of a day. Too conspicuous. Shows weakness.

More, I suppose, weakness.

The gleaming doors of the Montana wait for me as Chad, the doorman, holds the door.

"Welcome home, Miss Cranwell," he says, though I've only been gone a matter of minutes.

Home.

This place no longer fits such a description.

Bernie becomes engrossed in a particular smudge on his monitor as I pass.

"Snitch," I murmur as I pass him and catch his eye with a scowl as the elevator doors shut.

Inside my penthouse I drop my wet umbrella on the floor. Water splatters onto the tile and I blink at it, then step over it as I make my way to the kitchen.

Home.

More like the cold and lifeless walls and windows I've had to keep shut from the more desperate and willing of the paparazzi. Helicopter rides come cheap. Telescope and long-shot cameras even cheaper. And the number of residents able and willing to loan out their living rooms across the street in exchange for the excitement of telling tales and, if they're lucky, seeing their names in eight-point font in the papers . . . well. People were easy to buy. The bar was low.

I'm standing by the sink, halfway into last night's takeout when Serena swings into the kitchen, snatching the cold box of lo mein from my hands and tossing it in the trash can. She sets a hot cup of coffee in one of my hands and a paper bag in the other.

I raise my brow at the bag. The word *Buvette* flows in black script across the bag. The French bakery carb-loathing Serena only buys from when she's only exceptionally happy or exceptionally sad.

I'm about to be either thrilled or devastated by this news.

Scents of cinnamon and buttermilk and fresh bacon waft around me as she begins banging around the kitchen cabinets for silverware and plates.

"Murphy says he'll take the case."

No.

Serena pulls a plate from the cabinet and a spoon and knife from the drawer. "Now, he says since you signed every contract willingly it'll be tough, but—"

"He'll take it?" I say in a small voice.

Impossible.

After I've been turned down by every reputable law firm from Cortlandt Street to Tarrytown, *Murphy & Brown* will take the case. Her family's lawyer. One of the best.

"He's already reading through the emails between you and Bobby—"

But of course she somehow has my private email account information.

Sure she would.

"But before he really digs in," she says, grabbing the bag from my hand and tipping it over until two boxes slide onto the counter, "he recommends you start making some lifestyle changes. As in, immediately."

I let out a dry laugh, my eyes ticking over the mail table by the front door where PR packages and gilded invitations used to be brought in by the hour.

Today's mail?

Pizza coupons.

"Serena. What could possibly be more different than my life now?"

"He wants you to cut back on expenses. He says"—she pauses, giving me the side eye as if gauging whether my mental health can take it—"there's a real chance this could go sideways, and if you end up needing to pay out—well. He wants you to be prepared."

I squeeze my eyes shut.

We're talking about half of forty-six million dollars *and* my reputation *and* my livelihood. My job.

If I can't be proven innocent and salvage my name, any future in content creating will vanish. Leaving me, a girl with no college degree, no high school diploma, and no other skill set aside from what I've been doing the past fifteen years, with nothing.

Nothing.

How can I possibly ever be prepared for that?

And what could possibly work for another job? Where would I even interview? And for what? And who, after all this, would want me?

My temple throbs, as it does every time my thoughts take a cascading turn.

I can see the interviewer now, taking pictures of my résumé to send to friends so they can get a good laugh.

Work experience?

None.

Skilled in other languages?

No.

Can use Excel, PowerPoint, QuickBooks? Shoot, can add seven plus five without secretly using my fingers under the table?

No.

References?

Check the papers. They'll give you tons of opinions about me.

Because as it has turned out, aside from Serena in this city, practically no one has stuck around.

Even Jacquie, who was so supportive those first few weeks after the news spread, jumping into a manic game plan to get me telling my story for every broadcast, paper, and media outlet she could get me into, dropped me after the third interview. She saw the writing on the wall. She watched as the narrative against me stacked, my voice becoming smaller and smaller.

I suppose the desertion isn't surprising.

Most of my friends are also in my line of work. And when work and play mingle as ours do and your job relies upon your image and reputation, there is a real cost to associating with a notorious person.

Friends became slower and slower in answering my calls. Hedged more and more around the idea of showing up somewhere to share a meal. Avoided even visiting my home in private because just walking through the doors of the Montana would get them caught on camera.

Could I blame them?

Would I have done the same?

I like to think I wouldn't have, but then . . .

Even my followers abandoned me like the carcass of a Thanksgiving turkey after the meat was gone.

People, as it turned out, loved the story of the good little starlet.

But people loved the story of the good little starlet who deceived everyone more.

They liked me as America's sweetheart.

But they *loved* me as the nation's surprise villain.

It wasn't surprising, then, when people began to twist every caption I wrote and story I shared. It wasn't surprising when people started to nitpick every post and video, turning it around to blast messages I never intended.

I was no longer classy. I was spoiled.

I was no longer pretty. I was outdated. Pathetically trying to fit into a generation I didn't belong in.

Unintelligent.

Peppy to the point of exhausting.

Morose to the point of depressing.

Overnight, I became everything those in my business feared.

Canceled.

It came as no surprise, then, when Jacquie apologized as she told me she just wasn't "the best fit for navigating me through these troubled times" and that it was truly "in my best interest to work with an expert." Telling me she didn't have the "stretch to secure the brand deals I deserved given the current circumstance" but that "she wished me nothing but the best."

Her words sweetened with icing but bitter at the core.

All of a sudden I had no one.

No one but Serena.

"How exactly am I going to change my lifestyle more than I already have?" I ask weakly.

My whole body feels tired. An anchor attached to my feet, dragging me down as Serena sets a plate of brioche bread with berries and vegan crème anglaise before me.

"I have nothing," I continue, ignoring it. "Everyone thinks I intentionally sold their data. This isn't just some influencer losing it and driving through a grocery store in a golf cart naked."

Serena sighs nostalgically. We all remember Gary. He was a barrel of laughs up until the end.

"This isn't just another amusing bit of news they watch from a distance while eating popcorn. It's a personal hit," I say. "To *everyone*. *Everyone* feels violated. My reputation is gone *forever*—"

"Just because people don't believe you *yet*." Serena picks up my plate and, using it like a cattle prod, pushes me out of the kitchen. She sets it on the coffee table in the living room and moves toward the two-story windows and closed curtains. "It's temporary—"

"Nobody," I say, pulling my knees up to my chin on the couch, "bounces back."

"People do it all the time," she says flippantly as if we're talking about switching hot yoga bars. "We just need to have a plan. And step one of that plan is getting you to a place where you can save money *and* reshape your image. Cat, I've given this some thought."

I wince. This is the kind of tone that's landed me in Salvadorian taxis flying through stop signs with no heed to oncoming traffic all because Serena saw a video of black baby turtles from El Salvador hatching online, thought they were "cute," and decided we "absolutely must" visit.

"I think you need to rent out your apartment."

A shaft of light flows into the living room as she yanks one curtain back. I can't help noticing her little intake of breath and the way her hands clasp together as she looks over the skyline.

"My apartment . . . ," I repeat.

Had she said this a year ago, six months ago, even, perhaps, last month, I would've crumbled. I would've laughed at the audacity of such an idea. I would've told her she was crazy.

But now?

I scan the perfectly plumped pillows of the fifteen-foot-long sectionals meant for weekly entertainment. The sterile white walls of the expansive living room that echo the TV keeping me company late at night.

Feeling nothing toward it. Nothing at all.

From the white couches, to the perfectly laid dining table set for twelve, to the kitchen beyond. All new in planning for this purchase. So much research and mood boarding and color and product coordinating. So much excitement yielding such disappointing results.

No history or memories attached.

Just glass, marble, and walls.

What would it take to move? A few luggage bags of clothes and shoes. A few books and pictures.

"And," Serena continues, "you need to take up your uncle's offer."

This, at last, draws out some feeling. Like a needle jabbing you in the ribs out of nowhere.

"What?" I give a nervous little laugh. "Serena, you can't be serious." I pause, leveling my gaze. "Seriously. You can't."

She throws her hands in the air. "Now, I know it isn't ideal—I don't want you leaving the city any more than you do—but I've watched you the past few months. You're depressed. You spend hours every day on your phone torturing yourself, reading every post and comment about you out there. You stay inside all the time—"

"*You* just told me to get back inside," I counter.

"Only when you are *even worse* in public. How much do you want to bet the wheels of IG's algorithm are running manic right now over a picture of you staring at a bunch of newspapers in the rain, looking as guilty as Chevy coming home from spring break?"

Chevy was Serena's long-term boyfriend who made the mistake of getting frisky with another freshman on spring break ten years ago. Chevy was also the unfortunate long-term boyfriend who wasn't dumped by Serena but given a life sentence of frequent reminders of his grievances ten years ago.

"The thing is," Serena continued, "you're miserable in your apartment and—sweetie, I can't emphasize this enough—a *horrific* example out. You can't handle the judgment of other people—"

I start to interrupt.

"Not at this scale," she rushes on. "No one can. And the cost of living isn't doing you any favors while you're"—she pauses, as though trying to find the right word for *utterly rejected with frozen accounts and fired from everything*—"on sabbatical. You need to get out of the city. For that matter, you need to go somewhere as remote as possible from people who have modern technology. And I can think of no place better than in the middle of absolutely *Nowhere*, Utah, with your uncle."

"Kannery, Montana," I correct with a frown.

"Right. Sure. So rent out the penthouse. Do that job he offered for spare change. And stay far, far away from social media and online retail therapy while you're at it."

I look over at the portable hot tub yet to be inflated in the corner, all the while aware in the back of my mind of the vintage Marilyn Monroe lipstick I'm currently bidding for on eBay.

"So go kick back with family, get a reset, and let Murphy handle the rest. Believe me, Cat, I *hate* to say it and you know I'll miss you like crazy, but it really is what you need right now." Just as she says this she gives a mighty pull and the second curtain opens. Pointing, she begins counting under her breath the lounge chairs on the balcony.

"Or you're tired of me too."

"Nonsense." She waves a hand without looking at me. "I'm telling my only friend to move across the country. I'm miserable."

"You have a thousand friends, Serena."

"True. But none that I like."

I lean forward, elbows on my knees. A curtain of hair falls over my eyes, and I push it back. "So let me get this straight. You want to ship me off to the woods until this case is over and I get my personality back."

"I'd be lying if I said that part wasn't a little bit true too."

I squeeze my eyes shut as I count to twenty, taking in this news, trying to think.

Open them when it becomes clear that it's not helping.

That nothing I can do in this apartment will help.

That nothing I can do in this city will help.

My fingers find the necklace Uncle Terry gave me, and I start tracing the embossed rose on the front. "Where would I place an ad for the apartment? It's a bit last minute."

At this Serena swivels on her heel and faces me, her smile as radiant as when she discovered Dolce & Gabbana wasn't discontinuing their Blu Mediterraneo line after all. "Honey, I'm happy to do you the honor of babysitting your little place for a while."

I blanch. "You. Doing *me* the honor."

"Take over caring for the plants."

"They're cacti," I say. "They take an ice cube every three months."

"Collecting the mail."

"The pizza coupons."

"Just"—she inhales deeply while wafting her hands—"keeping the place socially happy."

As though the penthouse is a dog that needs company.

"Now." She gathers me up and leads me toward the closets. "I've already Venmoed you the first month's rent."

"I don't believe we set a rate."

"Oh, sweetie." At this she laughs, a honeycombed I-come-from-so-much-money-I'm-currently-doubling-whatever-you'd-ask laugh. "Let's just get your bags packed. And get you the biggest parka we can find."

CHAPTER 3

The Peanuts

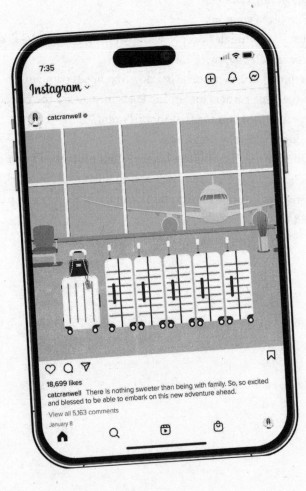

A side from the literal red and white flags waving the small, shaking plane to the runway, metaphorical red flags are everywhere.

The four men in neon uniforms brace their boots against the snow as they stand on either side of the runway, waving the plane in with glowing wands that are hardly visible against the blast of snow and darkened sky. The blinking yellow lights highlight the small airport vehicle as it moves parallel to us, its plow filling rapidly with snow.

A rolling sea of gloomy clouds follows from above, as though racing the plane toward the finish line.

Nails digging into the armrest, I clench my teeth with eyes squeezed shut as we land first with a shudder, then a squeak, and at long last a *thud*. My legs tremble with the reverberations of the wheels against ground, and I hold my breath—waiting in anticipation—for any signs of slipping against frozen asphalt and the inevitable flip, crash, and plume of fiery smoke as we meet our final end.

"You don't suppose I could have one more packet of these before we land?"

Incredulously, I open my eyes and look over to the man beside me who has managed to squirrel away nine packages of honey-roasted peanuts in the last two hours. Never eating them, mind you, but stowing them in coat pockets like he knows something about the end of the world waiting on the other side of those airplane doors that the rest of us do not.

Everything in this moment truly screams, *"This was a horrible, horrible mistake."*

The flight attendant, whose glossy lipstick and smile wore off nine hours ago, speaks from her strapped-in position across from us. "We've landed, sir."

He looks down at his coat pockets, genuinely affected by the news.

With lessening quakes beneath us, I brave a peek out the window. Visibility is terrible, nothing but sideways snow and a few streaking lights beyond. But it appears the worst is over.

The plane is slowing.

Though it's hard to tell, I feel us turning toward a small, snow-covered building.

Evidently I will live to see another day.

"Here." I slide my unopened packet of peanuts over.

The man's face brightens, just as the pilot's fuzzy voice comes overhead. "Welcome to Kannery, Montana. The time is 6:32 p.m. mountain standard time. Current temperature is a record two degrees, forecasted to accumulate eight to twelve inches in the next twenty-four hours. Looks like we're the last ones in before they rerouted planes to alternate airports, so stay warm and be careful out there."

As if on cue, I hear several jacket zippers around the plane zip up.

I zip up my own jacket as I move into the aisle.

It took several hours of research before Serena and I landed on this coat. It's a thinner material, a white, knee-length quilting that seems at first glance more suited to strolling through the floral market on a crisp spring day. Deceivingly thin. But when I reach inside the pocket and press the little button, heat instantly begins to flow from my neck to my knees.

I tuck my scarf into my coat, slip on my white leather driving gloves, and reach for my carry-on. I can do this. I'm a hardy New Yorker who has braced more than a few harsh winters in my time.

In heels, in fact.

I'd like to see any of these folks stride down icy crosswalks in stilettos while dodging taxis.

This will be even easier.

I blink at the blizzard out the window.

Absolutely.

No question.

Now, managing to transport six suitcases toward the car rental sign when there was no trolley in sight, that was another matter.

I struggle to push each of the white hardcase suitcases along the airport hallway like a mother duck trying to keep her ducklings in line. People around me scurry past, casting dubious glances at the girl in the snow-white coat juggling coffee and a slew of white suitcases down a hallway bordered on each side by hanging furs behind glass displays and educational pictures of hardy Native Americans past and present.

I keep my gaze fixed on the suitcases in front of me as I move toward the entrance of the airport, daring to look neither to the right at the market with its display of magazines (and my face, no doubt) nor to the left, where floor-to-ceiling glass windows display the sheets of snow beyond.

I can do this.

I am a grown woman.

I am thirty years old.

I have dealt with far more technical things than dragging six suitcases through an airport.

I pause in the hall, spotting the could-be humorous angle of my little tow-along, and slip out my phone.

Lighthearted.

Innocent.

Postable.

Serena pushed me to start posting again on my accounts. I'd stopped, overwhelmed by the onslaught of hate, wanting to remove myself from the trampling of people who waited rabidly for new content every day. Hungry for fresh pictures and words to chew on and spit out and then point at with disgust. Eager to get a conversation going in my comments about how horrible I was while hundreds and thousands jumped in to agree. It seemed every post I made only made my situation worse.

But Serena rolled out a PowerPoint before I left (complete with laser pointer fashioned inside a bright-red pen), pointing to stats as she broke down the analytics of a dozen canceled high-profile influencers, analyzing how and why either their crash was permanent or they were able to crawl their way out. Ultimately, it came down to this: keep posting.

And be happy.

Pretend what is going on is not in fact going on.

Focus on as many "humble highlights" as possible I could garner in a day.

Make my captions as unoffensively happy and relatable to the general public as humanly possible.

Throw in the "hiked-five-miles-to-school-uphill" kind of stories from childhood. Share the Louboutin leather studded purse Christmas gift, yes, but be sure to do so with a caption of how special it is given my childhood spent in poverty.

Show the other side of me (as though living in a national park is actually another side of me), making them curious and zealous to follow along and find out what exactly I'm up to, winning them over with my "down-to-earth alter ego" and, most importantly, proving to the world that I'm not guilty.

Because, as Serena has said a thousand times, guilty people don't carry on living life and sharing about it as though they were innocent (except for the stray psychopath).

Guilty people hole up when accused.

Innocent people shrug it off.

Guilty people stand in a rain shower while water drips down their umbrellas and strangers take pictures of them.

Innocent people go to bed with an easy conscience and demonstrate just how easy their conscience is by wearing sunny yellow sundresses and pointing out how pretty the flower in the cracked sidewalk is, all while comparing it to their lives.

So my job, aside from the literal job I took up with Uncle Terry, is to practice keeping on as usual. Just bright, and bubbly, and entirely unoffensive, and humble, and different.

I look at the line of suitcases from another angle—hearing the criticisms to come.

Who needs that many suitcases? Is that a Louisa Voeux? Just use an athletic bag like the rest of us humans.

Some people have real problems, sweetie.

It doesn't matter that these were given to me. It doesn't matter that this was—*is*—my livelihood. That my job was—*is*—to be a walking banner ad for these companies.

My confidence wavers. But Serena's words prod me on. It's this or hide altogether. I just have to press on.

At the last second I shift the angle of the camera.

Leaving three of the suitcases out of the picture.

Snap.

Satisfied with the shot, my white nails—done "one last time" with Serena in funereal silence—clap against the phone as I type the caption, then switch over to video and begin filming.

Just one video for stories.

Should I tag @LouisaVoeux?

No. They'd disown me.

Worse. Maybe make a public statement saying they don't want to be associated.

I swallow, fighting the heat in my chest at the thought.

"Catherine."

The video is still rolling as I look up at the sound of my name. It takes a second for me to register who spoke. Not just because I so rarely hear my full name spoken aloud, but because of the voice. I know that voice. I remember, vaguely, the low register and slight accent of that man's voice.

Uncle Terry's coworker, sitting on one of the benches, rises. He's wearing that same olive-green work uniform as three months ago, his badge flashing beneath his unzipped coat. Gone is his wide-brimmed hat, showing deep-mahogany hair sprinkled, oh so barely, with strands of silver. The colors match the beard, just thick and unkempt enough, by New York standards, to lie in that hazy field between unfashionable and fabulous.

Even now I see a few resolute snowflakes clinging to his beard.

That face.

Oh yes. I haven't forgotten that face.

"Cat, actually," I say, puzzled as he stops before me. I drop the phone to my side. "Uncle Terry's the only one who calls me that. So . . ." There's an underlying question in my words. "Good to see you . . ."

"Zaiah. And I'm giving you a lift," he says matter-of-factly. His eyes fall on the phone in my hand, the video still rolling.

I swipe the video off and stuff the phone in my coat pocket as the memory of our last time meeting returns. I don't know what it is about him, but he makes me feel like my hand is caught in a candy jar.

Only last time I was able to push against his antagonism by saving the day for him using the very means he clearly hated.

But now . . .

Well, now . . .

I see my own face on a magazine over his shoulder and my cheeks flare. "Oh, actually. I'm renting a car, though. I'm sure I told Uncle Terry that."

"Maybe in a few days. But today . . ." Zaiah holds out one hand toward the floor-to-ceiling windows. As if to prove his point, an airport worker below slips momentarily on the icy ground before stepping inside his blinking vehicle. "Terry would've come himself, but with the night blindness and"—he hesitates, glancing down at the row of suitcases—"he mentioned you might be carrying a heavier load—"

There it is again.

Judging with only the mildest flicker of his eyes.

"I'm staying indefinitely." I hold the handle of one suitcase territorially. "I had to prepare for anything."

"You don't need to worry about furniture. The cabin is furnished."

"Clothes, I mean." I narrow my eyes. What, did he think I packed a sofa?

I look at the array of suitcases.

It does rather look like a lot.

"And shoes," I add.

There's a long pause.

"Sure," he says, and positively looks like he wants to scratch the back of his neck while muttering, "*Women.*"

To his credit, however, his very *tiny* credit, he scoops four handles into his hands. The suitcases no longer roll at the pressed angle at which he holds them, and I try hard to keep my eyebrows from rising in quiet amazement as I watch him lift all four off the ground.

He takes a few steps—while I try to calculate exactly how many pounds all those hefty suitcases add up to—then stops and looks over his shoulder. "Ready?"

My eyes snap up from the suitcases. "Yes." I gather the single suitcase and carry-on in my hands. We move steadily down the hallway, past the last of the stores showcasing magazines and papers. But as we begin to move past the car rental area, I slow.

A line of people getting their keys and moving off with notable relief toward the exits makes me stop entirely.

I want that kind of end-of-a-long-journey relief.

I don't want to have to trek back here in two or three days.

Not to mention, *why should* I avoid driving a car right now when all of these people are considered perfectly capable? That woman with the cane is getting hers and looks not a day younger than ninety. I mean, the woman's seen the TV screen go from black-and-white to color. Her glasses are, quite literally, thicker than my cutting board back home. If they can hand her keys, trusting her fortitude and physical capabilities, surely I can trust myself too.

We're just a few feet off from the double doors now, and I stop. "Actually, Zaiah," I say, taking my hands off the bags. "I've already made the reservation. I'm just going to get my car now."

He stops with a look of disbelief as he faces me.

No, *disbelief* isn't the right word for his expression. Uncertain, as though maybe he's on orders from his boss about his to-be-handled-delicately niece and now doesn't quite know what to do.

I help him out. "I really appreciate it, but I can take care of myself. We get snow in New York too."

"You have a car in the city?"

"No, that's not," I begin, shaking my head, unwilling to answer that question head-on. "That's irrelevant." I shoot for another angle. "I'd hate to put anyone out by having to take another trip here in a few days."

"Oh." He sets the suitcases down. "Really, it's no trouble—"

I raise a hand, stopping him. Perhaps he's one of those men who needs to feel appreciated, that his toil is worth the trouble. Perhaps he needs reassurance that he'll still get that gold star for effort.

"I'll just follow behind you to the park," I say buoyantly. "That'll be very helpful."

For one long, long moment we are in a stalemate, him looking from me to my raised hand still in the *stop* position, me looking resolutely into his not-too-shabby green eyes above the blanket of a beard covering the rest of his face.

At last, while making clear from his expression that he can't disagree with my decision more, he turns the suitcases toward the car rental line. His voice is even lower, not quite at growl level, but close. "We need to hurry. The snow is coming quick."

I don't know why I need to feel this win with him. It must be something about how he so clearly disagrees with my life's choices (which I feel even more acutely given recent events), but I do. I take in a breath. "Terrific."

Twenty minutes later, I'm up.

"Name, please."

"Catherine Cranwell."

The woman typing away at her computer takes my ID in a way that makes it evident she does this a thousand times a week.

As her eyes flicker over from my ID to my face, she pauses. Her fake lashes quake as she blinks several times.

Looks back at the ID.

Then at me.

"Yes, Ms. Cranwell." She fidgets with the hem of her vest, in quite a new tone. Her fingers begin flying across the keyboard. "I have your vehicle ready. Should be in space 2B. Unless"—she pauses, and her fingers inch toward the walkie-talkie on her uniformed chest—"I can get someone to bring it out to you."

"No, that's all right—"

"Benny, bring 2B to valet," the woman is already saying into the walkie-talkie. She pauses, listening to his static voice and jumbled words. Her smile widens as she looks at me while repeating louder, "Bring 2B to *valet*."

I fold my hands together while we both listen to more cacophony of jumbled words and wind. "Really. It's fine—"

But she's already taking in a sharp breath, giving me a resolute, everything-is-totally-under-control smile and pressing her lips so close to the walkie-talkie they touch. Her words fly so quickly I can hardly make them out. "Benny-you-bring-2B-to-valet-*right-now-or-so-help-me*."

She drops her hand from the walkie and smiles as she staples several sheets together and places them in a folder. "It'll be right out those doors." She hands the folder to me. "Enjoy your stay in Kannery, Ms. Cranwell." There's a gleaming I-can't-believe-this-is-happening-I'm-absolutely-going-to-be-videoing-you-the-second-you-turn-your-back look in her eye. "Drive safe."

"Thank you." I pretend not to see the pictures she's begun taking of me from the phone peeking out from under her register. It's a terrible, up-the-nose angle.

After tucking the folder into the front pocket of my carry-on, I move to meet Zaiah a few feet off.

From the frown he's giving beyond my shoulder, I was right about the woman and the video.

"What kind of truck did they give—?" But Zaiah halts as the doors slide open and a whistle of snow flies past.

And there is the car sitting beneath the concrete cover.

Oh dear.

Its small oval headlights look like they're flickering in the onslaught of the slashing, horizontal snowfall.

Swiftly I unzip the carry-on and reach for the folder of papers. Sure enough, right above my signature is the name of the car: Mercedes-Benz E350 Cabriolet . . . Convertible.

The small white car purrs as a man steps out, holding the driver's side door open. It's stunning, melting like a snowflake into its surroundings, all except for the gaudy strings of chains covering each tire.

"You can't be serious."

There's something in the way Zaiah speaks—as though saying, "Fine. I put up with your childish shenanigans for a while, but now, *now* it's time to take over"—that slides like a bow across an out-of-tune violin.

It's that same look from our first meeting splashed across his face.

That hypercritical, disparaging expression as though I, Cat Cranwell, am the most ridiculous person on the planet.

Before this moment, I was going to point out this was a simple mistake. Was going to clarify that my virtual assistant always books me higher-end vehicles for trips—not only for the aesthetic in any photos and videos I take, but also because you can only make the mistake of being not particular and ending up in a junker on the side of a desert highway with one gas station forty-three miles away once—and had simply not taken the unusual location and season of this trip into account. That I just needed to go inside, explain the situation, and get something else.

And yes, maybe I'm hypersensitive and hyperaware given the onslaught of criticism directed my way lately, but I can already see branded across his eyes what he'd think, or say.

"You have somebody else book your trips for you?"

"You didn't think to double-check when you signed your name on the contract?"

"Have you *still* not learned your lesson about reading before you sign contracts?!"

I swallow down the humiliating truth of that last one that hits harder than the rest.

I can't show I'm that stupid.

I can't show to anyone, even just one person, that I would do that.

Which leaves only one thing to do in such a moment.

Lie boldly.

"Ah. There it is." Raising my chin, I press past him through the open door as if this is the best plan in the world.

As if everything is going exactly according to plan.

Absolutely. According.

"Thank you, sir," I say, reaching in my purse and, with a slight struggle, pulling out a bill.

"Oh good. White," Zaiah mutters, trailing me. "One ought to always get a car that is incredibly easy to get lost in the snowdrifts. Very . . . matchy."

"Careful. Aside from the kindergarten-level language, you're beginning to talk like a content creator." My smile broadens as I stare resolutely at the man taking my money.

Out of the corner of my eye, I see the shadow of a smile slip over Zaiah's face.

I pause.

Turn.

There's still fire in my lungs. Frustration at the judgment he dare pass over *my life*, shattered and crap as it stands right now, left to exhale and burn.

"Not that it matters, but I didn't *plan* this car," I snap. "My VA picked it out. It's her error, not mine."

"Thank you," the valet says, sidestepping as he eyes the two of us.

Zaiah looks startled by my response. Like he had just made a little joke and I had blown it out of proportion.

Great. Now I look tetchy and high maintenance. Like the villain.

Just *perfect*.

Snowflakes hit my cheeks and neck, and the wind slaps with a startling chill.

"Right. That's totally understandable," Zaiah says, clearly trying to mollify me, but it just makes things worse. "So I'll just . . ."—he pauses awkwardly, looking pointedly at the suitcases in his hands—"take these to my truck. They should fit more . . ."—he pauses again, seeming to be trying to tiptoe around with his words in such a way I won't blow—"comfortably."

With jaw clenched (or at least I think it's clenched—everything's going numb), I glance to the back of the convertible. I'd insist on taking the suitcases myself, but the car doesn't even look big enough to hold my purse.

"That would be terrific," I say. I sniff; my rapidly freezing nose threatening to drip. "Thank you."

As Zaiah drops my suitcases in the back of his truck, I turn the heat up as high as I can and try not to wince with each thud.

I feel my anxiety rising as I watch the parking lot dumping out the last remaining cars, and the freshly empty parking spaces filling with falling snow faster than seems possible. Even the car attendant who gave me my keys has given up videoing me from afar and is bundling up in her coat, dashing toward her car.

As Zaiah gets inside his truck, a man in uniform turns the lock on the airport doors.

The whole place has, quite literally, shut down.

Brake lights switch off and Zaiah's truck rumbles forward.

With wipers flying back and forth across the small windshield, I push lightly on the gas pedal and the tires begin to turn. My chest eases ever so slightly to feel and hear the crunch of chains gripping the snow-packed road.

"This is fine," I tell myself, exhaling a plume of frosty air that tickles my eyelashes. "This is just fine."

I follow Zaiah's blinking turn light out of the airport parking lot.

Ten minutes later, we hit Main Street.

The town is small.

A dozen brick buildings perch on either side of the street. Lampposts dot the sidewalks every few feet, holding snow-splotched American flags.

An overload of antique stores featuring gaudy brass lamps and old pictures in wooden frames. Two run-down upholstery shops either out of business or surviving solely by the scarcity of anything else in town. One yarn shop. Three buildings with windows covered up by boards.

But there is one little shop at the very end, with floor-to-ceiling windows rounding both sides of the street. Parisian lights are strung over empty bistro tables laden with snow. The gilded words *The Honeypot* sway slightly from a hanging sign beneath a striped black-and-white awning.

I make a mental note to visit what may well be the only thing in this town remotely connected to the twenty-first century.

This isn't so bad.

The road is covered in white but it's manageable, thanks in small part to the tracks of Zaiah's F250 with the words *US Park Ranger* across the sides.

The snow is coming down heavily, but not so much the wipers can't keep up.

I sink into the white leather, relief starting to set in.

The screen lights up on my phone in the dark car and I glance down, seeing the social media notification.

Ignore it, Cat.

Leave it.

My chest tightens, though, just a tiny bit. Just enough to make my anxiety rise without me quite knowing why. Just enough to make my eyes dart from the road to the phone, to the speedometer, then back to the phone and its glow.

The *come-hither* glow.

No. Just last week I saw one of those really awful commercials about texting and driving. I will not yield.

I purse my lips and look back at the road. As we move through another stop sign, I congratulate myself.

I mean, honestly, here I am in the middle of *nowhere* following the law, when just a few months ago I was in a plane with a friend (well, now deserted friend) who couldn't *stop* looking at his phone. And he was the one *flying*. At one point he was literally watching a TikTok of a girl flying a plane, while there we were *actually* flying a plane.

He couldn't even control himself over unimportant things, while here I am, dealing with the biggest crisis of my life regarding career, reputation, and *millions of dollars* hanging in the balance. And what am I doing? I'm obeying the law during those first critical minutes after posting. Those first critical minutes when feedback makes or breaks a post. And in this case, not just a post, but my life.

The stakes are high.

What if people are attacking the post from the angle of too many suitcases? It only takes one person to start a thread, to steer or skew the post to its will.

I should be on there, supporting the kind commenters with an overflow of gratitude that spurs them on.

My stomach churns, fingers gripping the wheel as we inch along.

My eyes flicker down to the speedometer.

Fifteen miles an hour.

Fifteen.

I could practically be running alongside the vehicle at this point.

I yank a glove off one hand with my teeth and with surgical-level precision and gamer-level speed I swipe and tap on the buttons as half a dozen screens pass by.

My eyes pinpoint the place on the screen where I see the number of likes from the previous posts. The little heart and the number below it that tells me how I'm performing.

Not well.

Not well enough when I'm calculating the time that's lapsed against the numbers.

I tap on the bubble for comments and begin to scroll.

A number of words catch my eye: *trying too hard.*

Wouldn't that be nice?

Expensive.

Phony.

Façade.

I exhale loudly, then faster than the speed of a bullet—and

certainly faster than the speed of this car—I begin typing responses, doing damage control.

I respond only to the kind ones, of course, carefully ignoring the haters while trying to inspire the positive people to come to my defense. To raise a war cry against the keyboard warriors.

It's only when I start seeing a few responses in my favor, a few banners rising, that I sigh and put down the phone.

Good enough.

I did what I needed to do.

We turn off Main Street.

Twenty minutes past the last streetlight, building, and stop sign, my nose practically touches the wheel. Every muscle in my body is taut as I hold my foot to the gas pedal. I gape at the small bit of road spotlit by my headlights, then up to the looming mountain ahead.

Its enormous body stretches to the sky, towering above with razor-sharp peaks that seem to glitter as they break through the clouds.

It looks otherworldly.

Beautiful.

Terrifying.

Not a soul in sight on this winding, tiny black strip of road rising higher and higher for miles.

I squeak through gritted teeth as the tires slip, yet again.

Forget the shaking plane. I'll take the shaking plane and nine hours beside the peanut-hoarding squirrel of a man over this.

Zaiah creeps along, but even so, I feel my little car losing its grip as the road ascends toward the great mountain.

I should stop.

I should stop *now*.

And then, suddenly, my worst fears manifest, and I feel the tires slipping out of my control.

My squeak grows into a scream as I hit the brakes and, for the second time today, squeeze my eyes shut.

Seconds tick by as I hug the wheel, waiting to feel myself slipping over the cliff and dropping hundreds of feet to the rocky depths below.

It'll be swift, at least.

Oh, I don't want to die!

And there it is.

BUMP.

I scream as the car bounces on something, then quakes.

Then . . . silence.

My heart thumps like the wings of a hummingbird. Maybe I'm hanging over the edge, teetering on the precipice before the weight of the car tips me forward and I plummet.

I will not look.

I *cannot* look.

If I'm really over the edge, I'd rather never know. Just kill me now.

Tap.

Tap.

I open my eyes slowly, first one eye, then the other. There's the mountain, still looming. The precipice is in front of me. I don't see any road.

Slowly I turn, and there is Zaiah, his breath fogging up the window as he's squatting down, peering at me.

And there, to my left, is the road.

The blinking emergency lights of his truck cast a red glow on the snow.

Oh dear.

I look to my right and see the headlight of the white convertible pressed against the guardrail, the body and back of the car turned sideways.

I look back at Zaiah's bearded face in the window and, if I'm not mistaken, see shallowly concealed mirth in his hazel-green eyes.

Wordlessly he pulls open the driver's side door. A blast of cold air hits me, and he reaches down, his face inches from mine, as he pushes the button for the trunk.

While he pulls out the carry-on and spare suitcase, I shakily step out of the car.

I'm alive.

I'm alive and well.

An absolute *idiot*, but alive and well.

I raise my chin and do the only thing I can do: walk silently behind him.

Just when I think he's going to let it go, let me keep what small dignity I have left as I slip and slide my way to his truck in gripless boots, he speaks as he opens the passenger-side door.

"Hey, Cat. Welcome to Montana." He laughs as he shuts the door.

Welcome to *his* world.

CHAPTER 4

The Cabin

see what you did there. Cute." There's a slight twitch of Zaiah's beard as he stares ahead, gripping the worn leather of his steering wheel.

The wipers are making mad dashes back and forth across his windshield, eager to sweep off the snow that's collecting quicker than they can handle. We're only thirty feet off from my convertible, and yet it's already just a big white plop of snow blurred into the rest of the scenery in the mirror.

"How long have you been dreaming about throwing out that comeback?" I click off the power button inside my coat pocket. It feels eighty degrees in here, and welcome at that.

"Hmm," he says, as though trying to recollect. "When was the last time we met?"

"Four months ago."

Like I'd ever forget that date.

"Four months then." There he goes again. There's that little curve of a smile on his lips.

I roll my eyes and settle into the seat, which is as warm as hot bread wrapped inside a tea towel.

The truck is old and unimpressive, but it blasts heat so powerfully through its vents it makes my rental look like a kiddie toy. There is nothing special about it; in fact, quite literally *nothing* is lit up on his center display. No red glow to say a passenger seat belt is on. Nothing to signal the airbags are engaged. No running display of music or Bluetooth or voice-command options.

For that matter, there's a high probability the radio doesn't work at all, given the rusty metal point where the knob was clearly knocked off some time ago.

But the tires are nearly as tall as me and the heat works and we're moving up the mountain at an impressive speed given the elements. Uninterested in looks, absolutely 100 percent practical.

This truck takes after its owner.

"So what about my car?" I ask. "Is there someone I should call to let them know it's there?"

He shakes his head. "No need. Scotty will tow it to the park tomorrow morning."

I raise a brow at his certainty and automatic response. We've only left the car ten minutes ago, and I have been in Zaiah's presence the whole time. Unless . . . "How will he know where to take it?"

Zaiah pauses. Glances over at me as if to say, "Do you really want me to explain the obvious?"

I blink back at him as if to say, "Obviously."

He exhales. "It's a white convertible."

"So?"

"Everyone knows Terry's niece is coming in from New York. I'm sure you'll find it outside your door by nine."

"Oh." I bite my lip. Look out the window. "Great. This is one of those towns."

One of those towns where word spreads like wildfire.

Zaiah frowns. "I think you meant to say there, 'Wow, I'm so appreciative that the citizens of this town will help me. What a considerate place these people call home.'"

I hear the rebuke in his words and straighten. "No, I'm not unappreciative. It's just . . ." I hesitate.

Oh, it's too late for this. Too late to argue. Too late to defend myself by breaking down what I meant.

I rub my temple. My head throbs too much to even want to

consider breaking into the depths of my sob story right now. Not to mention, there's more than a decent chance he doesn't care.

"I'm *supremely grateful*. That's very kind."

I stare out at the wall of darkness just beyond the guardrail and cliff. I'd be scared, but there's something in the way Zaiah's large, bare hands turn the wheel with ease, neither nonchalant about the storm swirling around us nor with a white-knuckle grip like the kind I so obviously had, that's comforting.

It's clear he knows what he is doing and has driven this road a million times.

But just then we swing around another curve hugging the mountain, and I feel a frog jump up my throat. I press my lips together, determined not to yield to my fears. And more importantly, not to yield to my fears after this true fireworks display of an entrance I've already made thus far in front of him.

I look down at the center console. Hunt around with my eyes for something to distract myself.

The inside of someone's vehicle says a lot about who they are, a hundred little details about a person's lifestyle and preferences. And as I look around, I feel like I'm gathering more data about this man's life in three minutes than if I read his profile on eHarmony.

An empty coffee mug sits in the console between us, the bottom rim holding the remnants of dark-as-night liquid and a few coffee grounds. Drinks coffee black. Noted.

The mug itself is charcoal gray, positively nothing to define it or give it personality. No top to protect it from sloshing around, as if travel mugs are unnecessarily fancy.

I set my venti coffee cup beside his. I've clung to it since the airport layover this morning. Only three sips are left in it, but I draw them out as if they're symbolic of my last remaining ties to society.

"You drink your coffee pretty quick?" I ask, partly because I'm curious, mostly because we hit a nerve-shattering bump and I feel the tires, mighty as they may be, slide.

Zaiah, amid recentering the wheel, tilts his head my way. "I drink at the normal rate."

He says it like he's not certain exactly what I'm getting at.

"Mmm." I press my lips together as the truck rumbles over another patch of black ice, trying my darndest not to grab the handle above my head. My eyes dart around for another clue.

He keeps a clean car, except for a cupful or two of dirt and gravel gathered on the floorboards, evidence of his job. A pair of aviators dangle from the mirror—nice enough to get the job done, not so nice as to carry a label. An old photograph on the dashboard of him standing beside a young woman, the photo so tattered and faded it seems to have become a fixture of the truck itself.

I point to the photo. "Who's that?"

His eyes follow the direction of my finger. He pauses, as though he'd forgotten it was there entirely. Replies reluctantly, "No one. Just someone I used to know."

There's silence, then to my surprise he makes a sudden move and pulls the photo off the dashboard. Sets it in the pocket of his door beside a crumpled wrapper as though it, too, will be tossed in the trash later.

So, old girlfriend. And here I am, witness to the moment he declutters her from his life.

This drive just gets better and better.

A rifle is locked into position behind our heads, no doubt part of his line of work. A drill and beat-up toolbox lie on the floor behind his seat.

"What projects are you working on?" I say, seeing the curve in the road coming up ahead.

It's a big one. I force in a deep lungful of air. Focus on exhaling.

"I'm . . . uh." He casts a look at me. It's clear he's catching on to my discomfort and processing how to handle me. "I'm working on a new run for a chicken coop."

"You have chickens?"

"Twelve."

"Any roosters?" I swallow and grip the seat as he turns the wheel and I see my seat heading straight for the cliff ledge. Here it comes.

"One. His name's Rocky."

"That's nice. How much longer do we have?"

My voice has hitched up and now sounds a little more like a chipmunk than I would've preferred. There's a mixture of something—concern? humor?—in his eyes.

"Two miles," he says calmly, as though he is completely oblivious to the panic attack his passenger is having in the next seat.

I take a breath. Two miles. I can do two miles.

What else falls into the bio for this guy?

"You don't travel much, do you?" he says.

I let out a tense laugh. "I travel quite a bit. Just not into places bent on killing me."

The tires slip as they climb over a particularly heavy patch of ice. The truck quakes and nearly pulls to a stop. Zaiah doubles his efforts in turning the wheel, all while working the gas pedal. As he finally pulls out of the slick patch, I add, "But no. My work is—was—based in New York."

I flush as I fumble over my tenses.

He raises a brow. "You're done working there entirely?"

"I'm on sabbatical." Sabbatical. It's a term I lean heavily on these days. Code for: lost everything in my life.

To his credit, he just nods as though this is completely believable and the girl next to him isn't using terms reserved for those with doctorate degrees teaching biochemical engineering.

At last a simple brown sign welcomes us to Kannery National Park and, without slowing, he turns the truck. We go deeper into the forest, and after taking a number of turns I could never remember later, Zaiah pulls into a little gravel driveway.

Here we are.

In the middle of *ab-so-lute-ly* nowhere.

I clasp my carry-on and stare at what Uncle Terry described over the phone as my "cozy cabin."

This is no cozy cabin. A cozy cabin is where I stayed with Serena on a group trip two Christmases ago, with a twenty-foot Fraser fir covered in more lights than the Rockefeller Christmas tree shining out of the A-frame for the world to see, smoky-gray leather couches positioned around a crackling fireplace covered in floor-to-ceiling river rocks bigger than my head, and hot tubs full of heavy mists and dripping hair and nighttime laughter that sent icicle crackles into the air.

This, though. Whatever *this* is, is not cozy.

Or even a cabin.

I look at the single cutout window that's smaller than they use in prisons. A hole in the floorboards of the porch is so big it threatens to swallow my foot whole.

Not really a tiny home.

Not a shack.

More like, if the three little pigs went into business but were rushed because the bank was getting tetchy about the building deadline for the construction loan and a wolf was on their tail, this would be a very realistic end result. A square house of logs the size of my closet.

I tilt my head. No. This has to be smaller.

I inhale.

It doesn't matter.

It doesn't matter.

Because no matter what, even if it were two sticks propped up against a tree, there is no way I will do anything after this whole road experience except look at this structure as if it is *exactly* what I was expecting.

And I'm just thrilled with it.

Just.

Positively.

Thrilled.

In fact, I'm going to smile now.

Despite the fact I have zero energy left after this day that never ends, I'm going to conjure up a delighted and approving smile.

Just for Zaiah.

See? I smile at the back of his coat as he works on the door. Smiling.

Mine is the third in a row of these structures bundled together, I note. And while others may be put off by the proximity to other "cabins" and people in a forest this big, seeing the other porch lights and signs of life inside is the only thread keeping me together right now.

I've lived thirteen years in a city of 8.4 million people.

At any given time there were at least a hundred people within screaming distance if I needed help.

And sure, I expected 95 percent of those people to, at best, whip out their phones and video whatever crisis I was in, but still. At least I wouldn't die alone.

A gal gets used to that assurance after so many years. The idea of being out of earshot of *anyone* in a forest like this would kill me.

I hear a snap in the distance and whip my head in that direction. Or grizzlies. I take a step closer to the back of Zaiah.

He stands beneath the small front porch roof held up by the bodies of knotty pines and works the key in the door. It's been quite the collection of seconds now, I realize, and the door seems to not want to let us in as much as I don't want to go. But at last it gives, making a tremendous creak as it swings open, and he takes a step inside and flicks on the light.

A moment later, I hear him mutter under his breath.

As I step inside I realize why.

"Jax said he just fixed this one up this morning," Zaiah growls.

"Who's Jax?"

"One of the interns."

"I keep telling Terry we need to get new heaters." Quickly Zaiah strides over to the tiny sink on the other side of the room and turns the faucet knobs. The faucet gurgles back but releases no water. He opens the cabinet beneath the sink and drops out of view.

I take the moment to turn around and take the cabin in. It is small, much smaller than I anticipated, but not nearly as horrible inside as it appears from the outside.

In fact, it's kind of like one of those secret clubs you only access by stepping over alleyway trash. The kind with rusted-out doors you have to knock on three times and give a special code word, only to discover once inside that the bathroom attendants are wearing Cartier earrings and the cocktails are forty dollars each.

An outdated but clean plaid sofa and wooden coffee table sit opposite a woodstove, below a row of hanging generic pictures of woodland animals offset by towering mountains and streams. An open door leads to a shadowy bedroom. There's a small dinette table in the kitchen beside half a dozen cabinets, a mini dishwasher, a stainless-steel sink with, apparently, frozen pipes, two brooms leaning against the wall, and a fridge—complete with a magnet featuring an illustrated pointing bear above the words *Kannery National Park Wants You . . . to Visit!* The place smells of a forest worth of pine and frost—neither of which is surprising since I'm boxed in by logs, and the two visible baseboard heaters look to be forty years old.

It also can't be a degree over thirty.

So. This is home.

About as cozy as living in a rest area would be, but not unimprovable.

Suddenly there are a few startling knocks and the faucet gurgles. Zaiah rises, hands on his hips as he watches and waits. So serious and so intent, I feel myself holding my breath alongside him. Moments later, water bursts forth.

We both exhale.

"I'll go work on the bathroom. Can you"—he hesitates—"take a look around? See if there's anything else you need?"

I frown, a sinking suspicion that was not at all what he originally wanted to ask. "What is it you wanted me to do?"

He shakes his head. "Nothing. I thought maybe you could work on getting the fire going, but I'll do it."

Of course.

Because Cat Cranwell is so obviously the girl with no skills who can't do basic adult things like drive in snow and is only out here because her doting uncle indulged in a little nepotism and offered her a way out of the city. He might as well have said, "You just sit there and try to look pretty. I'm sure that's all you can really handle anyway."

I tilt my chin. "I can do it."

"No, it's fine. Just give me a few minutes to get the bathroom faucet going and I'll see to—"

"I can *do it*," I repeat, and move for the stack of wood beside the woodstove. I drop down onto my knees, leaning back on my leather boots as I begin to stack the most promising wood in my arms. Dirt and wood splinters are quick to cover my white coat, but I ignore them as I look around the woodstove. There's fire starter beside it, but I glance around, going for what I know.

Ah.

A newspaper sits on top of the coffee table, and I lean over and snatch it.

Meanwhile, Zaiah stands beside the sink watching me, then rubs his face with his palm. He looks up at the clock and I can practically hear his thoughts. *It's nearing midnight. I'm exhausted. And I don't have the energy for everything that is this girl.*

"Listen, Catherine—"

"Cat," I say, not looking up.

There are several moments of silence, and as I begin tearing up the newspaper, I can feel his eyes on my back as he decides what to say and do next. Clearly my little pushback, however small, was enough to make him give up, because he walks past me through an open doorway and out of view.

By the time he returns, fire is licking the roof of the little wood-stove as I tidy up the area. The woodstove is decently sized for a cabin this small; already the temperature in the room has lifted a few degrees. It won't take long to get the small area up to a manageable level, but still, I'll have to get up at least two or three times in the night to throw on more logs.

All wearying facts given I was up at 4:00 a.m. and am already dead on my feet.

He halts as he enters the living room.

I see it on his face. His expression says it all.

"I didn't know woodstoves were a thing in the city."

Wrought iron poker in hand, I push a fallen log back into the center of the flames, then shut the door. "I had a life before the city."

For several seconds he stands there, watching my eyes, looking like he's trying to choose his next words carefully. It's clear enough that he doesn't want to offend, doesn't want to play any sort of game. That's fair. I don't either. And yet every word out of his mouth—even the unintentional ones, perhaps *particularly* the unintentional ones— rubs me raw.

"Looks like that life served you well."

Like those words.

Those exact, unintentional, and yet completely transparent words.

It's irritating, and not just because I know what he means: Whereas all your life choices for the past thirteen years have been flawed and pointless, thank goodness for the common sense bestowed on you by the life you were born into.

That's just mildly irritating.

What he's really done is worse.

He struck upon a topic far deeper. And managed to praise that which he has no clue of. My past. My parents. The life I escaped.

I place the poker back in its stand and rise. Press my lips together. Smile to dull the sharp edge of my words, to show him I am not aiming my weapon at him, but at what he just said.

"Actually, I wouldn't wish that life upon my biggest enemy."

\\\//

It's one thing to wake up in the morning after thirteen years surrounded by the cacophony of taxi horns, buses, and sirens. It's entirely another sensation to wake up to coffin-level silence because of a bird—just a single, solitary bird—in a world so quiet my eyes snap open like a roman shade at the sound of its *cah!* overhead.

Unsettling.

It's also unsettling to find oneself staring at a wall of logs instead of my penthouse's paper-white walls. But then my memory catches up and the past twenty-four hours—the tumultuous flight, the terrifying drive, the freezing shack of a cabin, and the exhaustion prompting me to drop into the first bed I came upon—all of it comes roaring back to me.

But to roll over and find myself looking at a dark-headed figure standing in the doorway is an entirely new level of scary.

I practically jump out of the sheets, and before I know it I'm sitting upright, holding the patchwork quilt to my nose like a shield.

But instead of reaching for a weapon of choice, the figure in the doorway also jumps, disappearing into the living room.

For several heavy-breathing seconds, I stare at the empty space in the doorway.

She peeks her head back into the room—a little squirrel-like, actually—and slowly, I lower the quilt from my face.

Our eyes lock for several seconds.

She seems to make a decision.

"Oh, hiii," she says overbrightly as she steps into full view, as though she just stumbled upon a friend on her way to being seated at a restaurant. "You're up."

I squint, then blink furiously as my vision is blocked by the wagging black centipede of plastic covering one eye. I reach for yesterday's lashes I neglected to take off. "Hi." I pause. "Who are you?"

The girl looks positively mortified as she watches me peel the lashes off.

"I'm . . . Mina Marsero." The girl lifts her gaze from the lashes in my hand and rushes forward, shaking my free hand. "Assistant junior park ranger, assistant junior wildlife instructor, and assistant junior secretary during lunch hours Monday through Friday."

Sitting upright in bed with one hand holding my wispy lashes, I look down at the other being shaken vigorously by the girl in front of me. There are a lot of assistants and juniors in that title.

Her skin is tan and smooth, the kind makeup markets kill for in their models. Her mahogany eyes are energetic, carrying a doe-eyed innocence bestowed only upon the young. She looks even younger than her age, no doubt, with the two tight braids resting on the shoulders of her ranger uniform and shining metal badge. It reads: *Kannery National Park*. And in the name slot: *Intern*.

"I'm Cat Cranwell. Nice to"—I pause, still not entirely sure what's going on—"meet you."

"Oh, I know."

My shoulders tense, as they have every single day anyone has referenced my current situation. Not that I was so naive that I didn't expect this. It's just . . . having a chance to brush my teeth before having to deal with it would've been nice.

"*Ranger Cranwell's* niece," Mina continues. "We're so excited to finally meet you."

There's a reverence in her voice at Uncle Terry's name. It's clear that, in her world, Terry is king.

"Oh." My shoulders relax. "Right. Yes."

"Not to rush you, but we'd better get a move on if we're going to make it to the staff meeting. I put eggs on the counter and have cold-brew coffee with"—her gaze reaches for the ceiling as she spouts the rest—"three vanilla beans, a tablespoon nutmeg, quarter teaspoon cinnamon, half-cup fat-free vanilla creamer, made up in the fridge."

My brows inch up. I raise a finger. "Um."

"I asked Superintendent Cranwell about you ahead of time," she says in a rush. "He directed me to your Instagram, and so after I downloaded it and created a username"—she pauses bashfully—"I'm @mmrangerproud22310. You may have seen me comment on your posts . . ."

She stops, her dark eyes looking into mine as though waiting for me to jump up and say, *"You're* @mmrangerproud22310? I've been *hoping* to meet you!"

"Ah. Yes. Mmrangerproud22 . . . and the rest." I nod a bit, because this seems the thing to do.

She beams in response. "Yes, well, anyway, I took the liberty of doing a little research. It took me a bit, but on your October fifteenth post three years ago you did say cold coffee with three vanilla beans, a tablespoon nutmeg, quarter teaspoon cinnamon, and half-cup fat-free vanilla creamer was part of your 'go-to' morning routine—"

This really was going a little too fast for me to keep up. "I'm sorry," I say and take a proper look around at my surroundings for the first time. The bedspread I'm holding is patched, covered in a dozen sewn pictures of mountains and creeks and woodland creatures. Where my calves and feet have been warmed at the bottom of the bed is a heavy blanket made of the hide of some animal—bear? bison? To my left is a small wooden dressing table, and on it a number of items. An earring tree holding a collection of wooden hoops and beaded earrings in blue, orange, white, green, and red. A half dozen frames filled with pictures of—

Oh no.

I swivel my head back to the girl. "Am I in your *room?*"

Mina looks down as if she were the one caught sleeping in somebody else's bed. "It's no problem. The couch is surprisingly comfortable. It's a pullout, you know—"

Before she's even finished her sentence, I'm throwing the sheets off me and jumping out. My hands struggle indecisively with the covers, at first trying to make the bed back up and then thinking that, of course, she'd want to strip the sheets and wash them instead.

"I'm so sorry." I pull off the corner of one sheet and move quickly to the bottom of the bed. "It was late and dark last night when I got in. I—I assumed—and here you are making me coffee."

"Well, sure," she says brightly. "That's what roomies are for."

I halt. Stand upright, a mash of sheets in my hands. "Wait. So. This is the right cabin?"

"Of course."

"This," I say, needing the extra clarification, "this is my cabin?"

She nods.

"But it's a one-bedroom."

"Right." Mina's brows crease together, like this is obvious. "Plus a pullout bed."

The pause between us lasts a couple hours. It must, because when I swallow, my throat has gone dry.

"Which is," I begin slowly, "where I will sleep."

"When you're not in mine, evidently." She grins at her own little joke.

So. My cozy little cabin is so "quaint" and "cozy," I'm quite literally sleeping on a couch.

With a puppy-eyed roommate.

And a salary so low I won't be able to afford the gas to get into town for coffee.

And I'm cold.

This time last year I was in Barbados, talking with my financial advisor about whether he thought getting a vacation home there would really be prudent.

"Roomies," I say, suddenly aware that Mina is waiting on me to reply. I look down at the wad of sheets in my hands. "Terrific. Roomies."

CHAPTER 5

The 9-to-5 Life

step inside the primitive log cabin that, aside from the sign describing it as the "office," looks no different than any of the several other log cabin–style buildings I've seen along our walk.

I clasp the thirty-two ounces of cold-brew coffee Mina insisted on pouring into a mason jar. My hand is freezing, begging to be tucked inside the pocket of my heated coat instead of holding the iced beverage. But with Mina smiling at me every five seconds as she glances from the drink to me, watching my progress, I hang tight.

I didn't have the heart to tell her I went vegan two years ago. So instead, I took every moment I could on the short walk through the woods to let out a little onto the snow as I went, sprinkling the path with iced coffee like a grown-up version of Hansel and Gretel.

Thankfully Mina is one of those people who likes to talk a lot, and as expressively as possible. Most of the walk she was so busy throwing her hands around while describing the "thrills" of her job that she didn't have the space to notice.

The weather is just as icicle-cold as it was last night, only now a little golden ball of sunshine shines overhead on the glittering snow.

Everything looks less ominous in the daylight. Even the three Dracula-fang mountains in the distance.

A young ranger, late teens to early twenties, with thin hairs of goateed chin quivering, speaks as I shut the door behind me. "For the hundredth time, that's *not* what happened. I *had to go to the bathroom.*"

A second ranger, far bulkier than the first, laughs. "That's the story you're going to stick with, Kevin. You stepped on that hose and threw two hundred programs on the ground while hightailing it like your clothes were on fire, all because you had to whiz. It had nothing to do with thinking you stepped on a snake."

Quietly, I step away from the door.

The office is everything and also nothing like what I expected. A bear rug lies on the floor, and dull, standard-issue waiting chairs sit in the corner. Official government posters hang on the walls, reminding people of commonsense rules: Do Not Feed the Bears and Leave No Trace. The air smells of microwaved ramen noodles, coffee, and like everything else here, wood.

All of this I expected, down to the little empty corner desk where I, presumably, will take up residence. Above it, an ancient-looking saddle, dark as espresso beans, hangs on the wall.

The younger ranger pushes up his bony shoulders. "I told you, Jax. *No.*"

It's only now that I realize something is slithering slowly on the bulkier ranger's open hand.

"Because that would be really, really stupid, wouldn't it?" Jax moves the small, vibrantly colored red, yellow, and black snake away as it tries to sneak its head inside his sleeve. "Given all the snakes are hiberating—"

"Brumating, you imbecile," Kevin interjects.

"—and you won't find a snake up and at it for a thousand miles. Well, except for Daisy." He moves the snake into the hand closer to Kevin, who takes three steps back.

"Stop it."

"C'mon, Intern Lilly. This is part of your job. You'll never make it to the big leagues with that attitude."

"Having a healthy respect for wildlife *is* my job." He takes another step back. "There is nothing in my job description that says I have to touch them."

"They aren't venomous and don't bite."

Kevin's frown deepens. "*Of course* they bite. The *Lampropeltis gentilis* species *rarely* bite. That doesn't mean they can't. And given you keep it up during the day, agitating its crepuscular and nocturnal habits, I wouldn't be surprised if it *does* get you, which you'd rightfully deserve." The snake's tail slowly lifts, and Kevin's eyes widen as he shakes a finger at it. "*Look at his tail. He's vibrating it! Now you've done it!*"

Jax lifts the snake to his face, looking at it eye to eye. "*Kevin. Six-year-old girls handle Daisy*—"

"Unlike you, I don't aspire to the lifestyle decisions of six-year-old girls—"

An elderly woman raps on her receptionist desk with a purple cane. "Boys, stop fighting before you scare off our company." She adjusts a tilted photo frame. "And get off my desk."

Jax, who to this point had been sitting on the corner of it, is pushed to standing by the butt of the cane. He and his coworker turn to see who's at the door.

Immediately the skinny, skittish ranger sees Mina and jolts upright as if his hand were caught in a candy jar. As for the guy with the snake . . . well . . .

"Well, hello there." His voice and the way he slides my way hit somewhere between used-car salesman and playboy. Or both.

His hair is military styled, short, black as the stripe on the snake's back. He's twice the size of his shorter, redheaded companion, but the color of their brown eyes and the hook of their noses are too similar to be coincidence.

Brothers. No question.

And I've got at least a decade on them both.

"Ranger Jax," he says, putting out a hand.

"Assistant," his brother mutters behind him.

A vein in Jax's neck pulses as he hears the word over his shoulder, but he ignores Kevin. "So. Have you by chance ever held one of the most beautiful, docile creatures of our national park? This is our milk snake, Daisy." He holds the small, coiled snake out to me. "Ah," he says, as the snake stretches out toward me. "She's taken a liking to you."

Apparently, he uses the snake for pickup lines as well.

"Mmm. Tempting," I say, making no movement.

"Isn't she?" And while his words mean the snake, his mischievous tone and eyes say otherwise.

I take a rather large step backward to make my position clear on using snakes to flirt or, you know, just flirting with this guy in general.

A door swings open.

"Catherine." Uncle Terry steps out from an office doorway. He's wearing the same olive-green uniform he always does. His bushy brows and mustache have somehow, beyond what would have seemed possible, gotten bushier over the last few months. And he's got a wipe in one hand and a rifle in the other.

So in Montana we clean guns at work.

Sure. Sure.

"I trust you had a good night's sleep."

"Terrific," I lie, walking past Jax (whose expression has coiled up like the snake in his hand) and going for Uncle Terry's free side for a hug.

Just then, Zaiah steps out of the door behind him.

"And Zaiah took good care of you." It's not quite a question, not quite a statement.

My smile remains plastered on my face as I release myself from his squeeze and look resolutely anywhere but at Zaiah. There's very little I'd prefer to remember about the chaotic day yesterday, particularly every embarrassing incident involving him. Even my own edgy tone at the end of the night I regret. "Yes. Yes, he did."

"Excellent." He nods.

Uncle Terry passes off the rifle to Zaiah and swivels me around to face the group. "Everyone, this is my niece, Catherine. She'll be doing the social media for Kannery National Park for the foreseeable future."

Except for Mina, who all but applauds, there's a mildly welcoming round of pleasantries.

I peek from the corner of my eye and notice Zaiah's stoic face.

"Peggy, did her name badge come in yet?"

Peggy sets down the cane she'd been using to nudge the curious snake's face in her direction. Pushes her glasses up her nose. Opens a drawer.

As she fishes around, I take her in.

She's an interesting combination of grandmother and fifteen-year-old-wrapped-in-a-vintage-coating. For one thing, she's wearing a graphic T-shirt of some sort beneath a red cardigan covered in beady-eyed cardinals. Her wispy white hair is drawn up in a clip, but her ears are adorned with beaded black, red, and orange hoop earrings so large they clatter on her shoulders. Her cane is an iridescent purple.

After some fishing, she sets a metal badge on the desk. "Came in on Tuesday."

Uncle Terry hands it to me.

I take it, seeing my full name (of course, because Uncle Terry seems to be allergic to my nickname) and the words beneath: *Senior Media Strategist and Social Coordinator.*

I press my lips together to keep from smiling at my uncle's gesture—particularly when everyone else's labels seem intended to keep them in their place. Even Peggy's badge says, *Secretary—Part Time.*

It seems he wants to make sure I feel as important as possible, even when there is no one to be senior over. I would bet money he spent more time than was prudent trying to figure out how to level up the job title of *Will Start an Instagram Account for Us.*

He looks at me with quiet eagerness.

"Wow." I take the badge and pin it on my coat. "This is lovely."

"And here is your desk." He moves a hand toward the desk in the corner. I look at the metal folding chair and ancient wooden desk, trying hard to think of something complimentary to say. "And right next to the heater too." I look at the baseboard heater, because really, heat seems to be the most important commodity around here.

"Yes!" he exclaims. "Moved the printer area for it. We've been having some issues with the heaters the past few days."

Peggy coughs.

"Months," Uncle Terry amends.

Peggy coughs again and Terry shoots her an annoyed look.

"Okay, years. Figured you of all people weren't used to this cold."

My grin stiffens. I mean, it's true, the whole place can't be warmer than sixty degrees with these ancient baseboard heaters trying to keep up, and equally ancient single-pane windows trying their hardest to keep the frost out, but still.

I can be tough.

I am *not* a delicate flower here.

Nobody needs to stare at me given recent circumstances, or go out of their way for me, or heaven forbid, pity me.

"Oh, it feels rather cozy to me." The reactionary words pop out of my mouth before I have time to stop them. Several brows rise as if to say, *Really?*

Zaiah's eyes, I can't help noticing, squint slightly like he knows he caught me in a lie.

Great. The only thing worse than admitting you set the thermostat to seventy-three degrees in your penthouse in winter is lying and saying you like freezing to the point of hypothermia within ten minutes.

I fumble to add, "It's just all so beautiful. The snow, I mean."

Several expressions ease.

"Yes, it is," Uncle Terry says proudly, giving my arm an extra squeeze. "Now that's the Cranwell spirit."

Suddenly, the phone rings behind him.

He looks back toward it, then to the group. "I'll need someone to give Catherine a tour around the park. Show her everything. From the reptile lounge to the picnic areas. Anything so she can get a jump on revamping our accounts."

"Now hang on." Kevin frowns. "What's wrong with our accounts? I don't see anything wrong with our accounts. They're just like the Glacier Boys'."

"They are *not* just like the Glacier Boys'," Mina says.

Kevin throws out a hand. "Okay, *fine*. They *are* different. They're fun *and* educational."

"*Kevin*." Jax groans and throws his head backward as if this is a daily argument. "Writing a series titled 'You Ask, We Answer: At exactly what angle do umbels of allium cernuum face downward?' is not fun. Nobody asks that, Kevin. *Nobody asks*."

"Some people don't *have* lakes full of rainbow rocks in their park to throw up on their feed every day," Kevin says. "Some people can't just post the same image of a bald eagle flying over Lake McDonald and get a gold star." Under his breath he adds, "Lazy bums."

Wow.

I don't know who the Glacier Boys are, but the national park competition is real.

"And that's precisely why Catherine will be handling *all* forms of social media from here on out," Terry says, redirecting the conversation. "This is her expertise. This is what our park sorely needs."

Kevin's gaze turns to me. He looks me up and down as if to say, "Really? Does she even know the life span of a bighorn sheep?"

I push a strand of would-be-better-if-I-hadn't-blown-a-circuit-this-morning curls behind my ear.

I can be outdoorsy.

I once made a New Year's resolution to walk instead of hail a cab every chance I could through winter—despite the elements. And I would've kept it up, too, had the smog and humidity not partnered up in attempts to kill my hair. (Which sounds ridiculous, I know, but when you are trying to do a shoot and Prada doesn't exactly want you associating their heels with your jungle hair . . .)

I also took a bird-calling class once as an *elective,* by *choice.*

Yes, it was technically in elementary school after-school care.

And yes, it was technically because Sophie Hunter was taking it, and she was the coolest girl in fourth grade due in large part to her plethora of Lisa Frank gel pens. But still.

I am quite good at discerning between the calls of a mockingbird and a cardinal.

Probably.

Almost definitely.

At any rate, Kevin's skepticism and Uncle Terry's unwavering confidence make me determined to do my best. He may not be paying me much (and that's really underplaying it), but the fact that he's acting like he wants me here—needs me here, even—makes me feel important.

And these days, I need that.

A part of me needs to feel like I have a place, a purpose.

And frankly, Kannery National Park is the only place I actually feel that.

"What about Cades Peak?" Jax says. "If she's going to be showing off anything, it should start there, right?"

For the first time Uncle Terry hesitates as he eyes me. He shakes his head. "Too cold for that. Just around here is good for now—"

"I'm up for going," I interject. "I'm happy to go anywhere." I look from Jax to my uncle. "And if it's somewhere important . . ."

"Better not this time. Let's just wait until it warms up."

I frown. "And when, exactly, is that?"

Silence.

I have a feeling I know the answer, and the answer is two to three months from now.

"Maybe when you get on something heavy duty," Terry says. "That jacket is awfully thin."

"This?" I look down at my white coat. "Oh no. This is really warm. It's battery-operated to stay at 98.5 degrees." I flip my coat pocket inside out and show him the button.

This seems to pique everybody's interest, because a moment later, they're shuffling forward to get a better view.

"Huh," Uncle Terry grunts, although I can still hear a little dubiousness in his voice. "Well, isn't that clever."

"Our aunt and uncle used to do the same thing with a heat lamp on their chickens," Kevin chimes in. "Worked every night until a blizzard knocked the power out. The chickens weren't acclimated and froze to death."

"Well, Catherine's not a chicken," Uncle Terry says, his bushy brows forming a straighter-than-usual unibrow at Kevin. He shifts to me. "Sounds like a plan, Catherine. You'll start by heading up to our jewel, Cades Peak. Who'll take her?"

The way he looks at the group, I feel a bit like I'm up for auction.

"Oh! I will!" Mina jumps on her toes, but Terry quickly dismisses her.

"You're working the visitor center for guests."

Guests? What guests?

"I don't mind taking her." Half of Jax's lips curl up in a smile.

Uncle Terry frowns. "Yeah, well, I do. Put the snake away and get back to trash duty."

I look around the room. It's down to Peggy—the elderly eccentric with painted-on eyebrows—and Kevin, who's refusing to make eye contact after the words "Cades Peak."

And, of course, Zaiah.

Uncle Terry turns to him. "You wouldn't mind giving Catherine a look around, would you?"

No, no.

Given we seem to be incapable of normal interactions, I'll go with the guy with the snake.

Zaiah's eyes flicker to me, then away. "I would, but I thought I was going to speak at the meeting."

Uncle Terry waves that away. "Miss the meeting. This is more important."

Zaiah's frown deepens. "On the contrary, I can't imagine anything more important."

Silence lingers between them for several long seconds.

Evidently, however, Uncle Terry isn't going to yield. "I'll give your speech."

Zaiah looks like he's about to interject when Terry presses on. "You show her everything. If she's going to get us on the map, she'll need to see it all."

Uncle Terry gives me a proud smile that's far too unearned and turns toward his office door.

So. The question is settled.

It's just me and him. Again.

Zaiah plasters on something that's a little less like a frown. Apparently it's the best he can do.

I do likewise.

"Okay then," he says. "Follow me."

CHAPTER 6

Cades Peak

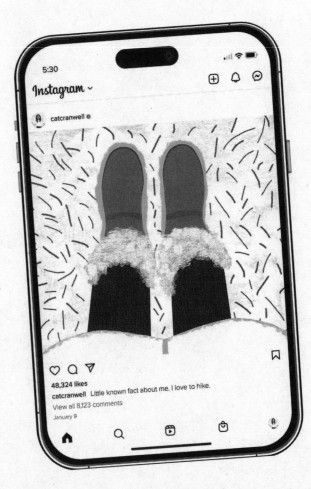

*W*hat is it with you all and your low prioritization of *body heat?*" I managed to keep my jaw shut when Zaiah marched right past the row of waiting vehicles outside the office when we left.

I stayed quiet when he started hiking twice as fast as I could through thigh-high snow.

I kept my mouth shut as we traipsed through the winter wonderland and he took a sudden turn uphill.

I bit my lip when it was only a matter of minutes before I was panting and then had to put forth all my energy into hiding the fact I was panting.

And snow fell in through the top of my boots, freezing my calves.

And my soaking-wet ankles went numb.

But finally, twenty minutes later and still no building, car, person, or living thing in sight—I snap.

I stop. Or at least, I am aware I've stopped because the trees have stopped moving. My legs long ago became two stumps.

My hands fly up. "Do you just hate me? Are you taking me out into the woods to kill me?"

Zaiah's boots pause at my words.

He turns and looks at me as though noticing me for the first time.

Both brows raise in puzzlement.

"I thought New Yorkers liked to walk. I thought that was your thing."

"Not when it's ten degrees and you've lost all feeling in your legs. Not then!"

At this his gaze drifts down to my legs—which beneath my

knee-length coat are covered by a pair of cable-knitted black tights and fur-lined tan boots. The fur is matted and jutting out in all directions with little frozen icicle spikes. It isn't my fault my feet are numb either. I learned my lesson the previous day and went for the warmest boots I could find. I think it's perfectly understandable I hadn't anticipated having to wade through snow up a mountain.

For the first time, Zaiah seems to notice this. His expression shifts into sympathy. Even a bit of embarrassment. "You said you liked the weather. You said you liked all the snow."

"That doesn't mean I wanted to take a fifteen-mile *bath* in it."

He glances around at the miles of trees around us. Puts his hands on his hips.

Stares at me.

My forehead wrinkles. *What?*

Starting at my boots, his eyes move up my body. But it's nothing romantic. No.

What he's doing is looking me over as though I'm a child who said I'm tired of walking (which, fine, I did say that), but we're in the middle of nowhere without a stroller and now he, the parent, has to decide if he'll just have to throw me over his shoulder and carry me.

He sighs. Takes a step toward me.

Hang on now.

I raise my hands. "I'm not saying I *give up.* I just . . . I just want to know how much longer."

Wow. I hear my own words. I've actually done the "Are we there yet?" thing kids do to their parents on a road trip.

He takes another step toward me.

My hands rise higher. He can't be serious. He can't really be about to haul me up like a toddler.

Absolutely not.

I don't care if I lose my legs to hypothermia, there is absolutely *no way* I'm going to be carried around on my first day of work.

I'd die of humiliation right here.

I open my mouth, about to tell him to "halt right there," when he stops just before me. Drops down on one knee.

What the—?

He pulls off one of his thick gloves, and before I know it, he's swiping the snow off the cuff of my boots. Then, the instant heat blooms in my cheeks, I feel him reaching one hand in my boot, his warm fingers against my pink, frozen-to-the-touch ankles. He scoops out slush from my calf and tosses it into the snow.

No, this is worse. Just throw me over your shoulder.

"I can do that. You don't need to do that," I begin faintly.

He ignores me. "We're almost there. Do you think you can make it a few more minutes?"

"Yes. Of course."

At this point I'd walk a hundred miles in the snow without complaining.

"You're underdressed for weather like this." He pulls more slush from my soaked boots.

I stand there, frozen to the spot—both literally and figuratively—arms dangling uselessly at my sides. "I thought I was working in the *office*. Mina said we were going to the *office*."

All the slush now gone, he puts his hand on the tights over my ankle. Squeezes. Heat radiates from his hand to my skin. His breath plumes in the air as he exhales. Waiting.

I both hate this moment and can't bring myself to speak and release myself from it.

Silently, he moves on to the next boot. Clears the slush and snow away. Warms me. "What happened to all your fancy gadget clothing?"

I purse my lips. He's irritating, despite how much I welcome his warmth. "I don't own battery-operated boots," I reply, as though the idea is ridiculous. "I'm not a robot."

"Just battery-operated coats then."

I turn my head to the right and stare resolutely at the bark of a tall, leafless tree. His hand moves to the other side of my ankle, and my ankle begins to warm as his hand cools.

It's a terrible moment, both loving and hating something so much simultaneously.

I give up trying to speak. Decide, instead, to file this away as another horribly embarrassing moment with Zaiah Smith, Week 1, I fully intend to pretend never happened.

As he stands at last, his knees are wet.

He doesn't act like he notices. Who knows, maybe he really doesn't. Maybe he's spent his whole life out here and his body feels the same way mine does on a spring day walking from West 81st Street to Amsterdam Avenue. It's just one breezy kind of day. I wouldn't be surprised. Even the ice crystals glittering on his beard look warm. Even the rosy hue on his cheeks looks warmed by the sunshine instead of windchill.

But as my eyes drift upward, they catch his gaze as he watches me. His irises, green as the evergreens around us, look not so unsympathetic and emotionless as his words. They're full. Thoughtful. Concerned. Even I can see in them as clearly as if he spoke the words aloud: "Sorry. I didn't pay attention. I didn't realize."

I stiffen.

So. He's one of those good ol' country boys. The kind who thinks it's his responsibility to make sure the lady is taken care of.

I wasn't aware they still existed.

In fact, I'm not sure if I should be offended.

If this were Park Avenue, the rule of thumb was to hail your own cab and leave him standing in a puddle of chosen words and public humiliation.

You need your girlfriends.

You need your coffee-shop barista who knows exactly what you drink.

But you certainly don't need a man.

A twig snaps in the distance, and I turn my head toward the sound. Nothing but a whip of cold wind burning my cheeks replies.

But this isn't Park Avenue, is it? This is the middle of nowhere, Montana, and if Zaiah for any reason left me here alone, I am fairly certain—no, entirely certain—I'd be a Popsicle in minutes.

I allow myself a small smile—small enough to relay the message back, and no bigger: *It's fine. Really. Let's just move on.*

Another thing I'd very much like to pretend never happened.

Ten more minutes of thigh-burning and feet-freezing hiking and we reach an opening between trees. A small wooden sign, half hidden by snow, says: *–des Peak.*

Here at last.

"I'll get a fire going." Zaiah strides through the opening between the trees, and I see it.

My breath catches in my throat.

Just beyond a row of small cabins is a cliff, and off that cliff is a view like I've never seen before. A winding river far below snakes toward the cluster of mountains I saw from a distance yesterday, but here they look even more staggering. Gargantuan. I feel like I'm at the end of the earth. Or perhaps in a Tolkien movie. Like at any moment I'll see a wizard breaking through the clouds, riding on the wings of a giant eagle.

"Unbelievable," I breathe.

I slip my phone out of my pocket and begin alternating between pictures and video. More for research for myself at this stage, to remember what I'm looking at when brainstorming a posting plan. Because I will be back, without question, for this million-dollar—no, billion-dollar— view. As I snap, something occurs to me, and as I turn in a semicircle searching for an answer, I come up short. "Where's the road?"

The break between the trees is only a couple feet apart. There's no route, as far as I can tell, wide enough for vehicles of any kind.

Zaiah doesn't answer. I turn back around and see he's already gone.

I move toward the cabins, and as I step onto the small porch of the first, Zaiah comes out, a bundle of wood in his hands.

"C'mon," he says gruffly, as though I should've been following him all along.

I follow him inside the first of the ten or so cabins, and the second I get inside and get a full breath, I cough. I can't help it. It's like my lungs are desperate to expel the moth-ridden conditions around me.

I cough again, almost certain I'm breathing the dust of moth skeletons. How is it possible that this is *worse* than the cabin I'm staying in? There is no heat, or heater for that matter, in sight. Zaiah has taken off his gloves and squats at the hearth, working to make a fire in a hole in the wall that looks like a blackened pit of ash. There is nothing in the single room of the cabin except two wooden slats in the corner, which, I presume, are supposed to be some sort of bunk bed. One tiny window faces the front of the area, with old chicken wire covering the window. No kitchen or bathroom in sight.

Just . . . a room.

"*This* is the jewel of Kannery Park?" I say, dumbfounded.

He hunches over as he arranges wood inside the small, vacant fireplace. "Not every place has to be covered in marble."

I frown at the memory of the way he looked around my apartment the first time he came. He had stared at the marble floors, counters, and walls of my kitchen as though I had willingly chosen to recreate a psych ward. As though he wanted to ask if I was allergic to a little color.

I purse my lips, then frown at another glaring thought. How *on earth* am I supposed to attract people to Kannery National Park when *this* is their golden goose? *This?*

It's impossible.

I might as well be creating a resort account for a cemetery.

The task seems insurmountable, but I lift my phone and begin taking pictures.

Dark floor made of ancient (and not ancient in a good way) wood. *Snap.*

Log cabin walls that look a hundred years old. *Snap.*

Creepy window trying to lock you in via chicken wire. *Snap.*

I take a step toward the bunk bed frames, camera raised, and halt. *Ohhh no. No thank you.*

Immediately, I step back.

I must've made my disgust audible, because Zaiah shifts his weight on his heels. Turns to look at whatever caused me to fumble backward. When he doesn't see anything, he stands. Moves to the bed frames.

"Ah," he says, when at last his eyes catch on it. He steps up to it and, to my horror, picks up the perfectly intact skin of a four-foot-long snake. The snakeskin dangles all the way down to the floor.

Then, to even fresher horror, he grins with absolute delight. Like he was just walking along on his merry way and stumbled into the best pop-up shop of his life. He unzips his canvas backpack and carefully winds the skin inside.

He sees my expression and pauses. "Do you want to see?"

If it was possible to recoil deeper into the wall, I would.

One side of his mouth tilts into a smile. "There's nothing to be afraid of with a skin. What you should be afraid of is that where there is a snakeskin, there is quite possibly the snake." He points to the wall behind me. "And just my opinion, but I probably wouldn't stick too close to dark corners if you care."

It doesn't help that just at that moment something grazes my leg. And yes, more than likely it was just some wood sticking out of the wall, but I wasn't about to take the chance.

I yelp and leap toward him. "I thought they hibernated," I say breathlessly, all but huddled at his feet.

Zaiah chuckles, a warm, breathy chuckle as he finishes zipping up the backpack and stands. I realize I'm standing far too close for medium-level acquaintances but can't budge.

"Brumate, and yes. They bunker down during the coldest months. Slow, but not sleeping. A lot of times that means finding their way into cabins. Mice follow the food. Snakes follow the mice. Especially the ones with kitchens."

"As in ours?" I say through a sharp intake of breath. That's it. I'm never going to sleep again. "Those snakes do that in ours? And mice? And *snakes*?" I circle back to the most important point. "In ours?"

"Well, not typically a venomous one like what we've got here." He taps the backpack on the floor with his boot. "Usually it's just a bull snake or a gopher. But a prairie rattlesnake like this one? This is the biggest skin I've seen. Kevin's going to be thrilled." He looks down. "How are your feet?"

It's hard to register his question, as the words keep replaying in my mind.

Venomous snakes.

Venomous snakes that are four feet long.

Venomous snakes that like to worm their way into my cabin while I sleep.

What did he say?

Right.

My boots. I look down. I momentarily forgot how numb I am. "Cold."

For the next twenty minutes Zaiah stokes the wet firewood until it crackles, and all the while I stand behind him, rooted to the spot. I'm not sitting in this room. In fact, I'm not going to sit in any building in Montana ever again.

Eventually, Zaiah turns to me as though he can hear my thoughts. As if I might as well have declared aloud, "I was absolutely unaware of this snake situation, and from here on out, I'm not touching anything."

There's a flicker of a smile beneath the beard.

"Prairie rattlers don't bother you unless you provoke them. So unless your name is Jax Lilly, you have nothing to worry about. Or, of course, unless they seek you out for body heat in the middle of the night."

I think I just vomited a little in my throat.

With *great* effort I clear it and force myself to change the topic.

"So what's the history with these cabins?" I lift my camera phone back up to resume picture taking. The angle is crap—I'm shooting too far away from the beds for anything decent—but there's no way I'll let myself be more than five inches away from Zaiah and his fire. "And where is the road?"

"There is no road. Cades Peak was built in 1946. They logged the trees on-site for building. Hikers start at the base of the mountain. It's Cades Peak Trail, 14.2 miles to this top. Where we started from the office was the shortcut. Just a little over two miles."

Two? It felt like twenty.

No road.

No trucks. So he wasn't intentionally trying to make my life miserable after all.

"So people hike up here? To spend the night?" I couldn't help it. Maybe it's the smell of dark, rotting wood, or the chicken wire over the window making the place feel like a prison, or, who can forget, the killer rattler likely coiled up somewhere in this room, but there's a tiny bit of a "But why?" in my tone.

Ripples form on Zaiah's forehead. He turns back toward the fire and throws a log in. A moment later he lifts his gaze to a crude wooden plaque above the door, featuring the words:

There is a pleasure in the pathless woods.

There is a rapture on the lonely shore,
There is society, where none intrudes,
By the deep sea, and music in its roar:
I love not man the less, but Nature more . . .
—LORD BYRON, 1788–1824

He turns back to the fire. "If you didn't understand why when you got up here, you never will."

The view. Of course he means the view.

"The view is breathtaking. I got that," I retort, cinching up my pride. "But if you're going to go to the trouble of making a cabin at all, I just don't understand what's so terrible about the idea of having a more"—I wave my hand around, searching for proper words to describe all this—"*livable* space while you're enjoying it. Is it so wrong to, for example, have a decent window?"

He frowns at me, as though I just dissed his mother. "Not everybody wants an Instagram-worthy stay. Sometimes that's *the point*."

All this feeling over a window.

A chicken-wired window.

But there it is again. Him getting his feathers ruffled over something more. Over me and my lifestyle and everything, to him, I am.

"Oh fine." I throw my hands up. "I get it. People feel like they can pat themselves on the back for living like they're homeless on purpose one weekend during vacation. There's something more validating about the experience if they're roughing it and not having cell service while doing it. But if that's the case, why have these cabins at all? Clearly you're winning more at life if you sleep in a tent—no, in a hammock—no, wait, on the ground. On the ground with nothing but some nice dry leaves to warm you. That's what *real* people do, isn't it? Not spending their lives getting free crap for a bunch of pictures?"

For the second time today, he looks at me with surprise.

And at a loss.

"The fire's ready. Why don't you take your boots off and get them dried up before we head down."

But I'm moving toward the door. My halfway-thawed toes cry out in protest, but my pride won't let me stop. "I have what I need here. I'll get a few shots of the other cabins and wait outside."

"Cat, no—"

"It's fine," I say firmly, and shut the door before I can hear, or say, another word.

CHAPTER 7

The Trash Cans

My toes didn't fall off.

It was touch and go there for a few hours while I sat on the edge of the yellowed tub of the little bathroom with my feet in hot water, Mina sitting beside me all the while (also with her feet in the water) working on elaborately woven roomie bracelets.

This was followed by an evening sitting upright on the pullout bed, vigilantly scanning the nooks and crannies for any snakes burrowing in through the walls. Cradling my phone against my shoulder as Serena lectured me on giving Zaiah "a hard time."

That's the thing about Serena. She prides herself on being an impeccable judge of character, and once she makes a judgment about someone, they hold that title for life.

To be fair, she hated Bobby. And was right.

Wasn't thrilled with my manager. And was right.

And absolutely detested Petra—my singer-songwriter ex whom absolutely *everyone* loved, down to the Queen of England herself. And sure enough, as we discovered when pictures surfaced of him with an entire alter-ego *life* in some off-the-grid community (complete with spare wife and two kids), she was right then too.

Which is why it was quite unfortunate that she met Zaiah on that night of my birthday launch party. And deeper into the land of unfortunate affairs, he was the only one to be seen eating her beloved grandmother's recipe of sauerkraut soup. Which she noticed.

"So he was trying to save your skin—your, I might add, income-serving skin that would do better without a bear slash across your face. Although . . . you probably could do something with that. It would really drum up the general public's sympathy for you . . ."

I jerk my legs out from under the blanket, where I can't stop imagining a curled-up snake lying at my feet. "Serena. I'm not going to play with bears in hopes of a sympathy vote."

"I'm just saying," she says, a shrug in her voice, "it's worked pretty well for that guy with the pencil incident."

"No."

"Fine. Anyway, from what I'm gathering here, you returned the favor of Zaiah helping you out, twice, by snapping at him on a mountaintop. Clever. You got a real instinct for survival."

I frown at a blob at the bottom of the bed and tear the sheet off for the third time, just to check.

Nothing.

"I don't know what it is with him," I say, drawing the sheets up again. "He just grates on me. I feel like he's a walking sign of judgment."

"*He* is?" Serena says incredulously. "Honey, you've got a whole country against you. They did a whole *SNL skit* about you last weekend, but you've got a problem with the guy picking you up from airports and saving you from losing your toes to hypothermia?"

I frown. "I didn't know about the skit."

"It was pretty funny, actually. We'll watch it when this is all over. You're gonna love it."

I let ten full seconds pass in silence.

There's a long sigh on the other end. "Fine. What did he say that was so awful? Dazzle me with his insolence."

"It's not so much what was said—"

"Give me direct quotes here."

"He accused me of not appreciating nature. He thinks I'm too shallow to do anything besides be glued to my phone all day taking selfies."

I'm halfway through angling the camera on my phone for a shot of my manicured toes beside the glow of the woodstove, when I hear myself and stop. I close the camera app.

"Did he actually say that?"

"He implied it. Heavily . . . *And*," I add, "he wishes I wasn't doing this job for the park."

"Did he actually say that too?"

"Not directly, but when my uncle announced what I would be doing to everyone, he didn't smile." I pause. "And I know that sounds a little ridiculous, but it was a moment to smile."

For a long moment, there's silence.

The room is quiet, but for the *ping-ping-ping* of the sewing machine behind Mina's closed door.

"Cat."

Her voice is motherly. Motherly enough I'm tempted to grind my teeth. Here we go.

"This isn't about Ezekiel—"

"Zaiah," I correct.

"It's about you. This happens every single time you find yourself in a room with someone who isn't tripping over themselves with excitement to meet you."

My shoulders hitch up as I growl, "It absolutely *does not*."

"I'm not saying you're narcissistic—frankly, if you were, that'd be easier to deal with. No, what I think—you wanna hear what I think?"

"No."

"What I think is that you're just absurdly, like next-level ridiculous, insecure about yourself. Honestly, you'd think after thirteen years of this you would've gotten over this terrible thing of pretending you don't do what you do for a living so everybody likes you. You want to be the most successful influencer in the world but also have absolutely nothing to do with it the second you're around a negative person."

"So you agree!" I exclaim. "You agree he's a negative person."

"I agree he is probably honest. And frankly, I think you should find that refreshing given how many crap friends we've seen flake out the past few months. An honest person who seems to at least *decently* like you is worth a hundred of those idiots." She pauses. "I'm sorry. But it's true."

I know it is. Painful as it is, she's right.

"Anyway," she continues, "my advice is the same as the advice you stoutly ignored here. Keep being you. You're a good person, Cat. Eventually he'll see that, too, if he's worth his salt."

"And if he's not?"

"He ate the sauerkraut soup. He is." Serena gives a long sigh. "Anyway, just something to think about while you're alone in the middle of the night warding off snakes."

I laugh. "You are both the worst and best friend on earth. You know that?"

"So I've been told. Now on to the most important subject of the evening. Did this whole blizzard hike do anything to your toes?"

I frown. Wiggle my toes on impulse. "What do you mean? Are you asking if I lost a toe? Yes, Serena. Thank heavens, only two."

"Terrific. I have a potential brand deal with Soren boots I'm working on. I ran into Claire Devont at Sabrina's gallery opening on Tuesday, and she said she was talking with Bryant Jennings at brunch the other day, who said that his contact at Global Media had talked about you and"—she paused—"the situation, and she said she actually felt bad for you and thought you were getting a bad rap. You remember Jules Lavender?"

"Maybe. Is she—"

"Anyway, so I got her info and jumped on the phone with her—"

My back shoots up. "You did *what*?"

"To see if she would be interested in working in some brand deals. And I showed her your new lifestyle shift—"

"Serena—"

"—and how you're going with a more rustic, down-to-earth vibe right now—"

"Serena—"

"—and she actually said that would be a perfect fit for a couple of brands she's working with right now."

"*Serena!*"

"And I'm battling it out with her—you wouldn't believe how much she's trying to take advantage of you, given"—she clears her throat—"the situation. But I think we really can secure some great spots for you coming up. I'm surprised, frankly. It's almost like we may have a way in right now precisely *because* of the situation. All these new brands may be opening up because they finally have a shot with you being in a lower bracket." She pauses. "Temporarily."

I jump up to standing. "I'm not sure I want to do *anything* right now—"

"Oh, right. You'd rather pay the lawyer with your ranger salary." She laughs. "Sure."

"I'm *serious*. My account's shot right now. I have no clue how anyone would react to me advertising boots or anything else, for that matter. And I can't risk losing Global Media's trust because I botch it up for the sake of twenty dollars."

"Twenty *thousand* dollars," Serena counters. "And consider it this way. You let them risk it with you, and you can pay to get that crappy heater fixed."

I glance over to the heater. It would be nice to be warm at least *some* of the time. "They'd really do twenty?"

"Honey, all eyes are on you right now. And that's not exactly considered a bad thing. The way Jules talks about it, if you went to jail right now for murder, she'd send matching boots for the orange jumpsuit."

I had to grant it was food for thought, and as I got off the phone and bundled more wood into the fire, the idea grew more enticing by the moment.

"Hey, roomie! Come in here!"

I open Mina's door. Her uniform and hat hang on the closet door behind her, freshly pressed (as it turns out she does this every evening in preparation for the following day), and from her perch beside the sewing machine, she holds up what appears to be a tube top for a newborn.

"What do you think?"

It's some sort of elongated mix of red, orange, and black fabrics sewn together. On the front is the figure of a bear.

A rather impressive-looking bear.

I take a step closer.

I'm not sure what the whole thing is, exactly, but the design itself is impeccable. At least a hundred different shades and patterns of fabrics are sewn together, tiny eighth-of-an-inch fabric here and triangles there that, when put together, form the most colorful scene I've ever seen of a bear reaching its arms up to the sky.

Like that mural I saw in a subway hallway once where hundreds of tiny individual headshots came together to form a single, enormous picture of the skyline with the word *Unity*.

This was like that. Only, even more impressive.

"It's . . . incredible." Still, I have yet to figure out what exactly it *is*.

Hastily, she picks up a mason jar and slides the piece over it. "A cozy for your cozy coffee!" she declares with pride.

"Ah!" I take it in my hands. "So it is!"

"I thought you'd like it for taking your cold brew to work."

"For me? That's so thoughtful." I turn it around, seeing another design of an arrow on the back. "This is really stunning, Mina. Like, you could sell these."

She shrugs. "I sold out last year at Powwow. I've thought about setting up at winter festival too—Kevin's mom sells antique spoon wind chimes—but I don't know about going into all that."

Maybe it's because I just got off the phone with Serena talking business, or the fact that the walls in the office are impressively thin and I discovered just how tight of a shoestring budget Uncle Terry, and consequently everyone, is on, but the wheels in my head start turning.

"Winter festival? Mina, you could do a lot better these days than standing at some booth pitching to one customer at a time. I'm talking widespread. With a little bit of branding, I think you could get a nice little business going on Etsy. People do it all the time. Call it Cozy Cans or something. I'm sure it'd do well."

"You really like it?"

"Like it?" I press it to my chest. "It's quite literally the most beautiful piece of artwork I've seen in my life. I mean that. You are really talented."

Mina's eyes do that thing they do when she's really adorably happy.

And then, just as suddenly, they give off a mischievous twinkle.

"Then maybe I'll just have to hire *you* to advertise." Mina stands up with all the enthusiasm of a nineteen-year-old armed with a fresh business plan.

I tilt my head. "What was that about advertising?"

"Well . . . the walls are thin. I . . . sort of heard everything."

Everything?

"You know." She looks at me a bit sheepishly. "What you charge for posts. The twenty dollars."

Twenty dollars?

"That'd be the cost of probably three of these beauties, but I couldn't go into this without supporting my roomie and *her* business too." She slips her arm through my elbow. "Roomies supporting roomies. Hey. I'll have to sew that on your next Cozy Cup."

Her glee is positively contagious. I dazedly follow her as we move into the living room and set up for the romcom of the night.

Twenty dollars for a post.

I smile every time the thought flitters in and out throughout the movie.

So sweet.

So utterly oblivious to both the perks and the pitfalls of the business.

And so sweet.

\| /

You look like u r feeling down. Pls take care of yourself. We love you!!!

I sit at my desk and stare at the post on my laptop.

Uncle Terry has been steady in his office all day. He keeps a surprising amount of meetings going, and the second he's off, his face droops and he spends the next fifteen minutes staring at spreadsheets deep in thought.

Across the room Peggy alternates between typing madly whenever Uncle Terry enters the room and playing Candy Crush on her phone.

The door has opened approximately three times today to visitors—which is approximately three times more than yesterday. Whenever someone does show up, the general protocol seems to be that everyone within earshot races to greet that person like we're welcoming the president. Regardless of what you are doing. Whether on a phone call or hauling trash.

I have spent the past two weeks since I arrived here at my desk building up the social media pages for Kannery National Park that were hitherto essentially nonexistent. (Although I have learned not to mention this around Kevin. I did once and received a lecture about how he can't control the world's *ridiculous* reaction of valuing a video of someone pulling down someone else's pants for a prank over the heroic efforts of the dung beetle.)

My work the past two weeks hasn't done anything magnificent, however. I've grown the account from about two hundred to twenty-three hundred, the engagement rate hovering at a decent, but not noteworthy, range of 3 percent. I've definitely not been successful in doing anything remotely able to, as Uncle Terry says, "put Kannery Park on the map." In fact, it's been a bit discouraging.

People have complained to me about this over the years, saying, "It's just so hard to get noticed."

I didn't get it before. I guess it's been so long, I forgot what it was like in the very beginning.

But I remember now. The memories come back.

Me at fifteen getting that used beater of a phone off an old boyfriend three years older and three *thousand* miles away from the kind of guy I should've been hanging around. Eventually he left, but his gift did not. I worked nights at a shabby restaurant to escape my life in a shabby home and scraped enough from work to pay for my phone bill and little else.

Social media for me at fifteen was an outlet. So little of my real world was worth sticking around for. So much of my life was gray.

I longed to escape it.

So I escaped.

Started posting little things.

Lip-synching in the corner of my dimly lit bedroom.

Dancing.

Just a young teen living her own personal talentless show.

Then a curious thing happened.

People started to comment. People started to follow.

At the beginning they may as well have been robots, because none of them felt real. Just a bunch of numbers. Just a bunch of names. But there was something about that boost, something about seeing the numbers rise that spurred me on, gave me an almost indescribable energy hit.

Seeing the little numbers rise to twenty thousand followers. Then fifty thousand. Then a hundred.

It was electrifying.

So I shared more.

Became more.

I started experimenting with myself. Noticed how people were attracted to the energy of the bright-eyed, excitable influencers. So I followed in their footsteps.

Began talking the way I *wished* I talked in real life. Began walking, laughing, dancing with the confidence I *wished* I had in real life. Had the bubbly personality I longed for. Tried out what it was like to be playful and attractive on-screen like I wished I could be in real life. I pretended I was an *it* girl.

And then one day, I wasn't just pretending anymore. I was an *it* girl.

You look like u r feeling down. Pls take care of yourself. We love you!!!

I look at the comment on my post, just one of hundreds filling the screen. It doesn't sting like that of the keyboard warriors striving to bring destruction to every happy person online. Those trolls I'm used to. They're mere sweat bees.

But this one, the one about me looking under the weather. One by @ginnylee1334, a devoted user who comments so frequently I recognize the tiny King Charles spaniel in the profile bubble. One who is faithfully kind to a fault.

It's about a picture of me standing in front of a waterfall yesterday—the highlight of a two-mile trail Mina took me (read: dragged me) on yesterday after all but dancing with glee at the "amazing weather."

It was forty degrees.

It rained on us twice.

She called it a sprinkle and sang about lemon drops falling on our heads.

But I went with her, and sure enough the waterfall she declared was *"so epic"* was indeed *so* epic. And with much prodding Mina did get me to stand in front of the roaring hundred-foot waterfall, grinning despite soggy bangs clinging to my forehead and mascara running down my cheeks.

And then late last night, I looked at that picture as I lay in my bed. I scrutinized it, then decided to post it.

Yes, my signature lipstick was missing.

My false lashes were beside my nightstand.

And the rain jacket I borrowed off Uncle Terry was so big it swallowed my body.

But the spray and power of the waterfall looked just so amazing. It was hard to capture on film, but it was truly iridescent.

Like a fairy world Mina and I had stumbled upon that no one in the world knew existed.

And I looked happy. Felt genuinely . . . happy.

It was me. It didn't represent all of me, sure, but a part.

And it was a real smile. A real, twinkly-eyed smile that somehow, despite my years of practice rearranging my eyes to look just so perfectly bright, my lips to show just the right amount of pearly brightness that effused joy, couldn't be perfectly fabricated on command.

It just couldn't.

My eyes may have looked a little smaller from the squinting, but they danced.

They gathered some laugh lines around my temples, because the laugh was real.

It was something I hadn't seen in myself in a long, long time. Something I hadn't seen in . . . well . . . years.

But instead of comments about my joy, or the waterfall, or the poem in the caption I'd shared from the cabin Zaiah took me to on top of Cades Peak, what did I get?

A well-meant worry that I looked sick. A hundred various comments along the lines of, *Wow, so that's what you really look like* and tirades by both boys and men about the deceit of makeup. Multiple accusations of catfishing.

I remember a time when I never got those accusations.

At fifteen. At twenty. At twenty-five.

I remember a time when, if I showed my bare face, I received praise.

Praise for going without makeup.

The comments, over and over, of natural beauty. Flawless skin. A thousand wanting to know what my secret was. Which makeup line I used. What my nighttime cleansing routine was.

The reality? Back in those days I lived off junk food, alcohol, and coffee.

Now? Now it's a mad race to put on as much face serum as possible. To try to slow down the inevitable. Push the tide back.

I open the top drawer. Pull out my lipstick.

Oh, the glory of being young.

"Well, well, well. If it isn't the prettiest girl this side of Montana here to distract us another day."

Red gloss has just covered my top lip when Jax steps out of Uncle Terry's doorway, Zaiah on his heels. I click out of my profile page and back onto an article about the Lyrid meteor shower for the upcoming newsletter.

I drop the lip gloss back in my desk and give the drawer a firm push.

"Hello, Jax," I say flatly.

"Jax. That's not how you talk to her."

"Sorry." Jax puts a hand on his chest. "Prettiest girl in all of Montana—"

"Try again." Zaiah's face remains expressionless, as though he's accustomed to having to steer Jax's misguided attempts.

"Prettiest"—Jax hesitates, looking from Zaiah to me—"prettiest girl in the *whole world*—"

"You're on your way to getting another citation."

"You are just so extremely pretty." Jax throws out his arms. "Like, *really, really pretty*—"

"Just go." Zaiah pushes open the door to Terry's office. "Go in there and have Terry explain to you, again, why you don't talk to female coworkers like that, particularly coworkers who happen to be your superior's daughter."

"Niece—" I interject.

"Niece," Zaiah says.

"Peggy says she likes it!" Jax says, all the while being corralled through Terry's door. "Tell 'em, Big Mama."

We all turn to Peggy, who's sitting at her desk across the room, munching on a bag of jelly beans.

She looks up. "I allow it."

A few more rounds of poor word choices and Zaiah gets Jax into Terry's office. Shuts the door.

At the same time, flurries scatter along the doormat and I turn to see Peggy has her cane in one hand and purse in the other. The front office door shuts as we see her through the window crossing the parking lot toward her car.

Suddenly, the room is empty.

Peggy is gone to lunch. Uncle Terry is in his office with Jax. It's just Zaiah and me. Reluctantly, I turn my gaze up to him. "Hello," I say quietly.

The greeting is left wanting, but at the moment I'm having trouble coming up with something better.

Ever since our mountaintop tension two weeks ago, I've done my best to avoid him. Really, based on both the airport fiasco and the hiking fiasco and even the fiasco of our first meeting, we are just too dissimilar.

No hard feelings.

Nothing to do about it.

We're just two completely opposite people who, for some reason I can't really pin down, just need to do ourselves a favor and never mingle. So that's what I fully intended to do.

Polite hellos and good evenings when needed, and otherwise, avoid conversation.

I'm not sure how long I intended life to go on like this, but I was thinking . . . forever.

"So," Zaiah begins. "I hear Mina roped you into a movie marathon."

Small talk. He wants to do small talk.

I know what this means.

Fine.

I can comply. "Yes, well, it's fun background noise when you're working on matching roommate bracelets."

He smiles.

"I'm running out of room, actually." I pull up my left sleeve, where four bracelets in an explosion of colors encircle my wrist. "Spring needs to come soon."

He gazes appreciatively at my arm for one-fifth of a second, then changes subjects. "I wanted to apologize."

Oh.

His abrupt shift into direct apology throws me.

After all, everyone knows small talk was created for two uses: time-filling conversation with people you're stuck in proximity to and don't really know or care to, and indirect apology.

Apologizing without really having to say anything that makes the hair on the back of your neck stand up or your palms start sweating. You can talk about how chewy the corn chowder was and with your eyes be saying, *I'm really sorry I stole your car and ran it into a 7-Eleven. Can we just forget it?*

And when the other person says, "It really is chewy, isn't it?" then you know all is forgiven.

This is what people do.

What you specifically *don't* do is rip the bandage off the still-raw wound and announce, "Wow. That really looks as awful as I remembered, doesn't it?"

Especially with someone you barely know.

Particularly with someone with whom you seem incapable of having a normal, sane conversation.

I tuck my hair behind one ear. "It's fine, Zaiah. So . . ." My gaze roves around for something, anything, to discuss. It lands on a box filled with shirts on the mail table. "What are those for?"

His eyes don't so much as tick over to the cardboard box that arrived this morning. "You were right. I implied some inappropriate things about you when we were at Cades Peak. We all take in experiences differently. You are . . . just as entitled to your opinions as I am to mine. I'm sorry."

For crying out loud, man, I'm a nonconfrontational person!

I swallow. His gaze is so unrelenting. His eyes don't dart away just as his words don't waver. He's not skittish at all. Me, on the other hand. I feel like a child who can't handle an adult conversation.

Pull it together, Cat.

I round out my shoulders, willing myself to sit straight. *You may have hit a few roadblocks, but you are* not *a child.*

I force myself to meet his gaze. "Thank you. And . . . I'm sorry as well."

I swallow, hoping desperately he's not one of those people who can sit comfortably in silence.

But sure enough, there he is.

Standing over me.

Looking into my eyes.

With those penetrating green eyes.

I blink and turn my attention to the Cozy Cup I'm currently pushing around my desk.

"I'm, um, going through some things right now. Life's been a bit . . . challenging lately."

And there he goes again. Just looking at me. Waiting in case there's anything more I want to say.

I shift uncomfortably in my seat.

I am not going to open up to him about everything going on.

I'm not.

"Anyway, thanks for picking me up from the airport and helping me to my cabin and showing me around. You've been very hospitable." I press my lips together, remembering the way I must've looked on the hike. "Even to a girl throwing a tantrum in the snow."

His lips curve upward. "It was no trouble."

And while we both know every interaction between us has been pretty much only trouble, I smile.

Just like that it's over. All of it just water under the bridge.

He nods to the box of shirts. "They're promotional shirts for the winter carnival. Kevin made them before you got here."

"Oh." I rise and move over to the box. Lift a flap of the cardboard. The shirts are olive green, the same color as the rangers' uniforms. The words across the front are the color of coffee with a splash of cream. The font is thick, squiggly, childish.

They're a little hard to see folded up, but the words visible seem to be, "Kannery National Park. So fun you—"

I take the top shirt from the stack. Unfold it. "KAN't resist."

"Wow." It's the best I can say. It's the only thing I can say.

It's moments like this that I understand why Uncle Terry turned my twenty-three hundred followers and average of forty-two likes from last week into a pie chart with the proud declaration, "With

Catherine's aid, we have already grown 200 percent." As though we are on the cusp of getting calls from *National Geographic* and the White House.

When Kevin was my predecessor, yes.

This. This suddenly makes sense.

I'm almost afraid to, but I flip the T-shirt over.

It can't get worse than the front.

It can't.

It can.

There is a giant photograph of one of the trash bins beside the parking lot. Overlaying the photograph (which is blurry, I might add) are the words, "Come! Don't throw your weekend plans in the KAN."

Oh boy.

"That one's for you."

"What?"

Zaiah's frowning at my expression. "He worked really hard on that, Cat."

Oh no. And here we're already doing it again.

I clear my throat. Clutch the shirt to my chest. "And it shows. It's just so . . . so *creative*—"

"It's awful."

"Yes." I exhale, dropping my head as I see the smile playing on his lips. "I mean, I've seen all kinds of drastic measures for attention work, but this . . . it's a pun using a *trash can*. You are quite literally aligning the park with trash. *Blurry* trash."

Zaiah chuckles as his crinkly eyes watch my tension ease. "Believe me. Aside from Kevin, no one will blame you if you accidentally *forget* it at home."

"No, no. I'm part of the team now. I'm all in." I frown, a new thought occurring. My eyes flick to the window, where flurries are being thrust by the wind so fast they move sideways. "So what's this about a winter carnival? Isn't that a little . . ."

117

"Crazy to do in the middle of January? If you haven't noticed, we're a bit limited on winter activities."

"You can't avoid it, so you all decide to embrace it." I scan the T-shirt again. "Interesting . . . You all couldn't go for a barn dance."

"That's Saturday. These shirts are mostly for the Thursday event."

He flips the T-shirt over, and sure enough, below the trash can is a running list of events beneath the words:

Kannery National Park
Official Sponsor of
Kannery Winter Carnival XXIII

Twenty-three years.

These people thought it was a good enough experience standing outside while their eyelashes froze off that they decided to repeat the experience. For twenty-three years.

I'm not exaggerating when I say I can think of fewer things I'd rather do less in my life.

"What's on Thursday? And actually . . ." I realize I'm holding up a T-shirt. A T-shirt. For an outdoor winter carnival. "These are terrific, but . . . won't our shirts be covered up with coats?"

Good grief, Kevin.

This group really needs a PR person, stat.

At this Zaiah's lips twitch. "Oh no, for that they're perfect. They're for the polar bear plunge."

CHAPTER 8

The Winter Carnival

2:55

Instagram ⌄

catcranwell ✓

♡ ○ ⫑   ⟋

82,345 likes

catcranwell Meet my ethically made, upcycled, stunning Cozy Cup handcrafted by authentic, indigenous artisans at Blackfeet Boutique. I have one for every day of the week—literally. Take the quiz at my link in bio to see which animal you should get on yours. #sustainablefashion #absolutemusthaves

View all 24,684 comments

January 27

*T*he world is selling out of mason jars because of you."

"C'mon, Serena. You know that's just an unlikely coincidence."

"No. You and your little buddy over there brought Cozy Cups into existence, and now the grocery stores can't sell mason jars fast enough. You two have drawn the wrath of canning ladies everywhere. Farmers are out in the streets rioting."

I squeeze the wheel and brace myself as the tiny Mercedes convertible falls into, and out of, the giant pothole the ten trucks ahead of me skated over with ease.

Mina yelps, as she does when we hit every pothole, which is about every twenty seconds.

A horn honks over the line. "Do you understand that you've brought orange in again? *Orange?*"

Nobody, and I mean nobody, can exaggerate like Serena.

"Where are you going?" I say.

"At first I thought it was just coincidence," she says, ignoring me, "but then I was at lunch yesterday with a girl who's a buyer for Ralph Lauren, and *she* said she was told by her uppers to buy big in orange. There's a whole group over there convinced it's because of *you*. She even asked me to ask if you could sneak her in an order."

Mina, who's been listening over the car speaker, turns her puppy dog eyes toward me, and I shake my head. Absolutely not. I've inadvertently ended up acting like her manager here, but the truth is, she cannot handle even *one* more order right now. I inhale and prepare to respond.

"It's pretty selfish of you really," Serena continues. "Just because there's an *infinitesimal* chance you'll end up in an orange suit, you go out of your way to change all the rules."

"*Prison?*" Mina hisses at me, her eyes widening.

I wave her down. "Stop, Serena, you're freaking Mina out. Nobody's going to jail." I pull the car into one of the last remaining parking spots. I may lose millions of dollars here, but nobody's going to jail.

I turn the ignition off and reach for the handle. The heavy, freezing wind whistles as it drives against the door, but with a heavy elbow, I lean in and push. The door gives, and I drop one boot onto the gravel.

I exhale, and my breath turns to icicles as it lifts like an icy balloon toward the silvery gray sky.

Ah. A perfect day for swimming.

"Listen, I gotta go." I swipe over to check the latest stats on my social media pages before powering down. "I'll let you know if I survive."

"I'll be thinking of you," Serena says, then adds with a hushed, "Yes. Gables . . . Oh? When did she get here?"

"What are you doing?" My thumb presses the alarm button and the car beeps in the most feminine way possible. Beside us, the horn of Jax's beat-up Ford blasts out one eardrum.

"I'm getting brunch with Gabby. The poor thing is on the verge of an emotional and mental collapse, so I'm sitting her down for a little life counseling."

I nearly choke on my own spit. "You?"

"Hey. The girl put up a video of herself prancing around her kitchen to share her recipe for strawberry cream."

"So?"

"That's all she was wearing. Strawberry cream."

I wince.

"I may not be a professional or anything, but you of all people know she'll be grateful down the road that *somebody* stepped in and slapped her."

This is such a signature Serena move.

Leave it to her to be the only one willing to notice someone spiraling and be the only one willing to do something about it. To state the brutal facts while refilling her wineglass, yes, but also hold her hand and help guide her out.

I could've used a friend like that in my early years.

I wish her luck, then end the call and take a breath. Look around.

Because I am going to jump.

In a lake.

Of frozen water.

I take in the cars and trucks filling the lot around me. Everybody is dropping clothes like flies. Stripping down to bathing suits and boots, heavy, excited breaths as they hop toward the lake, hugging their bodies with giddy smiles.

"We'd better hurry." Even Mina is stripping down, bright-eyed and bushy-tailed as she whips her hat off her double braids. She puts her coat and shoes and hat inside the car, leaving her standing there in the trash can T-shirt over her bare legs.

Insane, I think, pulling off one leather glove.

Everyone here is insane.

I drop my gloves onto the seat. Gradually slip off my white coat, inhaling sharply as the heat abandons me to the fate of the elements. I don't know which is worse, wearing this hideous T-shirt or being in a T-shirt in twelve degrees.

I pull an elastic band off my wrist and begin pulling my hair back into a ponytail.

"C'mon, girls! Stop primping and get over here!" Jax calls, waving to us from his huddle at the edge of the lake. Unlike the rest of the group, he's shirtless. Zaiah, the only one who seems to pull the shirt off, crosses his surprisingly muscular arms and gives him a look.

"Let's go, chickies!" Peggy cries, shaking her cane at us. "The fishes don't care what you look like!"

More than a couple people passing by raise their Cozy Cups at Mina in salute.

The fact that Mina's Cozy Cups have sold so rapidly is amazing.

We spent several evenings building up an online storefront, along with social accounts directing people to it. I was reluctant to even post it on my own accounts, convinced I would do her more damage than good. But after Mina repeatedly told me there was nothing to lose and batted her eyes about a hundred times, I gave in and we gave it a shot.

The results were shocking.

So amazing, in fact, she had to close the store and instituted a "feast or famine" situation where it opens back up only at certain designated times. She hired her mother and a whole host of women in the community who can sew in a pinch. Anyone who walks by our cabin these nights would hear the loud *pinging* of the sewing machine and even louder TV volume to make up for it. Even Jax and Kevin have started dropping in. Every night's a veritable sewing party.

And they sell out in five minutes.

I even suggested we try jacking up the retail price to a *ridiculously* high price one night just to see what would happen.

Sure enough, they sold out quicker.

People all over the internet are carrying them, proudly displaying their "original CC."

Mina's Cozy Cup covers have gone viral.

And true to her word, Mina slipped me that twenty dollars.

But what's just as shocking to me in all this is that it worked. It worked that *I* shared something, just like the old days, and people wanted it.

Serena was right.

The boot deal came through.

Serena apparently even "ran into" a tent company and there was some interest there too. (Although frankly, I have a hard time buying her story that she ran into the brand manager while getting her nails filled.)

It was relieving. There's a sliver of hope.

"So. You've been roped in to this fiasco, too, huh?"

I've stepped into the huddle at the edge of the frozen lake. Kevin stands beside me, chin quivering and skinny chest looking even skinnier without the bulk of his ranger uniform. His strawberry-blond brows are frozen. *Frozen.*

I draw in a breath for the lie. If I can even faintly get him to believe me, it'll be the performance of a lifetime. "No, no, I'm excited about this," I say, my teeth tingling as they flash freeze when I smile. Somebody next to me is slapping her thighs, *hard*, while hopping in place.

"What a great tradition." Even I don't believe my words.

Suddenly, a couple men in thick parkas drop a thick strip of carpet on the lake. They give it a push, unrolling it toward the center of the lake.

People seem to know what is happening and begin to follow.

I turn my head, scanning the lake's border.

Wait.

Where are we jumping?

We're jumping from the edge, right?

I squint at the small square cut out of the ice in the center of the lake.

Oh no. Oh no no no.

"That's it?" I point. "That's where we jump?"

"'Scuse me," one of the men in the parkas says, an aluminum pool ladder over one shoulder.

Half a dozen lifeguards are beginning to surround the area in the center, their heavy parkas hanging loose over their bare shoulders and lifeguard swimsuits. The water is the color I imagine when I think of the night the *Titanic* sank.

The color of night.

An inky black blue.

You couldn't see a person an inch below the surface.

Oh, this is a nightmare.

"How deep is that?" I ask.

"About forty feet, they say," Mina responds chipperly, as if proud to know and be able to relay such facts. "It used to be a town, actually. They just built the dam right over it back in the forties."

"A completely artificial lake." Kevin sniffs. "Absolutely destroyed the natural habitat."

"Go off the grid, Kevin, and you can talk." Jax rolls his eyes.

I swallow. "What do you mean? Like . . . they just covered an entire town with water?"

Mina nods. "We lose scuba divers every year. It's actually pretty dangerous diving down there because of all the old houses and trees and things."

Oh my *gosh*. This is seeming like the beginning of a horror movie more and more by the second.

We hear the first splash as someone jumps into the water, and Mina loops her arm around mine. Spotting an opening in the line, she simultaneously drags me while shouldering Jax. "All right, guys. Kannery Park represent. Let's *go!*"

What I want to do, what I feel very much like doing, is digging in my heels while Kevin follows along, giving a lecture on the negative effects of dams on the environment. But despite being five feet even and weighing no more than a hundred pounds, Mina has the strength of that elk rooted to the middle of the road last week despite how many times Jax honked his horn. And just as much stubbornness. I can just hear her now.

The pep talk about overcoming my fears.

The gotta-have-team-spirit slogans.

The very real possibility that she snaps her fingers and Jax throws me over one shoulder and tosses me in, all while yelling, "Kannery Park forever!"

And I want to have team spirit. And be fun. And maybe, just a little bit, I do want to jump in and get to experience the high of being part of a group. A team. I really do want to belong.

But the reality is, having sea salt waves crash around me while I laugh and hold up a tube of sunscreen for a shoot is one thing; jumping into water so deep and black and cold my heart might give out on impact is another.

A very different other.

I raise the phone in my hand. Put on my cheeriest tone. "Smile, everyone. I want to get some group before-and-after shots."

"Get your shirt on." Mina pushes the T-shirt hanging limp at Jax's side at his chest. "Let's get someone else to take it, Cat. You need to be in the picture."

"No, no." I wave off the idea.

Uncle Terry comes out of nowhere and reaches for the phone. "I'll take it—"

"*No!*" the group says unanimously.

The man has quite literally built a house by hand, but to press the giant and singular button on the screen would be too much.

"Really," I say. "I've got it."

I draw the camera up as the group bunches together. The line is moving quickly and starting to get away from us.

"But you're jumping. Right?" Mina says as I take several clicks on the camera.

I hedge. "I'm . . . not sure."

She squints. "You're not jumping?"

I get a couple more shots and scroll back through the photos.

Mina's brows are furrowed in all of them. She's giving the same face she gave when she woke up one morning last week to discover I'd cut the number of friendship bracelets I was wearing in half.

"Leave her alone." Jax peels the T-shirt back off. He smirks at me, scratching his bicep while trying to flex nonchalantly. "This'll get her a better view from the sidelines. Isn't that right, Kitty Cat?"

"Put that back on right now," Mina says. "If one of us has to wear this thing, we all do."

Kevin straightens. "What is that supposed to mean?"

"Hey, I'm just following the rules," Jax says, hands in the air. "No cheating by heating."

"*Diving* suits are heating. You know that. This"—Mina waves her hand at his six-pack—"this is just an excuse to show off in front of Cat. For the millionth time, *she's not interested.*"

"What was that supposed to mean about 'having' to wear this?" Kevin's voice is a high-pitched squeak over the others.

But as the group breaks into a scuffle, I just stand there, frozen by Jax's words.

Kitty Cat.

Not Cat. Not Catherine.

Kitty Cat.

He's seen it, then.

Been there, to the back rooms of the internet.

And found my old account. The first years when I made my first mistakes.

How I hit my first viral video.

And then bounced around trying a few different things, then hit a second.

Then a third.

And discovered a theme.

Consistent factors in the videos that set them apart from the rest. What it was that gave me virality.

My body. My fifteen-year-old, full, heart-shaped-lips body doing a little flirting with the camera.

Educational videos weren't for me. Trying to be funny was a joke. I certainly had no fancy house or child-prodigy skills to show off. Couldn't do a triple flip on command. Couldn't solve a Rubik's Cube in ten seconds. Couldn't make anyone laugh till they peed their pants. Didn't live in a castle.

Couldn't do anything, really, except be . . . pretty.

Show off a little skin.

Dance a little.

Wear a good deal of makeup to highlight all my best features.

And be . . . dumb.

Yes, it was ridiculous, but there was something about me playing dumb that worked. Pretend I didn't get the jokes. Blink my bright hazel eyes furiously with an airy smile on my lips.

Kitty Cat.

The beautiful young bombshell with the little brain.

And when I stumbled into wearing that seductive fan-fiction costume and people went wild? Well, I became every nerd's dream girl.

I jumped into the role. Watched in wonder as the numbers soared.

I tried not to look too hard at my analytics. The ratio of men to women following me was eighty/twenty. The biggest percentage of men watching were over forty.

And even though I dropped the handle and the persona and even my name eventually, there are still Reddit threads and screenshots and whole articles and fan pages serving as daily reminders of my cringey mistakes years ago.

That's the thing about the internet. Once it's out there, it's there forever.

And the higher you are, the farther the fall.

My cheeks blaze.

The reminder of my mistakes making me squirm all the way down to my toes.

Aside from Mina's little confession, no one has made mention of my social media.

Any of it.

And so far, everyone has done such a good job acknowledging that I'm good at social media without acknowledging the *why* behind it that I had halfway started to believe it. Halfway started to believe the lie that nobody here looks at me in the mornings walking in with my Cozy Cup of coffee and thinks, *There's Cat Cranwell. I can scroll back and know everything about her, from the date she posted about her first period to the disaster of her last boyfriend. What a mess.* That I really did have a clean slate. A chance to reveal to people whatever I want about my life, on my own time.

But of course not.

Of course.

"It's Cat, Jax," I say.

And for one long second as the group carries on, our eyes are locked. His goofy grin slips away.

He pauses.

Then he straightens.

In that moment I feel I get a glimpse of the man he will one day become. A good guy. A guy who may make some cringey mistakes, just like I did back then, but will come out just fine.

"Sure, Cat." He dips his head slightly. "Sorry."

He slips the T-shirt back on.

I give him a mild *thanks* of a smile, and he jumps back into the conversation going on around the group. It's just a hunch, but I feel almost certain he won't talk to anyone about whatever he's unearthed.

"You okay?" Zaiah stands beside me, his voice low. And while everyone else is knee-deep in argument, Zaiah is the only one looking down at me. His face pensive. Brow furrowed.

So. He noticed.

"I'm fine," I say quickly. I slip the camera into the pocket of my shorts.

"I'm up, boys!" Peggy cries, as the jumper ahead makes a mad dash past us, dripping wet. "Baby doll, grab your camera!"

I scramble to retrieve my phone and watch in silent wonder as she tosses her cane aside. She loops her arms around Jax and Zaiah.

She looks small and frail beside them, held steady by their strength.

Unbelievable. Zaiah really has managed to be thoroughly and truly attractive in these shirts.

Zaiah catches my eye, and suddenly I become very keen to discover the exact shade of the carpet I'm standing on.

The boys shuffle Peggy toward the edge of the ice like they're ushers at a wedding.

Jax tries to keep his feet on the carpet leading to the open waters. Zaiah seems indifferent as he walks directly on ice. Peggy, with her dangling hot-pink flamingo earrings, Bermuda shorts, and shower cap, inches along the carpet.

When they get to the edge, two lifeguards hand Jax and Zaiah bright-orange buoys.

"Long live Kannery Park!" Peggy cries and, without even a beat of hesitation, throws herself into the water.

It's both startling and amusing, watching Peggy thrash and yell, "Don't splash so much, Lilly, you'll ruin my curls!" Jax and Zaiah struggle to hold on to the buoys while dragging her along, and for a full thirty seconds my body fights between wanting to laugh and wanting to hightail it as fast as I can to the car.

Their heads and shoulders are the only things visible above the inky waters, not even a hint of visibility of Peggy's veiny legs or the mildly impressive six-pack Jax was so keen to show off earlier.

By the time Jax has hopped out and is pulling Peggy up while

Zaiah bobs in the water, helping from behind, I've decided running away is the best option here.

"You're up, roomie." Mina holds her hand out as though chauffeuring me to my limo instead of what it really is: the solo jump into black-water-above-haunted-town death.

I stare at the lapping water. Hear the hum of chatter of those in line behind me. Feel their eyes on me. The impatient, get-on-with-it stares.

I can do this.

An eighty-year-old with a cane just did this.

I *can* do this.

"C'mon, Cat!" Jax yells from the other side. His call is good-natured as he dances in place left-to-right, water dripping off his shivering body.

My eyes shift from him back to the water.

I know I can do this.

I *want* to do this.

I blink over to the group, all in their T-shirts, cheering me on. Welcoming me into their circle, into their world. Wanting me to share in their unity, their joy. Choosing me.

I *want* this.

I just . . . have to . . .

Despite the cold covering my body, stinging heat is radiating off my neck, cheeks, palms.

Everybody is watching me.

Oh, I can't. I can't.

My fingers curl into fists as I realize this is really happening. This really is going to be how it goes down.

Cat Cranwell failing again. Cat Cranwell so truly incapable of anything besides a lifetime of sitting there looking pretty.

"I'll do it."

I look up to see Zaiah striding toward me, barefoot over the ice. Water drips from his beard as he walks, eyes on me.

There's a question in my own eyes as I look from him to Mina, to the group, then back again. Do what? What is he trying to do?

"I'm already wet. I'll take the newbie."

As he steps up to me, it's not me he's looking at but Mina. "You can take the next one."

"Next one? What—?" I begin, but before I can finish asking he turns me by the shoulder to face the water. "First-timers' protocol. Our way of making sure you don't die. Ready?"

I look at the water. "Well, I—"

"Twenty seconds and then it's done. Get set—"

"Well, hang on—" I begin, then feel his hand grip mine.

"Go."

I hear his declaration a millisecond before I feel his jump, and the tug on my arm as it leads me to do the same.

Before I know it I'm in the air, hearing faintly Mina's triumphant cheer just before the splash as my body plunges into the water. And oh, does it plunge.

The glacial water sucks the air right out of my lungs as my toes, waist, chest, and head plunge into the belly of the whale, and for the longest second of my life, time stops. For one infinite moment it's just me submerged in a sea of silence. The only sensation is the prickles of a hundred thousand needles tapping every inch of my body. And his hand. The grip, the firm, stable grip, of his hand squeezing mine.

I emerge, birthed back into reality, and with it returns sound. Cheers of onlookers waiting their turn. Whoops and hollers from Uncle Terry. And Peggy. And Kevin. And Mina. And Jax.

I inhale loudly with a high-pitched wheeze with my first breath, my lungs aching with the pressure to expand. I cry out, feeling the adrenaline running through my veins, begging my arms and legs to move like the wind.

It's exhilarating.

Blinking the water from my eyes, I catch Uncle Terry attempting to snap a picture before lowering the camera with a puzzled expression. "Now that's not right. Mina, how do I get off this . . ."

My legs feel like they're foreign as they work to kick beneath me, just dead space. A smile erupts on my face as I begin to swim toward the other side. The splashing is loud, overtaking my eardrums. I wheeze with every terrifying, thrilling new breath.

But wait. Where is his hand?

I look down for it, and water splashes my face. I can't see my legs. I can't, in fact, see anything but a pool of black beneath me.

Nothing but water between me and the broken-windows houses, crooked trees, decaying barns below.

I inhale sharply, then feel a second later, as if he heard my silent plea, his hand on my hip.

Gentle.

Prodding.

I look to my right. There he is.

"Ready?" he says.

It's a steadying question, equal to his steady eyes on mine. He isn't splashing around. No. He's stoic, incredibly calm, as he waits for my reply. As if the water isn't freezing his bones as it is mine. As if he's immune to the icicles forming on his lashes and the air so cold it burns entering our lungs.

All I can think is, *He probably could've survived the* Titanic. He would've been that brandy-drunk baker who doggie-paddled for hours before rescue and made it. I look at him closer. Take in his steely, unwavering gaze. The pulsing vein following down his firm neck. Correct myself.

No, he wouldn't have doggie-paddled waiting for a rescue boat. He would've swum the whole four hundred miles to shore.

I feel my panic drifting away.

Feel the confidence return.

I really can do this.

I look at the ladder twenty feet off, bobbing quietly as it waits to be used.

With Zaiah beside me, I know I won't fail.

"Yeah," I breathe. My palms cup the water as I begin to move in an amateur breaststroke motion.

He pulls back as I reach the ladder. Waits while I pull myself out and my body shifts from freezing waters below to freezing air above.

Mina dives into the water behind me. Brave. Fearless.

It all happened in sixty seconds, probably less, and yet it felt like a lifetime.

I look up to Zaiah, teeth chattering. "What do we do now?" I say, and realize I'm panting.

A bemused smile passes over his lips as he watches me wrap my arms tightly over my chest, shaking from head to toe. My soaked, oversized T-shirt pulls over my athletic shorts, so long the shorts are hidden. My hair is plastered to my head, no doubt making me look like a soggy Yorkshire terrier.

My toes . . . Where are my toes?

I can't feel anything, now that I think of it, from the hips down.

"Now," Zaiah says, "for the fun part."

CHAPTER 9

The Boys

go for a week hearing about this polar bear plunge and nobody mentions *this*. Someone should have led with *this*. You know what, guys? You really are the worst at marketing."

"I told you about it." Mina's braids bob in the hot, clear water like two water snakes skimming the surface. "That morning I found you muttering to yourself about 'these crazy Montana people' in the bathroom, I told you about the hot springs. You just weren't listening."

I frown. "That was before coffee. You know I don't register anything before coffee."

Mina is a bit like that one neighbor I inevitably found myself in the elevator with. Like Mrs. Carry and the staggering amount of information I learned about everything from her grandniece's sixth birthday party to the effectiveness of her latest foot cream before the doors swung open. Mina essentially popped her eyes open with mouth chattering in the morning and didn't stop talking until ten seconds before she was asleep.

"Incoming!" Jax cries just before jumping cannonball style in the water.

Hot water shoots on Mina, Kevin, and me. Swiftly, I raise my phone high over my head. "Hey! I've got a phone here."

"Record this." Jax pulls himself back up the boulder and jumps back in.

"The internet doesn't *care* about your abs, Jax," Kevin says as Jax emerges.

"Well . . ." I say in a teeter-totter tone, but so quietly I won't get an earful from Kevin about the internet's standards or, worse, Jax mistaking my observation for interest.

"They care about the *habitat*. In fact," Kevin continues, "I'm not sure it's healthy for so many people to be in this at all. With the oils and soaps people use these days, all without any *thought* to what they could do to the environment—"

"Is that lady putting on sunscreen?" Jax says, staring off in the distance.

Kevin's head whips around. "Where?"

"Oh no, never mind. Just makeup."

"*What?!*" He bolts, wading through both current and crowd. "What kind? *Makeup?!*"

Jax grins as we watch Kevin move off, slipping this way and that as he goes. He turns to us. "You're welcome."

I lift my phone and pan around on video. It's surreal. I didn't even know places like this existed.

Surrounding us on all sides are mountains. The sky is the same color as the mountaintops, snowy white and clouded as far as the eye can see. Sparse trees dot the area here and there. But the truly magical part, the part that makes me never want to leave, is the hidden oasis between the mountains. Where we stand now. The springs.

Aquamarine water as stunning as in the Bahamas flows down the winding river, interrupted by large boulders. Steam rises from the hot water, misting the faces of people settled chest-deep in the river as far as the eye can see. The water is hot, as hot as any hot tub I've ever been in.

I've never enjoyed being in water so much.

I switch over to picture taking and snap a few shots of Mina's Cozy Cup I grabbed from the truck before the short hike down. My nails are starting to chip, and I angle them away as best I can while shooting the cup in my hand in the mist. I go back and review a few of the shots.

Oh, these are *great*.

This place is a brand-shot jackpot. It makes me want to stack on a dozen Neiman Marcus bracelets, splash on some Londontown pink polish, fill a Yeti with Yirgacheffe coffee, and throw a Kiel James Patrick rope tote spilling over with Costa sunglasses, Tavola sandals, and a variety of Reese's Book Club picks on a rock and go to town.

And that's just *for pictures with my hand.*

Imagine the bathing suit brands, towel companies, clothing lines, hair products, chairs, picnic packages, and, shoot, even board games when I included my whole person.

This is the postmodern version of finding a gold mine.

I want to go post these so badly on both Mina and Kannery Park's pages, I feel tempted to sneak out.

I hear splashes in the distance and set the cup down. Someone has brought a beach ball and a game has begun of bobbing it from person to person, keeping it above the water.

As I slowly make a panoramic video, I see Zaiah. He's standing with three other men, arms crossed tightly over his chest.

My phone stops on him.

He's frowning as he's listening to one of the men talk.

Wow. And here I thought at first he didn't like me.

I *seriously* underestimated the looks Zaiah could give.

This makes our first meeting look like he fell in love.

The group stands out in the crowd, partly because they look so rigid in a world of leisurely clusters, partly because of their builds. All of them soar a full head above the rest, wearing T-shirts and swim trunks like everyone else, but still set apart. More muscular. Standing straighter, like commanders of two armies meeting in the middle, conversing before the battle.

I lower my phone, squinting.

"Who are they?"

Kevin—who has his head trapped in Jax's armpit, fighting for his life—twists to look. Whatever he sees is significant because he slaps Jax in the stomach.

Somehow this type of slap is different than the other identical ones he's been giving his brother because Jax immediately halts. Looks over. He drops Kevin's head.

All of them frown as though smelling a landfill. There's a substantial pause before Mina speaks, and when she does, the words honest-to-goodness sound like she's a warrior having just discovered Orcs in the building. Gutteral. Low. "Glacier Boys."

"Glacier who?" I say, but Mina shushes me.

"They're coming," she hisses, and I realize then that all three of the men are headed our way. Kevin and Jax both visibly puff up their chests.

"Well, well, well, the Kannery Park group T-shirts rally around for another season."

The three men drift to the edge of the river beside us, stopping beside a large boulder planted in the water. The one in the middle seems to be some sort of ringleader. He's tall, his beard long and thick as though to make up for his receding hairline.

Distinct *West Side Story* vibes are coming off the two groups.

Really? Are we going to rumble at midnight? Is someone going to start snapping?

"Has the advertising worked?" one of the boys—I really couldn't call them men at this point—asks.

"Well, this is day one . . . ," Kevin begins. "I don't think you can really quantify any results yet—"

"Of course we have," Mina cuts in, and from the way Kevin suddenly yelps, I have a feeling some body part was just pinched under the water. "Several people—a *hundred* people—said they couldn't wait to visit. Said they've been trying to find somewhere secluded *and* beautiful for a week."

The man-child in the middle grins down at her, an amused tilt to his lips. "Really? A hundred people."

"Probably closer to two," Mina retorts, dark eyes daring.

He laughs. "Incredible. Makes me wish we had some ourselves."

"I'd be happy to help," Kevin jumps in. "I was a bit worried about the font at first, but—"

And there's the yelp again.

"But then, this past season we had the opposite problem. Three million visitors last year. A jump from 1.7." He sighs as though just thinking about it exhausts him.

"The traffic must've been brutal," I say.

What am I doing?

I'm actually *joining* in this national park drama.

The men turn to me. Seem to notice me for the first time.

The one in the middle drops his arms. Takes me in. "It is, actually. But then, 1,583 square miles of edge-of-your-seat views. What are ya gonna do?"

He shifts his gaze back to Kevin. "How many miles do you all manage again?"

"Three hundred fifty-three," Kevin replies proudly.

He gets a scowl from Mina and throws out his hands. "What? Even *that's* not allowed?"

"Ah." The Glacier Boy scratches his chin. "We have 1,936 miles total. Shouldn't be too bad. We may have to add two"—he looks Kevin, Mina, and Jax up and down—"or just *one* ranger. But that should be doable when we absorb your park."

"Will you post the job applications on the gov website?" Kevin asks, and this time gets an all-out elbow punch in the stomach.

Laughter ripples around the group, and somebody calls out the Glacier Boy's name. He lifts a finger as if to say, "Hang on. Just finishing up this very insignificant conversation."

"Take care of yourselves, kids."

"Careful now. Don't slip on a rock," Mina calls toward his back as he leaves with the other two.

"Now there's a thoughtful ranger," he replies with a laugh.

She stands in the middle of the water as they move off, staring at them with her arms crossed over her chest, the water up to her shoulders with her petite frame. A mouse glaring at the cats.

"Soooo," I say, my voice singsong. "What was that?"

"They think they're so special just because they have rainbow rocks," Mina snaps.

"Lake McDonald," Kevin corrects. "The colors of each rock are actually determined by how much iron is in them, and the oxidization by the air. It's quite stunning, actually."

Mina's brows are nearly touching her eyeballs as she swivels on him. "I'm not *trying to compliment* them, Kevin." She punctuates each word so intensely I have to wipe the smile off my face.

"Sorry. It's just . . . it's indisputable they have the best natural life."

"Excuse me," Mina growls. "They may have more land, but our 353 miles of undisturbed terrain is *a freaking masterpiece.*"

Kevin withers beneath Mina's fierce loyalty.

Several seconds go by, and he says, "I'm not saying I prefer their park to ours. I'm just saying it's—"

"It's what?" You would think he had just insulted her mother. "More beautiful?" She squints. "More . . . *breathtaking?* Say it, Kevin. Would you rather be working for them?"

"No. I mean, it's just . . . more well known. That's all. Just more well known."

"And we're a *hidden gem.*"

Nobody dares answer her, and for a while we stand with plastered smiles and bobbing nods at the adorable racoon who has bared both teeth and claws.

But then I remember something.

"What was that they were saying about absorbing the park, though?"

"Oh." Mina waves a hand as if that's insignificant. "There's a rumor going around that Kannery will be absorbed into Glacier if we can't get our visitor numbers up. But it won't happen." She sounds so certain.

"Why's that?" I say.

At this Mina grins as if it's obvious. As if, of course, I know.

As if I'm joking.

"Because of you, silly. You're our ace card. Our plan to save the park."

CHAPTER 10

The Moose

'm your *what*?"

My question throws Mina, because she darts her eyes to Jax and Kevin for support.

"Well . . ." She waits, it seems, for them to jump in. When they don't, she says, "Yeah."

"Mina." I inhale. "Do you realize I've only gotten the park two thousand followers in the past two weeks? *Two thousand*?"

"Twenty-*one hundred*," Mina corrects, lifting a finger. "In just *two* weeks. Imagine that many additional people coming every week! And you've only just *begun!*"

"Yes, but they're not all going to come. Just because they follow a yacht account doesn't mean they're going to buy the boat!" My eyes dart around for Uncle Terry. He's nowhere in sight.

I shift, looking around for Zaiah. "How long do we have? How long before they absorb the park? And wait—" I remember a tidbit the leader of the pack said. "So you're saying your *jobs* are on the line here? All of them?"

"Except one, apparently." Kevin looks hopeful.

"Lose the misty eyes, Kevin," Mina says. "You wouldn't make the long list."

"Well, they wouldn't give it to Zaiah if that's what you're thinking. He intimidates them too much," Kevin retorts. "And Terry wouldn't have a chance. We already heard how they feel about 'old folks.'"

Uncle Terry. I pull up short. Oh, Uncle Terry.

And Mina.

And Peggy.

And even Jax and Kevin.

I swivel around, squinting with renewed zeal. I need to find Zaiah or Terry now. I need to get a handle on exactly what situation I'm dealing with.

A pair of broad shoulders is moving against the current, away from the clusters populating the main area. Past the shorelines dotted with discarded shoes and keys.

Where is he going?

No matter. I'm going too.

"I'll be right back," I throw over my shoulder. I do my best to follow Zaiah's pace, but without Zaiah's tall frame, I find the current pushing against my ribs, slowing me significantly. I hold the phone above my head.

I need a new phone case.

Something more for looks than function was fine in the city, but in this job, I'm running daily into the hazards of snow, ice, and apparently even hot tub–temperature waters. The second I get back to the cabin, I'm ordering something heavy duty. Military grade.

I follow the river as it winds beyond the giant slate of river rock, keeping a sharp eye on the slippery rocks beneath my feet, hoping and praying with each step to find nothing slithering out from underneath.

Surely they can't live in these conditions, though? Surely a snake would boil to death?

Then again, last week Kevin told me a northern scorpion could live a year without food. *A year.* Just like that. Thriving on air. Anything in this part of the world seems game.

"Zaiah!" I call, just before he takes a turn around the hillside.

The current is loud, though, and the distance between us is growing by the moment.

"Zaiah!" But there he goes, around the corner.

I pause.

Check over my shoulder.

The beach ball bobs above the mist. People look small against the backdrop of mountains and sky. All of it is reminiscent of a scene from a movie. Watching the lackadaisical afternoon pass by.

I move toward the hillside. He can't have gone that far.

I turn the corner, and the river narrows.

I can see why the river is a local favorite. A wide river, opening up to a wide sky. Just enough boulders to hold drinks and phones like bar tables at a restaurant, all without overcrowding. An easy bank on both sides for getting in and out of the water.

Here, though, is different.

The river tightens.

Trees huddle close on either side, casting shadows over the crystal waters that, I can't help it, make a lot more snakelike illusions. I wince as I inch along, the arches of my feet repeatedly stabbed by the jagged rocks. There is no more commotion of people; the world around me is nothing but solemn stillness but for the gurgling waters when I first rounded the bend.

Mist still rises, though. The water is still unbelievably hot and refreshing against the nip on my nose and tingle of cold breeze against my shoulders.

It's still stunning here, just in an entirely different, more solitary way.

Where is Zaiah?

I begin to consider turning back. My anxiety starts to rise, not just because of the sudden isolation but because I'm not sure I want to run into Zaiah after all.

What if he's trying to find some silence on purpose?

What if . . . he snuck out here to use the bathroom?

I swallow the thought as I turn one more corner. If he's not there (or heaven forbid, if he's *doing something worse*), then that's it. I'm heading back.

I peek around a boulder, preparing myself for the worst, and then I see it.

The quintessential moment.

The quintessential shot.

A moose stands in the middle of the river just a stone's throw away, tall and majestic, a sight to be seen. Its dark-brown fur glistens as it hovers over the turquoise water, mist rising over his enormous nose as he leans toward it. Dark evergreens topped with snow shiver in the breeze, causing flurries to dance and swirl like powdered sugar around him. He gazes down with no awareness of the person who has just stumbled into his world.

My fingers tingle, activating, and of course, *of course,* I pull my phone up.

Quietly I begin to snap.

The pictures are unbelievable. They could rival a *National Geographic* photo.

Then I pause.

Consider the moose and the moment.

Flip the camera to self-facing.

As I snap, I angle my chin up to capture myself with the gorgeous creature behind.

I love this moment for what it is, absolutely. No question.

But I also have an awareness in the back of my mind of what it could be: a redemption opportunity.

People are going to love this.

People are going to eat this up.

I can practically hear the comments now.

The outpouring of praises.

Cat Cranwell. Adventurous. Carefree. *And* with freshly applied lipstick still in place.

The golden trio.

The thing all content creators worth their salt aspire to.

My heart is racing as I review the clip.

It was good, but it could be better. I shift, swipe a couple drops away from my cheeks, pull a few strands forward in front of my ear.

Smile.

Twinkle my eyes.

Press the button again.

Slam!

My breath knocks from my lungs as somebody yanks me off the river bottom.

I feel myself being lifted and seized backward. Water gurgles in protest as I'm dragged against the current. It only takes a glance to recognize it's Zaiah's arm wrapped entirely around my torso, pulling me back into his chest. The other hand presses over my mouth, clearly not to hurt but to keep me quiet.

Uselessly my feet dangle in front of me, bobbing like two buoys.

It's only until we are behind the boulder bordering the river that he stops.

The hot river water is loud, but not loud enough to drown out his hushed words. "*Geez*, Cat." His voice is low, growling. "C'mon."

Miraculously, I'm still clinging to my phone, the video still rolling as he slips out of the water and onto the bank. I scramble clumsily out behind him, ignoring the rocks that nip at my toes.

He crouches as he moves, keeping his head lower than the boulder between us and the moose.

I follow suit.

The sun dips westward as we enter the forest, the deceiving orange orb of the sun all looks but no results. My body tingles with the pricks of a thousand icy needles. A twig snaps underfoot and Zaiah turns, giving me a look.

Finally, the river so far away it's only a distant gurgle, he stops. In a thick set of pines he turns. "What—" he sputters, then stops. His fists clench as he inhales. Then he speaks again with what appears to be measured calm. "What were you *thinking*?"

Yeah. He didn't sound much better.

My chest tightens. The video is still running in my hand. I tap it off. "I gave myself some distance, Zaiah. I'm not an idiot."

"You were standing waist deep . . . *in water*. Ten feet off. That is *by definition* idiotic. We have warning signs all over the park literally depicting a tourist standing ten feet off from a moose. Have you not seen *any* of them?"

He rakes his hand through his hair and shoots his gaze away from me as he takes another breath. I've never seen him look so angry.

"I was quiet," I say defensively, although I can feel my ears starting to heat. "And I was a lot more than ten feet off. More like thirty."

"They can run thirty-five miles an hour, Cat. How fast do you think you can go *in water*?"

"I was *far off*," I repeat, jaw tightening.

"From that?"

I swivel around in the direction of the moose I had been taking pictures of. He's still standing in the middle of the river, tall and majestic, a sight to be seen.

"No." He turns my shoulder, redirecting me toward the bend where I stopped and began videoing. *"That."*

I halt.

Right out from the tree line, almost melted into the wooded background behind the water, stand two smaller moose, skinny-legged and heads bent as they chew on the pale-green river grass around them.

They look so small and helpless, not quite newborn calf level (or at least I couldn't imagine anything so huge coming out of a body), but a little older. Preadolescent.

Old enough and tall enough to be able to stand in the water

without getting their heads wet, young enough to still be hanging around their mom.

Mom.

My eyes swivel to the moose. The mother, not male, moose.

I see it now. No horns. And perhaps it's my imagination, but just a bit more feminine curve to her long snout.

A mother and her babies.

My teeth start chewing on my lip. When I turn and face Zaiah, my voice is weak. "I didn't see them."

If I'd expected that to bring some sympathy, for the frown between his brows to ease up or for him to say, "Oh! You didn't see them. That all makes sense now," then I was wrong.

If anything, he only seems more exasperated as he throws out his hands.

"*Of course* you didn't see them, Cat. That's the *point*. I saw you. Saw you so *dang* focused on getting a good *selfie* of yourself with the moose for your Instagram page or whatever that you didn't pay a *lick* of attention to your surroundings. They were *literally* three yards away behind you. Do you even know what could've happened if the mother saw you between her and her calves? Do you even understand how aggressive they can be? Just *one look* and that could've been it. You could've gotten yourself *killed*."

My gaze shoots over to the mother moose I had been taking pictures of so peacefully before.

Heat creeps up my neck, making it the only warm part of my body at the moment. The rest of me is starting to shake. From the cold. From the man suddenly yelling at me, calling me for all intents and purposes an idiot.

Calling me out for doing a stupid thing.

And being right.

"This isn't New York." Zaiah swipes away the water dripping down his beard. "Mistakes have consequences. Not paying attention has *consequences*. You gotta get off your phone because *real life is happening here.*"

A cloud billows up from his face as he finishes his rumbling words, and with them, he shuts his mouth as if afraid to say anything more. He looks away. Thunder in his eyes.

Clearly a hundred more things he wants to say.

"I know." I take in a shaky breath through my nose. Exhale. "I know that."

He's right.

But of course he's right.

He's right for insinuating I spend too much time on my phone. I know this about myself.

If he wants to know, I hate this about myself too.

But I can't escape it. This is the life I have chosen. Being on call to the public, prostituting myself out, divulging every word and thought to both everyone and no one in particular. This is what I do. This is my job.

I have no other skills, and I'm in too deep to change course now.

And would I anyway? Do I hate it all enough that I would really throw it all—*all*—away?

This life is my drug.

My world both thrills and kills me.

I don't know what Zaiah sees in my expression, but when he looks back, his jaw unclenches slowly. His eyes relent a little bit. "Sorry. I just . . . I would hate for anything to happen to you." He takes a breath. After a long pause, he offers up the faintest of smiles. "After all, my boss would kill me."

And that's when, looking into his green-as-the-forest eyes, I realize—these are the eyes of the person who not only saw me doing something stupid that put me in danger, but also waded straight into the line of fire to pull me out. Unarmed. With no means of winning that fight if it came to it.

I return a small smile. "It certainly would be tough to get promoted."

My words spell out a joke, but my eyes are saying *Thanks.*

And then I take it a step further, because somehow, it doesn't seem like enough.

"And . . . thanks."

He dips his head. "You're welcome." He looks down my quaking, shivering body, his own as unbothered as if it were made of stone. "We ought to get back to the springs."

I welcome the movement, and as we step over the rocky, thorny path, careful to give the moose and her young a wide berth, he stops several times, offering his hand. I take it twice, easing the pressure on my frozen, likely-bleeding-but-I-can't-feel-them-at-the-moment feet.

As we ease back into the springs, I ask, "So. What were you doing this far out anyway?"

"I spotted the moose family when I was talking with the Glacier Boys, and went to check her out. She looked pretty oblivious to the group, but still, I needed to make sure she moved off in the other direction."

I nod, impressed by how he silently went off to protect the crowd, all without their knowledge. It was a rather superhero-like move, come to think of it.

"That's a pretty notable thing to do, you know. Save the day and tell no one. You're a veritable Ranger Clark Kent."

He smiles but I continue. "What? I don't imagine anyone else out here doing the same thing. Kevin would scream and run while yelling out facts about a moose's antler size and life span. Jax would probably try to wrestle it to the ground to impress some girls. And, of course, get trampled."

Zaiah nods as though to say, "Naturally."

"And I have a feeling the Glacier men would somehow use them to trumpet themselves."

"Glacier Boys," Zaiah corrects.

I laugh. "Not you too. Surely you're too mature for this?"

"Not in the slightest."

I smile as we round a corner, then chew my lip as a question forms. I'm not entirely sure I want to know the answer. But I can't help asking. "So . . . Ranger Kent. The moose. Would you say they are the most dangerous animals out here?"

His response is immediate. There's no need to think before answering this question.

"No. The most dangerous are people."

"People?" I laugh, unable *not* to think of the tourists who have come through the office the past three weeks. That one guy who kept getting in trouble for feeding the deer his Cheez-Its. The group of nine-year-old Boy Scouts who managed to get one injured swinging marshmallow sticks at the campfire.

"You'd be surprised what we see," Zaiah says. "People like to do the worst in secret. And where's a better place for miles of solitude than here? The woods that offer peace for one person are the weapon that assists in another's homicide."

I raise my brows. His response had an intensity I wasn't expecting. "Murder? You've really seen murder out here?"

"I've been working in the park since I was eighteen. I've seen it all."

He catches my surprised expression and adds, "You should talk to Terry. He's done this forty-five years. Arrested more people, confiscated more guns, stumbled into—and survived stumbling into—more meth labs, broken up more domestic assaults, and got more injured hikers to safety from bite, poison, or fall than anyone I've ever met. I see the way you look at him. You think he's a teddy bear." He pauses. "And to be fair, he's becoming one a little bit more every year. But he's also one of the toughest people I know. You want to call someone Ranger Clark Kent? Name him that. Not to mention, he'd eat that title up."

I can't help it. I'm surprised by the reality check about his job.

For some reason—I don't know, probably because all I've done is sit in an office the past three weeks hearing Peggy directing tourists to the closest bathrooms—I've had the understanding that being a ranger is just about taking people's six bucks at the gate. Picking up trash. Shooing off the raccoons so they don't scare the visitors. And in the case of Kevin, explaining way too much to visitors about things they don't really care *that much* about.

I never thought about this other side of ranger life.

Being the law enforcement, and sometimes the only law enforcement, when there is no backup for a hundred miles. Protecting the wildlife, sure, and the trees from burning down by teenage pyro idiots with matches, yes, but also . . . what? Coming to the rescue of a fallen hiker? Stopping a domestic dispute? Making arrests? Protecting against potential *murder*?

Facilitators of peace.

Uncle Terry has those words on a coffee mug in his office, but the most peaceful thing I had been able to imagine was him fixing the snack machine before hungry hikers started a riot.

In this moment all the rangers gained something I hadn't given them too much of before. My respect.

And even, to a degree, my admiration.

I furrow my brows at the image of little Mina in her long braids trying to break up a group of backcountry poachers. "What about Mina? I don't—Should she—"

I mean, the girl is still *technically* a teenager. Out here in the woods. Doing all that. I'm not trying to be antifeminist, absolutely *not* . . . but still. She's a ninety-five-pound sewing machine.

Zaiah's voice almost explodes with a laugh. "Mina can handle herself just fine. If you want to lose sleep over someone, choose Kevin."

I grin. "I have wondered a little bit about Kevin. He just seems like he would make a great . . ."

"Anything else?" Zaiah nods. "He's an asset when lecturing in the tourist center, I'll give him that. But the actual walking outside part . . . well . . . we'll have to see."

We follow the turn in the winding river, see the clusters of people up ahead. Some are starting to leave, standing at the water's edge, slipping shoes back on. Several are trekking back up the path toward their cars.

"You like your job?"

I don't know that I specifically meant to ask him this question aloud. I hadn't intended to be so inquisitive, really, about his life. Or what he thought about . . . well, anything.

But I'm finding myself curious. *What exactly is going on behind Zaiah Smith's broody eyes? What exactly makes him tick? What kind of life does he lead outside these 353-square-mile walls? Who are his friends? Family? Just who is he?*

He pauses and looks down at me, seeming to note the weight behind my question. Realizing I didn't ask it flippantly, in such a way that "Sure" or "Oh, there are good days and bad" could sufficiently answer.

He hesitates, as though trying to decide on his next words. "I grew up in Brooklyn. Did you know that?"

Well. Of all the things he could've said, I didn't expect this. I feel like I batted a tennis ball at him, and what was lobbed back over the net was a lobster.

"No," I say, stunned. "I had no idea. So we're both New Yorkers."

"I am not a New Yorker." The rigidity in his voice is unmistakable. "That was a long time ago. And for me it wasn't . . . it wasn't a good experience."

I raise a brow. "I'd be lying if I said I hadn't noticed your distaste for the place roughly . . . hmm . . . every single second it's come up. You looked like a caged animal that night at my house."

"Well, forgive me for being a little preoccupied at the time. If you recall, I was kind of dealing with a situation."

I smile back at the memory, remembering how good it felt to put him in his place that night. A moment of glory.

"But aside from the hotel, yes, I'm not exactly a fan of the city."

I wait. A part of me, a very small part, wonders if he was going to add, "Or the people who live in it."

I can't help noticing he's stopped entirely now, in no hurry to get back to the group.

"Mind if I ask why?"

"It wasn't the best place to grow up."

"I get it. It's not for everyone—"

"On my street the buildings were so tall I didn't see the sun until noon. Two hours later, it was gone. No skyline like your fancy apartment. No room to breathe. Every morning my mom would open the kitchen window and I'd look out as I ate my cereal, staring at the graffiti on the back side of another building. And the smell."

I give a short nod. That was fair. There are always spots in the city where the pungency of a freshly urinated alleyway gets you. "It's not like living in a snow globe like it is here. I'll grant that."

"I spent eight hours a day strapped to a chair in school and the next eight hours before bed told to stay inside. My mom was too busy working to take me places, and where we lived wasn't safe enough for me to roam alone. And even if I did, I had no money. I was a latchkey kid, just like all my friends."

"So you came out here." I shrug. "I get it."

And I did. It made sense for him. Zaiah Smith was made for the mountains. He was made to roam. His job, quite literally, is roaming.

"When did you realize you wanted to leave?" I ask.

"In sixth grade we read *Hatchet*. I was the only kid in class who was sorry for the ending."

Vaguely I remember reading that one around the same time, but the ending is lost on me. "Which was?"

"He got rescued from the woods. Went back to civilization."

"Of course you were." I laugh. "When did you move out here?"

"Eighteen."

"Alone?"

"Yes."

I nod. "Impressive. Granted, I beat you by a year. But impressive."

He raises a brow. "You moved to the city at seventeen?"

"Yep."

"Take a bus?"

"Yep."

"Wouldn't that be something?" Zaiah clicks his tongue. "Maybe we were ships passing in the night."

I grin. Something about that idea feels cozy.

Out of the corner of my eye, I see Mina has spotted us. As she begins to wave us over, I can't help noticing Zaiah leaning into the boulder beside us, blocking her from view.

"What was your first bottom-of-the-ladder job?" he says.

"Ah." I shake my head. "Our common ground ends here, I'm afraid. I went straight into full-time content creating."

"You've never had another job?"

"Not in the city. I had a short spell hostessing at fifteen at a restaurant so bad it got shut down for spreading hepatitis."

His brow rises again.

My fingers skim the water. "I know. My résumé is incredibly intimidating. What about you?"

"I took the first job I could find. Became a busboy. Did it for about two years, until your uncle finally dragged me out."

I grin, completely unsurprised. "How'd he do it?"

"He used to come in all the time—"

There are three restaurants in town and one is connected to a gas station. So. Naturally.

"One day he told me through a mouthful of eggs that I looked like a rabid coon in that place—"

"He's always one for graceful compliments—"

"And that it was time to come with him. He was right."

I laugh. "So you just did. You just walked out on your job."

"I finished up the day, of course. If you haven't noticed," he says, a smile playing on his lips, "he's a rather influential person. How else would you explain how he got you here?"

Which reminds me, just as I feel the heat creeping up my neck at his gaze, why I am here. Really here.

"Oh, right. Yes. About that. That's what I was coming to ask you. I just heard that, apparently"—*unbelievably*, I want to add—"I have been brought here with the intention of saving the park. Is this true?"

Zaiah's easy expression tightens. His smile fades ever so slightly. "There are those at the office who are putting stock in this plan, yes."

"I can't do it."

"I'm not asking or expecting you to."

"But there is a plan to shut down the park if you can't attract more visitors?" I press.

He hesitates. "Yes."

"And we have until . . ."

"March twenty-first is when they say they will look at our numbers and make an official decision."

Barely eight weeks. Eight weeks to turn the park around and bring the numbers up. In the dead of winter.

I feel a rising sense of angst on their behalf. "What else are you guys trying to do, then? What else is part of your strategy?"

"Well . . . you've seen the T-shirts—"

T-shirts? Kevin's *T-shirts*?

He can't be serious.

"What about ads? Targeted online marketing."

But of course. They can't afford to fix the baseboard heat. How can they afford to throw money at some long-lead campaigns?

"And all of your jobs are on the line?" I look at our group in the distance. "Everyone's?"

Uncle Terry has done this job over the course of decades. *Decades.* Would they transfer him to another park somewhere else? Just after he lost Aunt Claire? This is his home. This is his life.

Not to mention Zaiah's. And Peggy's. And even Mina's and Jax's and, who knows, maybe Kevin's.

And for the second time this afternoon I am startled by Zaiah's hands on me, startled by his touch. This time it's gentle, just a single hand on my hands that have somehow, during the conversation, balled together and begun squeezing my soaked T-shirt.

"Cat. This isn't your fight."

I look up to him. Hold the wadded-up bottom of my shirt. "I know."

"It's not fair for anyone to put that expectation on you."

I nod.

He means it. He really seems to want to be saying, "Listen. If I lose my job, my home, and this life I love, so be it. You are not and never will be to blame."

"Still. I'd like to try to help. I'm afraid I won't be able to do much, but I'd like to try."

Zaiah opens his mouth as though to argue. But then hesitates. Exhales. "I'd be lying if I said I didn't see what you pulled off in New York. I don't like the means. For my own reasons, I don't like the methods—or what technology does to people. But if anyone can tip the scale in a moment like this, Cat, I believe it's you."

CHAPTER 11

The Lie

12:30

Instagram ~

catcranwell ✓
Kannery National Park, Montana

450,000 likes
catcranwell Move over Glacier National Park. There's a new-to-me park in town, and I am obsessed with this hidden gem. And truly, there is nothing like coming here in the magic of winter. Pack your bags now. You'll find me at the visitor center. I can't wait to meet you.

View all 34,006 comments
February 8

*H*e did it.

I stare at the teeny-tiny little notification among a thousand letting me know that @zaiahsmith1234567890 (only the most horrendous handle ever) has liked my picture. A notification I could have so easily missed, had I not seen how he had methodically liked every single picture of mine back to 2021.

Me. The only person he follows.

I don't know how it is possible, but this makes me flush more than the rather surprisingly moving poem by @catcranwellfan4eva (followed by a request to send a few concerning pictures, which promptly landed him on the blocked account list for life).

I look at the profile picture Zaiah has chosen. It's not of his face (surprise, surprise) but of a moose standing with head high among a smattering of trees. Not the same one we saw at the hot springs, but I can't help wondering: Did he do it on purpose, as a little reminder of that moment?

A little gesture saying, *Hey, I think about that moment late at night too.*

I swipe out of the app.

"Do you think I have a problem?"

"You have several," Serena says on the other end. "One being that you just encouraged everyone in the entire universe to visit you and become your BFF at that little park of yours. That problem?"

"No."

"Then you're going to have to elucidate."

"With my phone. Or technology in general. Do you think I'm"—my lips shift their hold on a couple of bobby pins as I pull one out and use it to pull back another strand of curled hair—"obsessed?"

"Sweetie, of course you're obsessed. Everyone in the world is obsessed. It's a universally accepted fact. We've all taken a vote and decided we're okay with it."

"Not everyone." I grab another strand and pull the second bobby pin from my mouth, watching myself in the bathroom mirror. "Zaiah openly said he doesn't like it. He said he doesn't like what it 'does to people.' But it's not all bad."

"Certainly not."

"I have to have it for the GPS, of course."

"Of course."

"And then phone conversations."

"Naturally."

"Texting."

"Without question."

"Shoot, look at Mina's business. Social media's been a game changer."

"Not to mention you've just used it to open up the gates to your run-of-the-mill psychos waiting to make a wig out of your hair."

"I'd rather not dwell on that part, thank you." I pause. "The point is, I'm using social media to *get* people here, and there's *power* in our globally connected generation, and it's absurd not to use it to better yourself and others."

I hear Bobby's words spill from my lips before I realize it. But this part, at least, is true. The connectedness and profits that can come from social media are unreal. I've gathered enough about Mina's current financial situation to know what a thousand, much less ten thousand, dollars can do for her. And where else could she build up that kind of business and opportunity for herself in this town? For that matter, name one way she could build up that kind of opportunity for herself with an after-hours side gig in addition to her true passion for the national parks?

This is good.

What I do and have done is *good*.

"I'm talking to you while shopping for a pair of suede sandals, ordering an Uber, and swapping out Tony's face in Photoshop with one of him actually smiling so I can post a picture of fondue night last night. I'm not arguing with you, Cat."

"It's just, you should hear him. You'd think I have a gambling addiction and am trying to win the world over to darkness. *Dang it.*"

The light above the bathroom mirror—and every light in the cabin for that matter—snaps off as I stand in the windowless darkness of the tiny bathroom, curling iron in hand. The phone on the small vanity glows, Serena on the other end.

I snap the barrel off my halfway-finished curl. Move toward the bathroom knob. I hate going outside to flip the switch on the breaker panel. It always creeps me out.

"On it," Mina calls, the floorboards creaking as she flitters across the cabin.

I exhale. "Thanks, Mina," I call out, and turn back toward the mirror. "I'm buying this place a new fuse box," I mutter. "Serena, what have you got lying around?"

I'm only halfway joking, maybe, as I stand in the pitch blackness in my bathrobe for the dozenth time. "If I can just get through curling my hair *once*," I plead to the walls of the bathroom. "I'm not asking for much here. Just *once*."

"I have three brands waiting in the wings. Portable toilets. Crypto coins. Lactation lollipops. Just say the word on any of them."

I pinch my lips together. I'm not going to utter a sound.

The lights turn back on, followed a moment later with Mina calling out, "Turned off the coffee maker. That did it."

"Thanks, Mina," I say back. Of course it did. Of course this cabin wants to withhold the chance at both caffeine and decent curls.

"So have you made plans to come on back yet?"

I toss a look over my shoulder to the closed door and tap the phone off speaker. I pull the phone up, cradling it to my neck, and continue in a hushed voice. "No. Not when there's this situation going on, I can't. It's overwhelming, though. Everyone here's got this unwavering confidence; meanwhile Murphy reminds me weekly that I'm on the brink of destitution. I can't pull something like this off for Kannery—"

"Sure you can. Don't underestimate yourself."

"Serena, ten seconds ago you offered me a lactation lollipop deal. This is how far I've fallen. Let's be realistic."

"I am realistic. Here's the thing. Murphy is fabulous, but he's a stick-in-the-mud. I think it's a calculated move, really. Keeping you depressed about your current situation is his insurance policy that you won't sue later down the road for false expectations in the tiny, *tiny* chance things go awry. He's neurotic like that. But look around you. Things are looking up. I even saw an article in *The Times* yesterday and you know what it said? It said 'Braswell's Club App Faces Hearing Due to Data Protection Authority Claims in Early April.'"

"So?"

"*So?*" she retorts. "So where's your name, Cat? Because it sure wasn't mentioned *in the entire article*. This is the beginning. People are starting to pull you out. Mark my words, it won't be long before you become the victim."

"I *am* the victim."

"Yes, yes. We know. But people are starting to believe it. Anyway, my point here is come back as soon as you can."

I chuckle quietly, winding up another strand. "What about my apartment? You're already done 'babysitting' it?"

"I found a roach in the cupboard last Tuesday. I haven't been back since."

I roll my eyes. Of course she hasn't. Of course she ran right back to Daddy's.

"I'm starting to go stir-crazy with just Chevy around."

"Serena. He is your boyfriend."

"And you are my friend who doesn't use my pearl mink floor pillows as a footrest while playing video games. He's becoming more optional by the day. You, I need."

I sigh. Even in the middle of 353 square miles of silent woods, I can't escape hearing the woes of life with Chevy.

"So. It's eight o'clock at night and you're primping. What's up?"

As I open my mouth to respond, she sucks in her breath. "Please tell me you aren't so starved for attention that those two rangers you talk about are starting to look *good*."

I laugh. "At this point, that's like asking if I'm interested in my nephews."

"I know where you came from. I know you may find it . . . tempting."

I frown. "For the millionth time, Serena, people in West Virginia don't marry their relatives."

"Fine. Who are you trying to impress?"

Steadily, I ignore her, setting my phone on the vanity and tapping to speaker again. I grab a new strand of hair and snap it into my wand. "Nobody." I wind up the section of hair, stopping an inch from my temple. "Really. Nobody."

And it's entirely true.

Yes, *technically* I was caught off guard by Zaiah's arms when he wrapped them around me, even more when he pulled me close and lifted me off the river bottom. *Technically* I found his strength and willingness to put himself between the moose and her calves for my sake appealing. But the thing is, I am human. I am female.

And frankly, my pool of available men has shrunk from four million to three, *literally* three—and that is a generous number given two of those include Jax and Kevin. I can't help noticing a man among boys.

But that doesn't mean I'm such a fool as to recognize how opposite we are.

Or to forget my life doesn't belong here.

And his, as he said in so many words, doesn't belong in a city, or with a girl like me.

"I don't believe you. *Mina!*" Serena shouts over the speakerphone sitting precariously on the ledge of the small vanity. *"Mina!"*

"Shh."

But a moment later Mina pops open the door.

"Hi, Serena." Mina leans down toward the speaker.

"Hi, darling," Serena coos. "How is all?"

"Pretty good." Mina takes a step deeper inside the bathroom that already isn't big enough for one. "Got another two hundred Cozy orders last night after Cat did one of her ads. Just trying to get a few done now before we go."

"That's fantastic and not at all surprising. So. Who is Cat trying to impress tonight? D'you know?"

"No one," I put in, at the same time Mina says, "We're just going downtown with the boys."

"Really? Which boys?"

She shrugs. "Kevin and Jax. Zaiah is going to drive so—"

"Is he now? Spending the evening with Zaiah, Cat? That brooding mountain man you always complain about who partners up with you in the town hypothermia games and casually saves your damsel-in-distress butt from straying moose on any given Saturday? That Zaiah?"

"I'm *not* spending the evening with him," I say, visibly pinking in the mirror. "We are going *into town*. And honestly. I've seen you take a shower and start your makeup from scratch just to hit up Panera with me. I'm just recurling a few loose strands."

Mina raises a brow at the very obvious complete makeover I've done in the past hour, and I resolutely avoid her eyes. "Anyway." I pull at the sleeve of the third sweater I've tried on this evening. "I'm bored. There is, and I can't emphasize this enough, *nothing* to do here."

"Not so!" Mina says defensively. "Our Snowball Cornhole Risk Blitz game begs to differ."

"I stand corrected." I frown at the mention of my entertainment source the past four painful nights. "We have Snowball Cornhole Risk Blitz."

People my age are riding the stock market waves.

Getting married.

Having children.

Me? I spend my evenings getting dragged outside with Jax, Kevin, and Mina, throwing snowballs as fast as I can to liberate Australia and finally lock in that sweet continent bonus.

So yes, when Zaiah stood next to his truck and offered to take us to the tiny, nearly nonexistent downtown, my own convertible beside his beneath a foot of snow, I jumped at the chance. Of course I wanted to get out.

Any sane person would want to get out.

Frankly, if Jax had asked me, I just might have taken him up on the offer.

These woods are the air Zaiah breathes, and in the past month I've realized what my air is. People.

Total strangers. Blocks of people. I need to see them. I need to be near them. I don't even need to talk to them. I just need to know they know I exist.

"Well, I'm proud of you for starting to get out there again. And to think, all it took was locking you up in the wilderness thousands of miles away for you to remember your social roots. This is progress."

"For the record," I say, "him teaming up with me at the polar bear plunge was only because somebody had to go with the first-timers and I was holding up the line. Apparently they want to ensure people don't die trying and blacklist the town."

"Not really," Mina interjects, inspecting a tube of lip gloss. "The town doesn't really care if tourists live or die. If you haven't noticed, everything's kind of go-at-your-own-risk out here."

I stop and turn, the final piece of my hair in midcurl. "Zaiah said someone had to go with me."

Mina shrugs. "I heard that. I think he just didn't want you to feel bad about being scared."

"He *lied*?"

Serena and I say this in unison, although she sounds absolutely giddy.

"Wait, so he did that just to make her feel better? Do you hear this, Cat?"

I frown.

My cheeks are beginning to match the color of my blush sweatshirt again. It's too hot in here with Mina and me crammed in like sardines.

I'm having trouble processing this.

"Mina, what does Cat look like? Is she blushing? How red? Out of ten?"

Mina scrutinizes me. "I'm going to go with seven."

"Cat, you liar. Mina, pay attention now." Serena's next words come with a sense of urgency, as if she's giving a super-secret combination to a lock. "Is she putting on the lipstick with the *007* on it?"

"It doesn't matter what lipstick I put on!" I protest. Okay, *007* is my lucky lipstick, and yes, *coincidentally*, I did happen to put it on tonight.

"I . . . I'm not sure." Mina looks uncertainly at the dozen tubes lying around. "There's a lot of lipstick here. Oh, this one?" She lifts the only tube without a top. She inspects the label. "Yep."

"I *knew* it!" Serena cries triumphantly.

"Really, Serena. This is *nothing*. I'm just excited to go out—"

"Excuse me, Cat. I'm in the middle of a conversation with Mina."

Mina's mouth opens, but I snap the phone off the vanity before she can say another word. Or worse, hear another word from Serena and get any ideas. "We-gotta-go, it's-getting-time, I'll-call-you-later, have-fun-at-hot-yoga, bye," I say, all in one swift blend of words before Serena can get another word in edgewise.

"Mina! Call me! My number is—!" Serena cries, just as I hang up and swiftly turn my phone to silent.

Mina's mouth is drooping slightly as she watches me pocket my phone.

After several seconds, she points to it. "So. How do we want to play this? My role is to . . ."

"Ignore everything you heard and pretend it never happened."

Mina nods. "But you do know I . . ." Her words trail off with a meaningful look.

"Know something may be going on that I'm not prepared to discuss? Yep."

Mina clicks her tongue. "Okey-dokey, roomie. Then I say we get going."

As I'm taking a step to follow her, I turn toward the mirror and carefully sweep a few loose curls to the side of my face. Pick up the lipstick tube with the gilded number *007* across the side.

And hesitate.

I slide it across my lips one more time. Nude. Just a touch of pink. The perfect choice for trying without looking like you're trying. A master of deceit, aptly named.

Why?

Why am I doing this?

Of course I'm not really doing this to impress him. At this point I'm pretty sure that if I wanted to even get on Zaiah's radar—*really* be on his radar—I'd have to throw away my phone, makeup, and 99 percent of my clothing; take up making deer jerky and canning on the weekends; and start going on long walks while reciting Thoreau.

Basically, I'd have to just not be me.

Mina's words, however, play over in my mind. *"I think he just didn't want you to feel bad about being scared."*

As does the feeling of hovering over the black water's edge, aware of everyone's eyes on me, feeling the pressure to jump from everyone around and yet paralyzed with fear at the inky water crashing against the frozen corners of the hole in the ice.

And the relief—the total, all-consuming relief—at Zaiah's sudden presence. The way he took hold of the moment. The press of his strong fingers still wet from his previous jump wrapping around mine. Steadying me with his firm, unwavering grip. Looking me in the eyes and telling me that it was time to go. That he was right there with me.

The only one in the crowd to see me, the real me, the quaking little girl on the inside, and come to my aid.

Lying about it, even.

For my sake?

For my sake.

I look in the mirror and rake my fingers once more through the curls of my hair. My liner is almost indistinguishable as it melts into my lash lines. No falsies today, but instead three meticulous rounds of mascara. Bronzer just barely around the cheekbones. Blush light as rose petals spotlighting the few freckles on my cheeks.

My green eyes sparkle against the swoop of my auburn hair above one brow. Ever-so-slight curls twirl down to my shoulders. I wear a simple light-pink sweatshirt and jeans above dark boots.

One cheek shows a little pinker than the other, and I raise the heel of my palm and rub until it's buffed to match the other side.

I look ready.

I look . . . I hope, lovely.

With one hand on the knob and the other on my phone, I slip over the password and reflexively check my socials once more before I open the door. News floods in through a quick scroll. In the span of a minute, I take in the fact that an acquaintance from high school had her baby, a tsunami hit off the coast of Japan, my doorman's mother passed away, a light acquaintance adopted a shelter cat, a girl I don't remember had a miscarriage, and war is on the horizon on the other side of the world. A thousand bits of news and emotions and pieces of people's lives all taken in, ingested, in the span of a minute. A thousand emotional peaks and valleys with very little time to process one before experiencing the next.

My chest tightens ever so slightly as I bounce from one to another, a small part of me wondering, *Are we meant to know every thought, deed, traumatic event, and triumph of every person in this world?*

I tap over to my home feed, then to my most recent post. The likes aren't as high as they should be. The comments, on a quick skim, are weak. Internet-troll comments small but mighty.

Hmm.

I smile and snap a selfie of myself in the mirror, then a second and a third.

I hear Mina's footsteps coming toward the bathroom and quicken, feeling the sense of urgency as my fingers slide madly over the screen. Cropping. Editing. Typing a thoughtful caption. My brain stretches to think of something witty and cheery and short and on-trend all without looking like I'm trying too hard.

Something that'll cause people to comment back and engage, thereby pushing the post out to others, without sounding desperate for that exact thing.

I feel the hunger, the desperation to get it out into the world, to redeem myself, all the while knowing my window for the night is closing. Knowing that if I don't get it out now, I'll have to do it later.

And when exactly will that be?

In the truck on the way into town with Mina and Zaiah?

No.

I did that all the time back home with friends—in the taxis and the Ubers we always concentrated on getting that last post in, responding to those messages, just scrolling. But with them? No.

They don't get it. This is a town of people who set their phones out of sight during meals with company. This is a town where if you look at your phone in the middle of conversation they stop and wait until you look up to resume.

They'd do something worse than judge me if I finished this post on the way down. They'd pity me.

Poor Cat. Always glued to that phone.

I hear Mina's footsteps nearly at the door and press Post.

Swiftly I slide the phone into the back pocket of my jeans and open the door with my other hand. Mina's eyes are curious. "You . . . ready?"

"Yep," I say brightly and stride toward the door as though she was the one slowing us down.

CHAPTER 12

The Flat White

O at milk flat white, one pump of simple syrup. *Thank you."*

The hushed words come on an exhale as I stand before the forest-green barista counter and look over my shoulder, watching Mina with her arms and legs wrapped around three freed-up barstools, snapping like a tiny Chihuahua at people who come near.

She was so proud of herself for unearthing my caffeine recipe from years ago, I haven't had the heart to tell her about my vegan lifestyle yet.

The Honeypot turns out to be exactly as lovely as I wondered it might be, and given trucks, vans, and even snowmobiles line the snow-covered street, I'm not alone.

There's a sign on the door stating the hours, but beside it is a Post-it note with hand-scribbled words: *If lights are on, come on in.*

A hum comes from a massive, expensive-looking black espresso machine grinding beans on the counter. Several old leather couches and bistro seats line the narrow building, with exposed brick on both sides. For once in this town, something besides country music is playing over the speakers. I vow here and now to clean the mountain of snow off my car and make the trek downtown once a week, come what may.

Some things are worth risking sliding off a mountain in a convertible.

This is one of them.

The building smells of cologne, mud, and coffee beans. The earrings of several women across the room glint beneath the industrial-looking pendant lights. As do the freshly cleaned belt buckles adorning several men's pants.

So.

This isn't just the place to get coffee.

It's the place to get a date.

"I'm the *same way!*" I hear Mina exclaim from a distance. "I remember exactly where I was the day I heard the gray wolves were delisted from the endangered species list. I cheered hearing how well it went reintroducing them into the wild. It's something you just don't forget . . ."

A man who couldn't be a day under fifty opposite her nods fervently as he slides his cup, and arm, closer to her on the table. Kevin turns beet red as he watches.

Hang on.

I turn around to Zaiah. "People *reintroduced* wolves to this area?"

Zaiah, just finishing his own order behind me, sidles up to the waiting area at the end of the bar beside me. He grins. "They almost went extinct."

"And that's . . . bad." I shake my head. "Honestly, do you all realize there are other things to do than try to get yourselves killed *All. The. Time?* It's like all you guys want to do is freeze to death or drive on ice sheets or, oh dear"—I throw my hands up—"life's getting too boring, let's just throw some wolves into the mix and hope for an earthquake."

I finish with a flourish and slap my hand on the counter harder than I intended. Cheeks warm, eyes bright. It was good to get out like this. Coffee shops, restaurants in general, are my element. I understand the rules of order here. I feel at ease with the unspoken etiquette.

That plus the company of the evening makes my blood pump faster. Makes me feel alive.

Still, that may have been too much. Am I too much?

But there Zaiah is, nothing but a bemused smile on his lips as he watches me.

But I suppose I'm not the only one to show off a new part of me tonight. It's surprising seeing him like this too. Clad in that hideous green uniform? Constantly. But tonight he wears a plaid button-up beneath a sage-green sweater. His brown hair doesn't hide under that stiff, wide-brimmed hat but sweeps to the side, the front-most section rolling like a wave.

A mountain man, yes, that part of him is inescapable, but one who looks like he could be picked up by a scout for L.L. Bean so they could take shots of him holding stacks of wood while staring off into the distance. A mountain model.

A new thought forms and my stomach churns. *Is this what he's doing too? Dressing up like all the other guys in this place and going on the hunt?*

I clear my throat and press on. "But really, Zaiah. Wolves. *Wolves.*"

"I'd worry this will keep you inside, but then we have those pesky rattlers to deal with. So . . . it looks like you're pretty stuck."

The barista sets a coffee mug on the counter, and Zaiah picks it up and holds it out, handle forward.

I take the mug. The handle is hot, hot enough my eyes can't help flickering down to Zaiah's large, callused hands that took hold of the mug itself without flinching. Making sure I didn't take the mug by the hot end, making sure my fingers didn't get burned. Quietly, subtly considering me.

Stop, Cat.

If this isn't next-level overthinking, nothing is.

The perfect, foamy hot sip of flat white slides over my tongue and rolls down my throat. My insides shudder like an old car finally oiled. This has been too long.

Zaiah seems to pick up on this, because he nods to the drink. "Not the same as Peggy's Dollar House roast, eh?"

"Not the same species."

He laughs, and my fingers tingle, desperate to stretch toward the phone in my back pocket. Snap a picture of him like this. Capture the way he stands there, crow's-feet around his eyes, layered sweater, rolled-up sleeves, low laugh. Not for others but just for me. A way to remember the fleeting moment.

But of course I can't.

For so many reasons, I can't.

I tuck my free hand in my pocket, push it deep down in case it tries to betray me.

"So. I just discovered you lied." I feel my phone buzz inside my pocket and ignore it.

If I was expecting him to be confused about what I was referring to, I'd be wrong. Because the second the words come out of my mouth, he replies, "I did. But it was a well-meant lie."

I raise a brow. "Would that stand up in court?"

"Without question."

Mina—whose male companion is now standing a few inches off her, trying his darndest to sit in the chair beside her she's protecting with her life—looks around him and waves toward us. She points to the seats, and I nod as though to say, "Yes, coming right over."

Neither of us budge.

A girl reaches around me, picks up her coffee.

I move out of the way. "Somehow I expected you to be the George Washington type. The scout's honor, never-tell-a-lie-even-if-it-causes-me-to-be-run-over-by-a-train kind of a person."

His lips twitch. "Seems you come with a lot of preconceived notions."

I hold back a laugh. "I think we both know that statement goes both ways."

Somebody else steps in for their drink, and he slides it over without looking at him.

"For one thing," I say, "I don't think I ever thought you'd be the kind of guy to wear . . . well, that."

"What's wrong with what I'm wearing?" He frowns as he looks down.

"It's a cable-knit sweater. Honestly, if I had to wager on it, I would've nailed you for a furs guy. A live-off-the-land, sweat-of-my-brow person. Instead here you are. Commercial clothing. And"—I squint at the contents of his steaming mug—"is that *whipped cream*? You are a *whipped cream* guy?"

"I enjoy it on occasion."

He says it with such simplicity that it suddenly makes sense. No games about playing to stereotypes, just doing what he thinks is right and simple. Of course, then. Of course the whipped cream.

In my periphery Mina begins to make a little walking demonstration with her fingers, followed by pointing at the barstools. As though we must be confused on the exact process of walking and sitting.

Neither of us move.

"So. You joined Instagram."

His face doesn't move a muscle. "I don't recall that."

"ZaiahSmith1234567890. The worst username, for the record, I've ever heard."

"I'm sure there are dozens of Zaiah Smiths out there. And just as a thought, whoever did make that username may have done so because every other number combination was taken."

"And this fellow liked every one of my photos." I break into a grin, seeing at last a shift in his expression. "Are you blushing?"

"It's hot in here. There are too many people."

I laugh. "Right. I forget your cap is at six."

"Hey, guys. There are a couple chairs open over there."

We both turn toward the barista, and I'm surprised to see several cups have gathered behind us. The barista is no more than twenty, but even I can see the little knowing smirk through the curls falling over his eyes. He slides a cup between us to the customer behind.

"Oh. Sorry, Zach." Zaiah nods to the middle-aged woman who just picked up her cup and gently touches the small of my back as he guides us forward. "Sorry, Mrs. Givens. We just got caught up."

"No problem at all, sweetie," she replies, and of course, *of course,* she's now giving a suggestive little wink.

Does this whole town know what's going on with everybody over *everything*?

Mina at this point is throwing stranded-on-a-deserted-island-looking-at-a-passing-plane waves.

"We should go," I say. "Mina's going to break something."

"Of course." But we're only a few steps toward the table when he pauses. "Don't you have millions of followers? How is it *possible* you noticed?"

This time it's my turn to flush. "I may have checked for your name a couple times."

More like a couple times an hour the past two weeks.

So. Zaiah Smith looked through my account and liked a hundred pictures and posts, not because he wanted to be noticed but because he wanted to be supportive. Quietly supportive.

My steps slow to the point the couple we are inching past look up at us, clearly thinking we're trying to listen in on their private conversation.

"So . . . um." I clear my throat. I'm not sure I want to hear what he thought about my account. It's intimidating. Like saying, "Hey, so you read my entire diary last night. What did you think about everything I've done or thought the past ten years? Are you still interested?" But the curiosity is killing me. I have to know.

I try to keep my tone as nonchalant as possible. "So what did you think of it all?"

He nods to the couple as if to say, "Mind your business and we'll mind ours."

"I understand the six suitcases now."

Great. That's what he got from it all? I own a lot of clothes. I'd be annoyed, but he's doing that mischievous twinkle-in-his-eye thing that makes me struggle momentarily to take full breaths. Where his mouth says one thing and his forest-green eyes say something completely different.

There's a long pause.

Finally, he exhales.

"It's impressive. I don't think I could do what you do in a million years. I'm actually a bit intimidated by you, to tell the truth."

A laugh hiccups in my throat. "Me? No way. You're the one who shoots bears with bows and arrows here." When he starts to object, I jump in. "Don't try to tell me otherwise. Peggy explained how we got the bear rug in the office."

"It was with a crossbow. And the bear was getting aggressive with the tourists. I had to do it."

"Fine. *Crossbow.*" Like the crossbow was any *less* impressive. "A pathetic *crossbow.*"

He smiles and shakes his head, but I can't mistake how his chest puffs up just a tad beneath his flannel.

He takes a few more steps. Pauses. "I did wonder about that rémoulade you made for those crab cakes, though. What did you use instead of dairy?"

"Oh." He's referring to the story I posted last night when the group (aka Jax and Kevin) came over for dinner. "I just whipped up a vegan yogurt. Two cups of cashews. Some apple cider vinegar. It turned out really well. Even Jax ate it."

I pause.

What is that look he's giving?

Is he . . . feeling *left out?*

"You know," I continue, "our Snowball Cornhole Risk Blitz nights are pretty off the hook. It's exclusive, but I know someone who may be able to get you in sometime."

He shrugs, but I can see the way his eyes light up. "Oh, I don't know. I hear the venue is pretty small. And cold."

"True." I raise a finger. "But the chef is first rate."

And not to brag, but it's true. While the games are played and the sewing machine *pings* and a movie hums in the background, I seem to have stumbled into being the in-home chef. The praises are pretty effusive, which is nice but unsurprising considering menu selections prior to my arrival seem to have revolved around gas station hot dogs, popcorn, and grilled cheese.

"So Jax really eats your food? Even though it's all vegan? I have a hard time believing that."

I nod. "He hasn't clued in yet. Last week he told me my BBQ ribs were a bit chewy, but that's as close to being caught as I've come." I glance over to Jax currently eating his way through three breakfast sandwiches stacked together. "And don't you tell him yet either."

Zaiah raises his unoccupied hand in surrender. "You won't have any trouble from me. I'd like to see this ignorance firsthand anyway. You take partners in this risk cornhole game of yours?"

"Yes. You can be mine if you like. I'm a weak link, though. You will, without question, be dragged down by me."

His laugh is deep, warm. "You really know how to sell yourself. I'm in. Partners."

"Zaiah Smith," a voice behind us booms. "Just when I thought I was going to have to come and drag you down here myself."

I glance over to see a man roughly Zaiah's age. His beard is equal in thickness to Zaiah's—which isn't saying too much considering beards in Kannery seem to be part of the dress code, as commonplace as trucks and *My Kid's Chicken Can Beat Up Your Kid's Chicken* bumper stickers. He's wearing a light-khaki Carhartt jacket.

And yes, he's notably handsome too.

Not in the same way I'd have to admit that Zaiah is handsome, but a little more city smart: a healthy mix of knowing both how to handle himself in the elements and also how to hop on a subway. Someone who can make it in both worlds.

Except—I note both of his hands on the handles of his wheelchair—perhaps with a little more effort. There's a makeshift platter on the handle of one side of the chair, and a carafe half full of coffee resting on it.

Zaiah looks visibly startled. "Mark."

He hesitates, then leans down into an awkwardly given man-pat-slap-hug.

Straightens.

He looks around, like he's trying to find an extra chair to make himself eye level. When none present themselves, he resumes. "Heard you went out of town for a while. When did you get back?"

"Last Friday. I was hoping to make it back for the winter carnival but got tangled up and had to miss. Heard it was a heck of a turnout, though."

Interesting.

In Kannery, a heck of a turnout equals the same number of people a neighbor squeezed inside her eight-hundred-square-foot apartment for her New Year's party last year.

His gaze shifts to mine with interest. "And who do you have here?"

If I'm not mistaken, I sense Zaiah hesitate.

"Oh." Zaiah shifts to me. "Cat, this is Mark Huddleston. We were busboys together at that diner I worked at when I first moved out here. He poured me my first cup of coffee." Zaiah raises his cup. "And still does. This is Cat—"

"Nice to meet you," I say, cutting Zaiah off before he can finish giving my name.

For heaven's sake.

Never after your first five million followers say your first and last name in a room full of people when you'd rather not be noticed. These are elementary-level rules even techy eight-year-olds know.

"She's started doing some work at the park," Zaiah adds.

"Terry's girl, eh?" Mark holds out a hand and shakes mine. "I've heard good things."

My eyes flicker down to the tray attached to his chair. "So. You work here? It's quite the place."

"Own it. And thanks. It may not be the vibe some locals were going for around here, but I like it."

"Seems to me everyone in the town likes it." I scan the room. "You could heat the whole place up with the body heat."

He laughs, and his blue eyes twinkle. "You caught me. That's the real goal here. Save on heat expenses."

I laugh, and then I see it.

Zaiah shifts on his heel. It's a subtle shift, and frankly, did I not make it my job to know exactly how many lights were in a room, their wattage, and the exact degree I needed to incline my head in order to highlight my best features at all times, I would've missed it.

But I didn't.

I'm an expert in this.

And without question Zaiah, whether he even realized it or not, shifted.

Just the slightest degree toward me. Just the slightest degree toward boxing Mark out.

Mark is either oblivious or, more likely from the way he seems to keep his eyes trained on me so resolutely, doesn't care.

"So you're Terry's famed niece," he says, without breaking a smile.

Ah. So he does know.

"I was just in the city a few months ago for a trade show," he continues. "I went in for CFIR. It's an independent coffee retailer thing. Just a good ol' swap of best techniques and industry gossip." He waves a hand nonchalantly. "Probably sounds pretty lame. But I did snag that beauty when I was there." He points backward toward the counter. "Cost more than I'm worth to ship it here, but she was worth it."

He looks so admiringly at his lady—the black espresso machine with glinting antique gold knobs—I have to smile.

"Well." I raise my cup. "This is the best flat white I've had in a long time. I commend you for your conference-attending efforts."

He claps his hands together and calls over his shoulder to no one in particular, "You hear that, everyone? A bona fide New Yorker appreciates my coffee."

"Good, because the service sucks!" a voice in the back calls out.

A chuckle moves around the room.

He ignores it. "Wanna take a shot at the machine?"

I look up at it with interest, then to the line backing nearly to the door. "I'd love to. Doesn't seem like you guys are slowing down, though."

"This ungrateful lot? They can wait."

He laughs jovially, and I find myself drawing near to him and his confident, easygoing attitude. And I would indeed like to take a shot at the espresso machine, actually. I always wonder what it would be like when I see baristas dashing about, pressing buttons and cranking knobs.

But there's something in the way Zaiah slowly pulls into himself, his hands moving uncertainly into his pockets.

It's a new look from him, that uncertainty.

Endearing in a way. Makes me feel protective, even.

Although, of course, there's nothing to feel protective over.

I will be returning home in a matter of months—weeks, perhaps, from the way my image seems to be gluing itself back together.

Still.

I am stepping backward before I know it, and in an instant, I sense the pressure drop out of the air like a balloon.

"I'd love to . . . sometime." I leave it with an obscurity that can mean anything from "I really would love to but I have to go" to "If this is your invitation to something more, I'm halting it now."

"But I have to do some rescuing," I say. I tick my head over my shoulder toward Mina. The man is now hanging over her shoulder while she holds her phone.

I squint. No, that's not her phone. It's his.

"I can't remember offhand when the next meteor shower is, but I definitely know the best spots around the park," she says.

And there he is, smiling down at her like a vampire floating overhead.

Good grief.

Kevin! I glare at him as he stands beside her, nervously twitching but making no attempts at interception.

"Just call me next week," Mina says. "I'd be happy to help you scout out the best ones for when your fiancée visits. What a *sweet idea*! That's exactly how I'd want to be proposed to myself."

"Hang on." I hand off my mug to Zaiah. "I gotta intercede before Mina gets herself kidnapped. It was nice meeting you, Mark."

As I elbow my way through the crowd, I notice Zaiah has jump-started toward the duo as well. And while he may have the height advantage, I have had years of experience slipping through crowded rooms. I reach the table first, snap the phone out of Mina's hand just as she's passing it back to the man, and bare my teeth while I method-ically delete her number.

My eyes stay trained on his. My grin is overbright. "Hi," I say, fingers mechanically flying across the screen. "I'm going to give you one chance to tell me who you are"—I swipe my own phone out of my pocket, snap a picture in the time it takes him to blink, and tuck it back inside—"and why you are asking a teenager to get in a car with you at night in the middle of nowhere—"

"I'm not a teenager," Mina cries. "I'm nineteen—"

"That counts," Kevin interjects. Oh sure. Now he's all talk.

"And Paul's just about to get engaged!" Mina adds.

"Well, Paul. That's terrific. Marriage is a beautiful institution." I put my hand on the back of Mina's chair. "Now never talk to Mina again."

His receding hairline turns the color of beets. "This is a public establishment."

"Nah, bro." Mark wheels up beside Zaiah. "I run this place. You'd better move along."

Paul's eyes swivel from Mark, to Zaiah, to me, his previously pale skin turning redder by the moment.

Mark, Zaiah, and I stand in a row by the window, arms over our chests as we watch until his truck's headlights reach the end of the road and turn.

Eventually, Mina clears her throat behind us. "He seemed really nice—"

"We will talk more about this when we get home," I say.

I spin around to Kevin. "And *you*."

The lecture lasts for several minutes, Mark steadily refilling my coffee as I slosh it around with "And another thing!"

Going over the basics of stranger danger. Cuing in on the signs of stage-five creepiness. And overall, just telling Kevin to man up.

The horror stories to back up the warnings aren't hard to find; I just scoop from the top of the bin in my memory.

By the time I'm done I realize the shop has quieted down significantly.

The espresso machine grinds quietly for a single customer.

The snow outside the window has stopped.

The room is nearly empty.

"Right." I lower my finger at Mina and Kevin, who look like scolded puppies. I reach in my pocket and give Mina my debit card. "Now go get yourselves hot cocoas for the ride home. I'll be right there."

The two skirt off, and as they do so, I turn around.

Zaiah and Mark are still here.

"Sorry," I say a bit sheepishly. My face is hot. "I just . . . They needed to get a little reality check."

"You're a good breed, Cat Cranwell." Mark tips the rest of the coffee in the carafe into my mug. "You'll always be welcome in my establishment."

I laugh. It was nice to feel so openly welcomed. So openly liked for being, well, me.

"Thanks, Mark. All creeps aside, I think you have the finest shop in town. I fully intend to come down more often."

"Excellent," he says, his grin broadening. "We need a designated bouncer."

His eyes flick from me to Zaiah.

For a moment, there's silence.

And then he nods, a respectful sort of nod, and wheels backward. "I'd better go start breaking down the machine. See you soon, Cat. Zaiah, don't be a stranger. It's nice having you around again."

As Mark wheels off, picking up leftover coffee mugs from tables as he goes, Zaiah turns to me. His voice is quiet. There's a respect in his voice I haven't heard before. "You've had quite a few scrapes in life. I wouldn't have expected you to be so . . ."

"Street-smart?" I say, filling in the gaps. "Yeah. Well. You kind of have to be if you're going to do what I do. Take the good with the bad."

"How do you sleep at night?" His question is sincere. Curious.

I laugh. "With three security guards, five locks between me and outside, and a hidden panic button GPS on my wrist."

He gives a curious smile, and I pull up my sleeve. Show him the charm bracelet with the button attached. "I've only had to use it once, but it's handy. Calls the police straightaway and gives them your location."

The smile in his eyes dies away.

"It's not that expensive, really." I shrug my sleeve down. "And frankly, given what I saw tonight, you can bet I'll be gifting Mina with one."

Zaiah gives a breathy chuckle. "Seems you've given a lot for this job of yours."

Now it's my turn to pause. I twist the mug in my hands.

Not really sure if this is something I want to say.

In fact, these are words I never say.

"No. My life the past thirteen years has been all threats and failed attempts. My life before that wasn't so lucky."

A crease forms between his brows as Zaiah's eyes darken.

I halfway expect him to jump in, asking me what happened, begging for details. But he doesn't. He just leans against a barstool beside the bistro table, watching me, a look of patience on his face as if he has all the time in the world if I want to share. Or don't.

A light turns off, signaling it's officially time to go.

I don't know why, but I feel compelled not to leave him hanging. To tell him the rest of the story. So he knows. This is me. This is also me.

And what do you think of that?

I turn my head and pull back my curls from behind my ear. Run my finger down the smooth scar falling along the back side of my scalp. The thin, raised scar never grew hair back. It's almost invisible to the untrained eye, even when I put my hair up. But here, now, I pull the part up just right so he can see.

"How did that—?" he begins.

"Beer bottle. My father has impeccable aim," I say wryly. "I was all the way across the room, and yet . . ." I shrug. "Not quite fast enough that time. A friend got my call and took me to the hospital. I took the bus to New York from there. Never went back."

Storm clouds churn in Zaiah's eyes. His hand releases the mug on the table. He shifts and takes a step forward, getting a better look.

As he does I take in a breath of him, the sudden scent of something beyond just cold and pine. Something distinct. Something that tickles my nose.

Cologne?

Zaiah put on cologne tonight?

I feel a tickle along my spine as his hand touches my hair, pulling it back.

His face hovering inches above mine.

That hard, handsome face of his is cold as steel as he traces the wound that required thirty-two stitches, following it all the way down to the nape of my neck.

Something catches in his throat as he finishes. The whisper of a growl in his chest. The rising of anger. Fury.

He clears his throat.

There's something about his breath this close to me, his concern hovering over me, that makes my knees threaten to quake. "Terry never knew?" he says quietly.

I raise a brow. "Do you honestly think he wouldn't be in jail right now for murder if he did?" I laugh lightly. The air crackles a little with Zaiah standing so close. It's making me feel a little dizzy, actually. A little bit like my feet are having a hard time finding the floor.

My mouth opens, searching for something—anything—to say.

And whereas I feel myself loosening, Zaiah's fingers tighten around my curls. His hand clenches, fingers sweeping the back of my neck momentarily, before he lets go.

Takes a step back.

And there it is. Fire in his eyes.

"That's a horrible thing to have experienced, Cat. I'm so"—he swallows, his Adam's apple running down his throat—"I'm so sorry."

"You weren't there. There's nothing to apologize for."

It's surprising to see him like this. So affected. Such strong emotion running across his face.

And yes, I've had over a decade to deal with the facts of my childhood. Yes, he's only hearing it now. There's something to be said for shock factor.

But I guess I just didn't expect him to take it so seriously.

To care, really, in a world full of tragic people and problems, about me.

About the things of my past.

So much.

Nobody—not even Serena—has ever cared quite so much. With looks to kill.

Part of me shivers under that look. Shivers in a way that makes me want to shiver forever.

"I haven't told Uncle Terry much. He knows enough to know it was worse than he feared, but we sort of leave it at that. I don't want him to feel responsible for the decisions I made. I—" I take a breath. Did I just share a secret with Zaiah? "I hope you understand."

The music clicks off, signaling with certainty that it's time to leave.

He nods, and I know that's as good as his word.

"I see you doing that all the time." He looks at my fingers running over the locket from Uncle Terry. "He must be very special to you. Now I understand why."

"He's all I have. I'd do anything in the world for Uncle Terry." My chest feels tight. A lot more than I intended has been shared about my life; it's not a bad thing, but it's just . . . heavy. I need a break. I need to talk about something else.

"So what was that about not being a stranger? Mark made it sound like you stay away from this place. What, you just can't bear to leave the woods?" I say, half kidding but also hoping, a bit desperately, that that's not the truth after all.

I like the woods. The forest is growing on me, admittedly. But really, you can't be a hermit *all* the time. I realize even as I'm saying it, I'm measuring him up with a questionnaire as if to see just how compatible we are. It's not just a question out of idle curiosity.

Part of me is saying, "But seriously, Zaiah. How much time do you *really* spend outside of society? Because I can't—I'll never, ever be—the girl cooking up deer-jerky stew alone in some cabin *all* the time. You can't expect that of me."

But then he swallows.

And I see him pull back.

Everything about his body language screams, "I'll allow you to share your secrets. You can do whatever you like. But I'll be keeping mine."

"It's a great place," he says. "Mark—Mark runs a good shop. I just haven't had the time to get away lately." He pauses. "When we lost half our paid staff last year, it came down to just me and your uncle." His eyes flicker over to Mina, Jax, and Kevin, now standing by the door. "Those three are young and a handful, but they've also been what's made it possible to survive the past year."

I frown. He's trying to distract me from the heart of my question. He's trying to pull my heartstrings on another topic.

I won't take the bait.

I feel foolish, sharing something with him when he so clearly is uninterested in doing likewise. Like I've stretched out my hand for a handshake, only to have him stare at it, then retreat.

Together we move toward the counter and I set my mug among an empty dozen. "Right," I say. "With any luck we'll get the park back on track soon."

\\//

The coffee has been cold for a while now but I press the takeaway cup to my lips and take a thoughtful sip. I'm bundled up in four thick blankets and bearskins, per usual for my evening routine when the temperature dips down into the single digits and the baseboard heaters fight their nightly battle. My knees are tucked in at my chest as I sit up on the pullout bed and watch the flames lick the roof of the little woodstove. Mina went to bed an hour ago.

Days go by easier. It's easier not to think about the crisis overhead or the fact that Bobby went missing the day after everything exploded. It's easier to focus on trying to find any viral way (any, any at all) to discuss the generational effort to restore whitebark pine without putting people to sleep. It's easier to enjoy watching the sideshow of Jax sneaking behind Peggy's back and pouring the pot of coffee out every single time she refills it. It's easier to watch her chase him out with her cane when the jig is up.

Mina isn't alone; I too have my floating vampires hanging over one shoulder. Mine are just financial.

I take another sip.

Maybe I was fairly hard on her tonight about that. But the girl is nineteen years old. Beautiful. Innocent. More unique and fascinating and just a delight with every passing day. My, well, my roomie.

And just . . . well, the protective side of me took over. I'm not always going to be around. And here she is, living out here all alone. I need to know she can take care of herself.

A flash of light reflects on the window beside the door and my eyes automatically flicker over. It's too late, though. The light has come and gone, but I frown anyway. It was probably just a reflection off the flames in the woodstove, but the angle felt off. The light was more of a silvery white than orange.

I push the blankets off.

Pause a moment.

Stand up.

Listen to the world of silence but for the crackling flames.

Tap.

What's that?

Not an animal. Just the lightest of taps on the exterior door.

Tap.

Tap. There it goes again.

I move to the back of the door, out of view from the window.

Put my ear a little closer to the wood. Listen.

Tap.

A pause of three or four seconds.

Tap.

Why, it almost sounds like gravel hitting the door.

My hand is just on the handle, ear pressed against the door, when I hear an absolute roar over my shoulder and feel my body thrust to the side.

"Ahhhh!" Mina cries, throwing the door open. Her waist-length hair is unbraided over her nightgown, and around her waist is a pack with a series of items—*Is that a knife strapped onto her ankle?*

As I watch, stunned as I hit the wall, she leaps barefoot into the blackness, holding out two giant cans of bear spray.

Leaps.

"Mina!" I scramble to my feet. I look around frantically for something, anything, that could possibly be used as a weapon, then grab the first thing I can find.

Somebody yelps in the distance, a man's voice, as I run onto the porch.

Zaiah's truck spews gravel as it slides to a slushy stop in front of the cabin, and before I know it, he's thrown his door open and is running through the beam of the headlights, rifle in hand.

And there's Uncle Terry, peeling up in his truck behind.

The screen door of Jax and Kevin's cabin next door slams and there they are, halfway dressed but aiming weapons.

A man scrambles to his feet behind a tree but only makes it a few steps before Mina pulls herself off the snow and leaps on him with the agility of a mountain lion. I know because last week I saw a mountain lion.

Right now, I'm not sure which of the two I'd rather go up against.

"I yield! I yield!" the man cries. It's a little hard to hear, though, given his entire body is spread-eagle, facedown in the snow. And Mina's sitting on him.

Wait a minute . . .

I know that voice. That nasally, high-pitched voice. "Adam Adams?" I move closer.

And sure enough, there he is, his Panasonic camera with a dozen special parts and pieces littered around him in the snow.

"*What are you doing?!*"

But, of course, I know what he was doing. Just like he tossed around that fabricated story about his cat getting run over at my launch party, the ridiculous man really would do anything for a good shot. He would've just *loved* a picture of me standing on the porch of this little shack, accompanying some dramatic headline about my becoming a wild mountain woman.

After Uncle Terry handcuffs Adam and hauls him off, all the while asking why he has such a stupid name and how he decided to do such a stupid stunt and saying how he should be left out here in the cold for the night to learn his stupid lesson . . . and so forth, there's a moment of silence.

When the brake lights pull out of view down the mountain, Mina turns. Her arms are crossed as she frowns at me. Her eyes flicker down to the object in my hands. "Really, Cat? A lamp?"

I look at the table lamp. The white fabric shade knocking slightly in the breeze. "I didn't want to come out empty-handed."

"And what were you doing with your hand on the knob?" Mina throws her hands out. "Were you actually going to *open the door?*"

I shrug, avoiding her gaze.

"Have you *never seen any movie ever?*"

And while I receive the blunt end of a fifteen-minute lecture by Mina, getting everything from "What happened to all your street smarts, roomie?" and "Of course you had to live in one of those high-security buildings. Otherwise *apparently* you would've gotten yourself *killed*," Jax, Kevin, and even Zaiah stand around her, lips clamped shut as they try not to smile.

After my toes are almost certain they are going to fall off, she exhales, finally running out of steam. She looks at me. Gives one more shake of her head. Points to the door. "C'mon. Let's get you some tea and tuck you into bed."

The group begins to disperse, and I'm halfway up the steps when I pause. Turn. "Wait. So how did you know to come so quickly, Zaiah? Did someone call you?" I flick my eyes down the road. "And Terry?"

Something was oddly suspicious about all this.

Zaiah, who is locking the rifle back into his vehicle, hesitates. Then he points up to the closest tree. Then the second.

I squint at the blinking red lights.

"Terry said they were for the eagle cam," I say. "For their nests."

In the distance, Jax explodes with laughter.

Zaiah grins. "Yeah. Well. Have you seen any eagles?"

"Wait." I hold up a finger, whirling around to confront each face. "So . . . wait."

"It's for you, you beautiful nitwit," Jax says, a comforter over his shoulders as he stands shivering on his porch. "He wanted to take some extra precautions for *you*."

"And you all just . . . decided to come over if something happened?" I look, stunned, to Zaiah, seeking clarification with my eyes.

But Zaiah just shrugs. "We're rangers, Cat. You may have had some good security in the city, but here? Here you've got a team who's got your back."

CHAPTER 13

The Supportive Niece

*W*hen I said that I would do anything for Uncle Terry, I meant I really would happily do anything.

Except this.

And yet . . . here I am.

I grit my teeth as I stand beside the black Jeep, then swig another bit of Pepto.

"Hi, Brody. Yeah. Long time." My voice rings with the smoothest, happiest tone it possibly can. So much so I find I'm standing on tiptoes as I try to keep up the ethereal tone. A tone that coos, *No, I have not been all but hung up on by creators trying to distance themselves from me as much as possible the past five calls. No, I am not getting more scarred by the moment putting myself out there and getting doors slammed in my face.*

Brody has 7.2 million followers among his accounts. Smaller than me by a few million, but then, he doesn't have several million at the moment trying to knife him in the back.

Brody is your typical Hawaii-based, abs-of-steel-meet-humor content creator, using both his six-pack and his baby blues along with his mildly humorous videos for a winning combination.

He's five years younger than me.

Run-of-the-mill in the creativity department.

Sticks mostly with regurgitated trends. And when running low on ideas, simply lifts up his shirt in the mirror for a selfie to see him through the dry spell.

Oh, and he has not so subtly asked me out on two occasions.

Both times I politely turned him down with distance as an excuse, and both times he took it fairly well.

"Cat Cranwell." It's loud in the background on his side of the phone. A hum of people and clattering plates as though he's in a restaurant. "So. Where is this mysterious place you've run off to lately? City girl has gone a long way off from New York City. It looks from the videos like you might be inching closer to my world every day."

My fabricated laugh tinkles as I turn in my boots, following the six-foot or so path I've created in my pacing. I appreciate, though, that he hasn't brought up the elephant in the room about my life.

"I am getting closer to Hawaii, it's true."

"Getting your fill of nature, too, from the looks of it. You know the offer still stands to come out for that kiteboarding lesson sometime. We could make a great team of it."

Zing.

And there, so casually proffered, is the magic word I wanted to hear.

Team.

He's up for partnering.

For whatever reason, whether because day by day I'm making a little more progress crawling out of the pit I fell into or because of lingering feelings, Brody is willing to have his name associated with mine.

He hasn't shut the door on me entirely.

Which means he may be up for a project idea.

And some bartering.

"Actually, Brody, I did have something in mind I wanted to ask you about . . ."

And as I break into the same pitch I've thrown to half a dozen other creators the past three days, I try hard to ignore the plethora of distractions around me.

Keep my head down from midday sunshine that makes the snow covering our surroundings shine like crystals. Avoid catching the eye of any overfriendly locals I've come to know from my frequent trips to the coffee shop of late.

And I have made frequent trips to the coffee shop.

It wasn't three days after I talked to Serena about my coffee shop experience that she called to say she had just so happened to talk with a Jeep company and was able to work out a partnership with a rental in exchange for the occasional snowy, grinning-as-I-lean-on-the-side-of-the-machine, dramatic-backdrop-of-mountains-behind-me posts. It was a miracle, given my last collab ended up featuring a portable nursing pump even though I am neither nursing nor with child, and I quickly snatched it up.

For a couple days I watched the weather, and the *second* the clouds let up, I took the afternoon off, pushed all the snow off the convertible, and drove it (very, *very* slowly) down the mountain.

I swapped the adorable, impractical car for the rugged, towering machine. The tires themselves come to my waist. The treads could cradle a small child.

When Jax saw me driving back up to the office, tires chewing up gravel and spitting it out, his jaw dropped. Apparently I had secured one of those military-grade, all-but-bulletproof Jeeps rumored in dark corners and alleyways to successfully roll down the side of a cliff without a dent.

In fact, those were the first words out of Jax's mouth when I stepped out of it. *"Cat.* Wouldn't that be *so cool* to video you . . ."

The answer was no, for the record.

A resounding no.

So while the Jeep may have been overkill (and unfortunately now forces me to shoo off all the males in town like fruit flies), the new drive was worth every single brand post. I didn't even mind telling people how wonderful it was as an all-terrain vehicle. This is one partnership where my zeal on-screen is genuine.

It gets me to town whenever I want.

It gave me instant freedom,

And now I suddenly have more options than just Snowball Cornhole Risk Blitz for entertainment. I've actually had some adult conversations, and that first sip of coffee was like I'd swallowed a cloud in heaven.

It was a beautiful thing.

"I don't know, Cat. I want to, I really do, but I'll have to talk with my manager . . . I'm not sure I even have the time. I'm hitting up Thailand at the end of March," Brody begins.

My hand grips the phone tighter. I swivel on my heel in the snow.

It's time to throw the sucker punch.

"I'd be happy to help you out sometime, too, Brody. Anything within my power you can think of. Just say the word."

There's a long pause.

It's a risky thing, offering whatever I have.

Used to be, that offer would've really meant something.

Now, though? Now there is half a chance he'll laugh in my face.

After a pause so lengthy I begin to question if the call has been dropped, he exhales. "Tell you what. I do this for you, and when all the Bobby stuff is over, you give me another call. Maybe you'll come out for that kiteboarding session."

I press my lips together. Smile, touched at what he is saying. He believes things will work out for me. He believes this whole Bobby lawsuit mess will all pan out. Even if Bobby is nowhere in sight and there's a court date looming.

He's willing to extend a hand on that bet.

"I really appreciate it, Brody. It's a deal."

I get off the phone and log in his name beneath the tiny but growing list of influencers willing to make the trek out to Kannery National Park to shoot some content and promote it on their channels in the next month. I'll have to throw in a bit of my own reserve cash for the partnerships.

And Brody, along with three other full-time travel bloggers with decent lists, is now my biggest catch.

I'm doing this, though, for Uncle Terry. For the way I come into work and there's a wrapped-up breakfast sandwich—sausage thoughtfully already taken out (I never have the heart to mention the dairy)—from the local gas station sitting on my desk. No explanation. No acknowledgment. But his door is open and there's a wrapper on his own desk and crumbs in his beard.

I do this for the way he and Peggy keep a steady word game going on their phones, and how throughout the day I'll hear one of them mutter from their office desk about the other being a cheater.

I do this for the way he lit up seeing my new promotional material for the national park (complete with nice, normal T-shirts), and for the way he gazed in admiration at a postcard I created from my shot on Cades Peak, then launched into a story of the time he and Aunt Claire camped up there for their twenty-fifth anniversary and had a run-in with some hikers wearing nothing but bandanas on what turned out to be Naked Hike Day.

Kannery Park is a precious place to him. This job, these people, truly have become family.

And for him, and for Mina, Jax, Kevin, and Zaiah, I put myself out there, place my bets, hoping their jobs and this place can be saved.

Announcements come over a megaphone, and I pause to listen.

This is, for the record, the strangest event I've ever heard of.

Huge haystacks surround the outside of the winding track of snow, several children sitting on them, eager spectators. A dozen snow-covered mounds dot the track, jumps two or three feet high. Red rings like those kiddies use to dive with in the pool dangle from posts around the track.

Parked vehicles are everywhere, truck beds dropped as people mill around, throwing on blankets and setting up lawn chairs for their viewing experiences.

A huge rust-colored barn sits off to one side, crackling bonfire beside it.

There are no signs detailing what to expect from this place.

No flyers or banners or anything official to scream, "This is an approved event. Please come."

No. It's just a good ol', passed-through-the-grapevine, everybody-hop-in-your-trucks-and-bring-your-casserole-for-the-potluck backcountry weekend.

Kind of like those street races in *Grease*. Only, apparently, with horses. And skis.

My fingers tingle, taking in the bright, shiny black Jeep among the rows of trucks covered in haystacks and blankets. People left and right hold steaming cups of coffee. Kids hold cups with hot cocoa. The perfectly ancient barn. The flickering orange of the flames. Horses everywhere. Cowboys in denim and boots and wide-brimmed hats abound. All on a crisp layer of snow.

If I had the time, I'd grab one of those hot cocoas the kids are running around with. Pop the lid off. Stuff it with an extra layer of marshmallows for a photo.

Instead I lean my elbow on the front of the Jeep, ensuring my red nails are front and center as my hand pulls back my shoulder-length curls and rests on the side of my neck.

Click.

Click.

I flip through the shots as people around me settle into their seats and a girl no older than thirteen begins a wobbly, *"Oh, say, can you see?"*

My white coat goes down to my knees, heat radiating from the shoulders of my sleeves down. My curls ripple neatly down my back beneath my snow bunny–white beanie. Mascara is extra thick and extra black in contrast, striking a match in my hazel eyes, making them almost glow. Signature red lipstick applied. Simple gold studs in ears.

Aside from the troubling lines around my eyes and my hands that keep looking like the Sahara Desert no matter how much moisturizer I apply, I look nice.

Good, even.

I would prefer to drop a decade, but I suppose this is the way it is.

I smile a little to myself as I hear my own thoughts.

I'm not perfectly accepting of my aging status—online purchases of miracle-working beauty regimens are a current weakness—but I do feel less of an edge out here.

Something about not being so surrounded by mirrors helps. And models. And mirrors and models at the same time.

I've seen Mina get ready for work, and there are days she doesn't check herself in the mirror once. *Once.* Not even to brush her teeth. She just stands there, toothpaste on the precipice of overflowing from her mouth as she jabbers on about some kids' hiking tour she wants to start or sings about tulips.

Not worried about her hair. Just living.

It's rather freeing here. Taking off some of that pressure.

My phone rings.

It's Mina, guaranteed about to tell me to hurry up.

I spot the haystack just as she's setting a picnic blanket on it and she and Kevin sit. As I walk, I see Zaiah at the other end of the ring, someone tying a rope to his saddle. Uncle Terry, meanwhile, paces while on the phone behind him.

Zaiah's wearing a tan cowboy hat and a matching denim jacket. It looks tough, worn at the elbows and along the sleeves, with the collar extending up to his Adam's apple. He looks different.

What is it?

As if hearing my thoughts, he looks over, and we lock eyes.

His beard. He's trimmed his beard.

Not entirely, but enough that it looks . . . well . . . really, *really* good.

He holds the reins lightly with one hand, the same casual

confidence and familiarity as he had driving us around those icy roads my first night.

Then he gives me the slightest dip of his head. Smiles.

I give a little wave.

"Well, well, well. Look who's come out to see the show."

I turn my attention away and break into a full-out grin.

Mark is sitting on a sleek black horse, one so large I have to crane my neck ninety degrees to see him. He's gone all in on the cowboy act, too, I see. Shiny silver stars on his boots glint in the sunshine. His Carhartt jacket matches Zaiah's but in a crisp, black style. No signs of wear and tear. Not even creases yet along the elbows.

A rather well-chosen plaid collar peeks out from the neck of his coat. He, too, holds the reins like someone who's spent his life in the saddle—only this saddle fascinatingly slips all the way up his back, along with a tan strap that hugs his middle.

A clever saddle for adaptive riders, and I'm glad to see he looks as cheerful and carefree as he always does. "So you're riding in this crazy race too?" I say. "What is this thing called?"

"Skijoring," Mark replies. "It's something else. You'll love it."

"So, what . . . you just steer a skier around?"

Mark slaps a hand to his chest as though shot. *"Please,* Cat. You can't speak about such a treasured event with such flippancy. I am *the guide."* He presses his fingers together like an Italian chef I knew once who used the same motion while speaking about his secret sauce. "My role is to *carry* my comrade to victory through a series of precise, death-defying tasks. One ill-chosen step and"—he snaps his fingers—"that's it for Pooh and His Pals." He drops his hand. "And yes, technically I suppose I steer a skier around."

I laugh. "That's your team name? Pooh and His Pals?"

"Absolutely not. We are not children. We are the Honeypot. But you may refer to me as Pooh, as I am the ringleader."

Ah, of course.

My eyes flicker almost unconsciously over to Zaiah, cheeks warming as I see him still watching me. He looks like a man trying not to care that the girl he likes is laughing with another man. "So you're our competition, I take it?"

"Unfortunately . . . that is the case."

"And Zaiah is going against you?"

Mark nods. "Even more unfortunate for me, that is also true."

I laugh. "Well." I stretch out a hand to shake his. "I wish you all the best, Pooh of the Honeypot and His Pals."

"Pooh and His Pals of the Honeypot." He pulls open his Carhartt and plaid shirt to reveal another poorly made T-shirt with a crudely drawn bear beside a pot of honey.

I raise a brow. "Seriously? So this must be a thing then. You all revel in poorly made T-shirts."

A skier yells Mark's name across the field and he picks up the reins. "I'm up. Make ours next year and you'll have coffee on the house for a month!" And with a pull on the reins he turns the horse toward the area where all the horses and riders are clustered.

It really is like a rodeo, I realize, watching a man on skis settling into a gated enclosure.

A few minutes later a woman steps onto the snowy track and raises a flag.

She drops it at the starting cry over the megaphone, and the gate opens, revealing the skier inside.

Mark gives a yelp and the horse charges.

Children on haystacks cheer as the man clinging to the rope swings around the track. Mark checks over his shoulder, grinning wildly, and swings the horse to the right just in time for the skier to hit the sloping hill and go flying.

The skier—one of the baristas whom I now recognize made my latte just yesterday—reaches for a hanging red ring and snatches it just in time.

Wow.

So. This is fun.

I lift my phone and shoot pictures as the horses and their hooves pound against the snow.

Mark really knows his way around the track, and as the pair race around, gathering rings and flying, I find myself cheering and clapping with the rest.

"Stop it," Mina hisses, dampening my claps by covering them with her hands. "We're supportive but not *too* supportive."

She watches Mark and the skier with aloof eyes, careful to keep her face as placid as possible despite some surprisingly quick turns that gather cheers.

I laugh, clapping on.

As Mark and his "pal" finish—beating the score of the previous rider and putting the team in first place—I press my fingers to my mouth and let out a high-pitched whistle.

The announcer steps back out into the middle of the track with his megaphone, staring at a sheet of paper in his hand.

"Representing our beloved Glacier National Park," he says, as Mina elbows Kevin to make room for Peggy, "we have the Glacier Boys eyeing the prize."

A round of cheering ensues. Mina's and Kevin's hands go limp.

"They've put up a good fight the past two years, always comin' in close but never close enough to take the crown from Kannery National Park. They're looking strong today, though, folks. Will this be the year they take home the saddle?" The man with the megaphone steps off the track, just as two of the men I remember from the hot spring wave to the crowd. They look pretty chuffed up about the attention, waving about ten seconds too long.

Peggy rolls her eyes as the one on the horse begins pumping his arms to encourage more cheering.

"Billy Joe!" she calls out, cupping her hands around her face. "You stop that foolishness and get on with it!"

His pumping stops at her voice. He drops his hands. Lifts the reins and gets into position.

"I've been his Sunday school teacher since he was a little boy," she says to me. "Since Sunday school days he always tried to hog the show."

The flag drops and the boys kick off with a start, fast enough to compete with Mark and his team. I'm getting pretty invested in watching the pair round the track, when Peggy's phone starts to ring.

Her hands scramble in her jacket pockets, and she pulls out her phone. "Hello?" she says. She pauses. Listens.

My attention turns from the race as I see her expression shift. "Oh. Oh no. That's too bad. Does he need someone to take him?"

She pauses.

Nods.

"What's going on?" I say.

She hushes me, and a minute later she ends the call and slowly rises to her feet. "Jax hurt his ankle doing a practice jump. I'm going to give him a lift to the hospital."

"What about the race?" Mina's attention shoots to Peggy. "We can't compete without a skier for the race."

"He will be fine. Thank you for asking." Peggy rolls her eyes, earrings dangling, as she turns and hobbles off toward her truck.

"What should we do?" Mina calls after her.

"I think that's fairly obvious, isn't it? One of you will need to fill in!" she calls back, just before prying open her truck door, tossing her cane in, and hoisting herself inside.

Mina looks shell-shocked as Peggy's truck rumbles out of the field filled with parked vehicles. She gazes at Kevin.

"Don't look at me." He shakes his head.

I don't blame him. I've seen Kevin trip on his way to the bathroom.

"Well, I can't," Mina says. "Sliding on sticks isn't my game."

Right.

The irony of her saying that while a skier yips after snagging a red ring in the air.

I frown. "So I guess we'll have to forfeit?"

The world, if it were possible, goes silent.

There's a crackle in the air as Mina's shoulders stiffen, her back to me.

Static.

Just like I would imagine one feels right before being struck by lightning.

Mina turns to me. Quite slowly, I realize. A little bit scarily. She looks as if I have all but slapped her on the back. As if I have just succumbed to some terrible, unbelievable betrayal.

"Cat." Her voice is carefully measured calm. "We cannot forfeit. This is the Tenth Annual Skijoring National—"

"Is it really a 'national' race when it kinda has the invented-in-our-backyard vibe?" I say.

"—Race, and *we* are Kannery National Park, two-time leading champions and rightful owners of *the* original 1910 saddle owned—"

"Allegedly," Kevin puts in.

"—by none other than President William Taft's personal secretary's good companion's brother, Johnathon King. The man who rode out on horseback through this land—"

"Also allegedly."

"—and came back to tell his brother, who told the personal secretary to the president himself that he should do all within his power to protect this area. The man who convinced—"

"More or less," Kevin chimes in.

"*—President William Taft himself* to sign a bill into law making Kannery National Park—"

"—and more well-known Glacier." Kevin raises a finger.

"—into a peaceful park and protecting over 353 square miles of pristine field and forest—"

"—and more impressively, Glacier's 1,583 miles," Kevin says.

Mina's all but standing now as her voice and sense of justice rise. "And we *cannot* sit *idly by*, watching"—she narrows her eyes in the direction of the Glacier team—"*those boys* take what has been rightfully ours through the sweat of our brow—"

"Technically, Jax's and Zaiah's," Kevin says. "Although we are proud supporters—"

"—by default. Due to an unfortunate circumstance out of our power."

Oh *my gosh*.

Mina is holding a fist to her chest now. Chin raised. "This is not just about the saddle."

Are her lips quivering?

Are Mina's lips actually quivering?

"It's about honor. And we cannot let our park, our beloved, cherished park, be swallowed into that hole of Glacier and swept aside."

Silence follows.

A couple of the kids on a haystack near us begin to clap.

"So . . . you want me to give it a shot?"

True, the words pop out of my mouth before I really think them through, but still. The lip quivering.

It's actually quite effective.

Mina clutches my hands. "*Yes.* Yes. Of course. *You*, Cat. *You* do it."

I can't help but laugh.

Any possible thoughts of wimping out and retracting the idea are really out of the question when she looks at you like that. "Now, there's a real likelihood I'll end up falling on my face out there." My fingers start to ache in her vise grip.

"There is no honor in falling. Just failing to take the risk," Mina says with dead seriousness.

"Right. Terrific."

I manage to pull my fingers away before Mina crushes them in her eager gratitude for the honor of a job she's not technically getting paid for and the possibility of keeping the dirty leather saddle over my head another year—my seat from which, for the record, I have looked up and seen the "Made in China" label.

Still.

There is a sort of adrenaline pumping in my veins as Uncle Terry helps me borrow all the gear I'll need, and twenty minutes later, I'm outfitted and guided into the starting area full of horses and skiers.

"What are you doing?"

The large brown snout of Zaiah's horse notices me first, followed by Zaiah in the saddle.

"Jax hurt his ankle and I can't say no to Mina, so apparently I'm saving the park's honor." I lift my poles with a hopeless shrug.

Zaiah gives a surprised expression. His gaze shifts momentarily to Uncle Terry, as though wondering if he's going to stand up and say anything.

"He found me all this," I say, answering Zaiah's thoughts and nipping that idea in the bud.

Zaiah scans my ensemble, from the goggles from Big Joe's Fly-Fishing to the Uncle Buck's Gas Station and Market bright-red skis and black poles. I'm still wearing my white coat. I opted to keep my small, thin leather gloves since those from Genie's Book Barn were XXL.

The goggles are much too large, and most unfortunately a little wet (I try not to think about it) from the sweat of Big Joe, who used them in his race fifteen minutes ago.

"Is that . . ."

Zaiah pauses.

I know what he wanted to finish that sentence with: *wise.*

It wasn't too long ago we settled into our nonverbal, unofficial agreement, and it's clear he doesn't want to break it. He's not allowed to question my ability to do anything while out here or make disparaging remarks about my use of social media, and I'm not allowed to do anything, well, stupid.

A horse and skier swing by for their second turn around the track. It's quite a different viewing experience from here, standing so much closer to the track as the skier flashes by.

It's all quite quick, isn't it?

Much quicker than it looked on a haystack thirty feet off from the real thing.

But here . . .

I squint, trying to calculate how easy it'd be to get trampled here. Is it actually possible? If a horse is going thirty miles an hour, and a skier fifteen feet behind is catapulted thirty degrees into the air, how high of an incline does said skier need before she is thrown to her death?

It's like an SAT question created by a morbid mathematician.

And here it is: the first moment in my life where paying attention in geometry could've come in handy.

I flinch as a wave of snow sprays my way and the skier flies in the air.

Not just in the air, but in the air at quite the swinging angle whilst trying to grab a second red ring.

"What I don't understand," I begin, "is why every social activity in your state has to be something like *this.*" My voice is rather higher pitched than I'd intended.

I glance over to the several people lined up beside their horses and riders, readying themselves to go. All men.

"Ha!" The rider of the galloping horse prods it on with a squeeze of his legs, and the skier bounces as he lands on the ground with the sudden jerk of the horse's draw in the opposite direction. His left ski lifts off the ground for one precarious moment, ski facing north, horse and rope drawing him east.

The position looks just like my friend's five years ago, right before I watched her knee snap at the force of the unforgiving angle. She tore her ACL and had to be airlifted.

I squeeze my eyes shut for several seconds, not interested in watching something gruesome I'll never get to unsee (again). But when I open them, there he is going strong around the next turn.

I release a breath I didn't know I was holding.

"Cat."

See Zaiah's piercing gaze.

"I'm fine. Really."

"I appreciate what you're doing, but it's really not a big deal to forfeit," he says.

I hold back a bark of laughter. "Try telling that to Mina. If I don't at least try, I don't think she'll let me back in the cabin."

The man with the megaphone calls over the crowd, "And now for our reigning champion, the team that has won two consecutive years in a row, our beloved local park . . ."

I bend down. Grab the rope attached to Zaiah's horse.

"If you need me to stop, just raise your hand. Okay?" Zaiah's dark-green eyes are so intense, so probing as he looks at me.

I find myself having to swallow before I give a little shrug. "Sure. Yeah." My voice is quiet. Squeaky. I clear my throat. Try again. "C'mon, Kannery. Let's represent."

CHAPTER 14

The Tenth Annual Skijoring National Race

I stand at the starting line, clutching the red rope and staring at the closed metal gate like a bull at a rodeo moments before it swings open. This has to be how bulls feel.

Heart pounding.

Sweat starting to itch my thighs.

Restless legs as I wait in this bizarre Montana version of a Kentucky Derby meets Jet Skiing meets skiing.

Swept by the intense hush of the audience into feeling this is all somehow very, very important.

Ears attune to the breathy exhales of Zaiah's horse as it jerks its head against the reins, also impatiently waiting on the call to run.

Eyes attune to Zaiah as he sits on his horse, holding the reins with steady hands.

His broad shoulders poised and still as a statue.

Focused.

One.

Two.

Three.

I breathe the numbers slowly, forcing myself to focus on something besides my own heartbeat knocking against my rib cage. Knees bent in position, I tell myself to think about something besides the rising temptation to drop the rope and call it quits now.

Then the voice cries through a megaphone, "Gooo!"

The metal gate is thrown open and Zaiah's horse launches toward the track.

My shoulders jolt as I'm swung forward, locking my knees in a bent position as my skis begin to slide over icy snow.

The crowd is already whooping and hollering.

None, though, so loud as Mina. *"Go! C'mon, team! Go! Go! Go!"*

It's a loud cry, impressive given the distance—until I see she's no longer on the haystack but running alongside the track, cheering us on with raised arms.

"Go, Cat!" she cries, running. *"Go, Zaiah! You. Can. Do. It. C'moooon!"* She's shaking the gate. Actually shaking it.

I swipe spraying snow from my goggles with my forearm and grin. The snow-covered ground is packed tight, despite the dozen or so sets of hooves that have trod upon it today.

My legs burn in that familiar way that they only do when on a pair of skis, and I settle into position as the first jump comes into view.

Here we go.

Zaiah whips his head back, making sure he's guided me in line with the ramp.

I take it and then follow the incline.

His eyes are still on me, he in his cowboy hat craning his neck around as he watches my first jump.

My first reach for the ring.

I let go of one hand on the rope in the air.

Loop my hand through.

Feel the ring slide up my arm.

One down.

Cheers erupt as I land. A massive smile overtakes my face.

Kevin's standing beside Mina now as close to the track as possible, Mina clutching her hands. *"Gooooooo!"* she screams, then makes massive, elaborate sweeping motions with her arms.

Two more jumps, and I see what she means.

I hear the cadence of Zaiah's horse. The *clop, snap, clop, snap, clop* of his run.

My eyes tick to the giant clock beside the stands.

It's fast. Yes.

On par with several of the teams who've gone before.

But not fast enough.

"Speed up!" I yell, and Zaiah looks back.

I yell it again, and see in his eyes the hesitation. Feel it, even, from his legs pressed against the horse through the rope, to my hands, to my own burning thighs.

The doubt.

The decision of whether to trust the words of the petite girl in the white leisure coat or his own instincts.

I raise my eyebrows.

He shakes his head at me but turns forward.

Snaps the reins.

The extra energy is immediate.

The thrust of power almost overwhelms me.

I see now how Kannery has held the title the past two years.

I bend my burning thighs deeper, preparing for the turn in the track.

The snap into the air is like nothing I've ever felt before, and I almost miss the ring, but I grab it by the tip of my thumb, and it rolls around like a Hula-Hoop along my arm until it reaches my shoulder.

I drop it, and a boy runs inside the track behind me to pick it up and place it again.

We round the track for our third and final loop.

"Ten seconds to gain on our current first-place holders, the Glacier Boys!" I hear over the megaphone. "Will they do it?"

Mina is clutching Kevin's arm, screaming maniacally as we pass.

Feeling my arms as tight as rubber bands, I yell, "Give it everything! Give it all you've got!"

Zaiah doesn't look back, but I know he's heard me by the way he drops his shoulders. His grip on the reins is tight. Both boots tap against the sides of the beast, quick as Morse code, giving the horse the go to give it his all.

It's exhilarating.

This sport is exhilarating.

My arm connects with one. Two. Three more rings.

As my skis land with a shaky *thud* on the second-to-last jump, the last ring comes into view.

"Ten, nine, eight," the announcer calls over the megaphone, counting through excited breaths of his own as his eyes bounce between watching the clock and us. The number of seconds left if we want to beat the Glacier Boys and win.

The final ring is still over ten yards off.

Mina is screaming her head off in my periphery.

Even Uncle Terry has taken off his cowboy hat and pressed it against his chest. Watching like he's seeing something miraculous.

My arms don't have any fight in them.

I'm barely hanging on.

But eight seconds.

I can do anything. Anything. For eight seconds.

I let go of the rope with my left hand and reach forward, gaining a foot as I grab onto the new bit of rope.

Let go of the rope with my right, do the same.

Reach. Pull.

Reach. Pull.

Reach. Pull.

Until the horse's pounding hooves are just a few feet in front of me, beating the ground just below.

Zaiah whips his head back and does a double take.

Sees how I'm now just a few feet behind him and adjusts the horse, going straight for the on-ramp themselves.

They race up and jump.

Me after.

The ring dangles, and I swoop my arm through.

A strong swoop.

It hooks up to my shoulder immediately.

"Unbelievable! And we have a winner!" Megaphone Man cries as we land.

The crowd goes absolutely wild.

"Give it up for a *tremendous* ride from Zaiah Smith, senior park ranger, and"—he tilts to the side as Uncle Terry mutters something—"Catherine Cranwell, senior media strategist and social coordinator extraordinaire!"

Mina has her arms wrapped around Kevin, dragging him up and down by the neck as she jumps.

I gulp air as my skis slow to a stop.

I drop the rope and for a moment feel dangerously close to throwing up.

After snapping off my skis, I sit on the ground, panting.

A moment later I'm all but knocked sideways by Mina, followed by an eruption of pats on the back and congratulations.

The attention feels overwhelming, and I look up, dazed by both what I just accomplished and the number of new people in my face. Something about it is different from the many, many times strangers have gotten in my face. Something about it feels . . . startling.

New.

I look into their eyes, and I realize what it is.

They don't want something from me.

They're not hovering over me, trying to get a picture to show off for social clout or trying to make friends hoping I'll help them climb the influencer ladder. They aren't congratulating me in order to get me to post about their shoe business or Jeep business or hotel. They just are . . . happy for me.

Just because.

"All right, everyone. Make way. I'd like to congratulate my partner now."

People part as Zaiah makes his way through the crowd.

He stops over me, cowboy hat tipped down as he looks into my eyes.

One *heck* of a smile on his face.

A smile of pride.

A smile of pure joy.

I begin to lift myself up on my elbows, but they ache so much I smile and leave them limp at my sides. I shake my head. "Sorry. Your partner will just have to lie in the snow until she freezes. I've given everything for the park, including my arms."

"That's too bad."

I nod.

And without a second's hesitation he drops down. Reaching one arm under my knees, he wraps his other around my back until his hand grips my shoulder.

Lifts.

I'm raised like a child into the air.

The crowd, as if it were possible, gives another round of cheers.

"Winner's gotta get her arms back," he explains, stepping out of the circle. "Now if you'll excuse us, we'll be making our way to dinner."

I laugh as we move through the crowd. Although at his words I feel my whole body flushing, from the tip of my nose down to the heavy ski boots still on my feet. Either that, or my battery-operated coat has malfunctioned and I'm now burning alive.

Dinner.

CHAPTER 15

The Confession

*W*hat exactly does he mean by dinner?

Did Zaiah Smith just declare he was taking me to dinner?

For that matter, did he just skip the part about asking me altogether?

Cat Cranwell?

I could have him know that I have never been so insulted in my life. Make him aware, as I can guarantee he currently is not, that I have been in no fewer than eight magazines in the past two years, targeted solely on the topic of my relationship status. Marriage proposals slide into my DMs daily.

Daily.

And this man thinks he can just take me on a date without my permission?

This man?

This . . . one.

Zaiah's chest smells deeply of leather, his Carhartt jacket rough against my cheek. Leather and hay and aftershave and sweat, not the kind that makes you yearn to find a polite way to hand over some deodorant, but the kind of sweat of a day of hard work. The kind that mixes so perfectly with the other scents, you think, *Well of course. It wouldn't be perfect without it.* There is a difference.

Yes.

I suppose I can do dinner.

People are giving one another knowing looks as we pass by. Commenting, "That Terry's girl?" and elbowing others to pay attention to the scene unfolding.

Zaiah either doesn't see it or doesn't care.

I flush all the more.

Like a child, really. As if I've never had a grown man pick me up and carry me.

Which, now that I think of it, I never have.

But we're not heading in the direction of the far-off mountains. We're here.

In a crowd of people encompassing essentially every citizen of Kannery itself.

And people are staring.

"My boots are over there," I say, and when he walks me over and sets me gently on the ground, I give a feeble, "Thanks for the lift."

As if he were a taxi.

I reach for my boots, feeling the growing need to do something. Say something. "Your arms must be killing you."

"That was incredible," he says. "You were incredible."

Our words emerge simultaneously, and I smile as I register his.

"I discovered skiing when I was twenty. I'm a sucker for a good ski trip."

"Colorado?"

"Sometimes." I hesitate, uncertain how he would take it. Should I say the full truth? "Mostly Switzerland."

The finest crease forms between his brows, but there's no "Are you serious?" escaping his lips. No need for me to ball up like a hedgehog to defend myself. "I've heard Switzerland is beautiful. I've always wanted to go."

No criticism. Just honesty.

I exhale just a tiny bit, and the tension in my shoulders eases. "It is. It's breathtaking."

He pauses. Nods. "I'm not a big traveler. Not intentionally. Just I never have found a place I'd rather go than right here."

"What a surprise. You?" I say with a smile. "Let me guess. Once you got out here, you've had a hard time leaving. Saw these big, beautiful mountains and just couldn't let go."

"More like, I weigh the cost of a few days away, and it never quite seems worth it when I have this here." He smiles. "So yes, in a way, I suppose I got here and couldn't let go."

I laugh. As I finish lacing up my boots, I feel something funny in my coat. What is that?

Oh yes. It's the wind, a twenty-degree wind getting through the barrier.

I reach inside the pocket as I stand. My thumb and forefinger find the button and press.

"You seem more related to Uncle Terry than I am. What about family, though? Your mom? Do you keep up with her?"

He raises a brow. "Yes."

But there's something in the way he looks at me, amused about something I clearly don't know.

"There's my girl!" Uncle Terry departs from the group of men huddled around the bonfire and walks over the snow my way.

He gives me the hardiest pat on the back I've ever felt. The kind of slap that would dislodge a chicken bone from one's throat. "That's the Cranwell spirit. Now how about the champion's dinner?"

And as it turned out, Zaiah did not skip the moment of asking me to dinner and all but throw me over his shoulder like a caveman declaring his girl. Apparently what was known to every person at the skijoring event, except myself, was that after the Tenth Annual Skijoring National Race was the Tenth Annual Champions Potluck, and *of course* that's what my skijoring partner was referring to.

A good ol'-fashioned chili potluck in a barn.

Uncle Terry proceeded to spend the next two hours touring me around to every single person he knew—which turned out to be everybody in the entire town. Around and around we went, like little dolls twirling in an open music box, him rehashing the same play-by-play we had all seen and experienced a couple of hours prior. He laughed often, a boisterous growl of a laugh that roared up to the rafters where cats with curlicue tails walked along them like balance beams.

As the line at the long string of food tables died down, he only seemed to grow more and more excited with each retelling.

I didn't mind it, despite the way the heavy scent of chili and cumin and roasted tomatoes was doing strange things to my stomach. Actually, I found it all more exhilarating as the evening wore on, with the way Uncle Terry put his hand on the back of my shoulder, guiding me to another person he noticed in the crowd, saying, "Oh, John! John! Have you met my niece?"

The way he embellished a little bit more every time he told the story.

The way whomever he was speaking with didn't question the details of his embellishments, despite the fact they saw everything with their own eyes.

He was proud of me, not in the way a few ill-fated boyfriends had been in the past.

No, like a dad would be. A good dad.

Like Serena's father after she sailed to the bottom of the black diamond last year in Zermatt.

Or the face he gave her when she just stood there in the living room, sharing the details of her ordinary day.

A good father.

Somebody who makes it his job to know his child's weaknesses and guide her through them but chooses to rejoice in her strengths as well.

Just rejoicing in her existence.

It was a completely foreign feeling. And I relished it.

But there was still a point when food became a necessity.

"Here. The Crock-Pots were getting low." Zaiah moves beside

me, holding out chili in a paper bowl. On the plate beneath it are no fewer than five golden-yellow cornbread biscuits.

I smile as I take it, turning away from Terry's latest rendition of how I flew over the horse to reach victory in the nick of time.

"Thank you," I say. "Four pieces of cornbread are certainly not going to be enough."

"I saw you sneak that third breakfast sandwich at lunch the other day. I figured I'd play it safe." He scans the plastic round tables. Most are full of occupants. Every table at least halfway full. His eyes trail toward the open barn doors to the dark night and flickering blaze of the bonfire beyond. "Care if we . . . ," he begins.

"Please," I say, and follow him out the door.

Night has fallen, and the second we get outside, I realize so has the temperature. There's a sizable bonfire to our left. A couple mingles around it on one end, but frankly, they look so invested in each other, I am fairly certain they wouldn't even notice a bobcat beside them. The sky above is blanketed with glittering stars, so bright even the locals who have spent their whole lives beneath such beauty admire them with frequent gazes upward.

We walk over. Grab a seat in the middle of the log on the other side of the pair.

The chili smells heavenly, but I try to ignore it and pick up the cornbread. Tear off a piece.

"It's meatless—or rather, um, vegan."

I raise my brow. "No way. A guy just told me he named his favorite calf Chili last year. In honor of today. When he cooked him."

"That man would be Larry Rush, and yes. It's vegan chili."

I pick up my spoon. Prod around, looking for clues. Sure enough, the meat seems to have been replaced with cubes of zucchini and small bits of carrot.

Apparently my feeling of elation is evident on my face, because his smile deepens.

I blow off the steam of a spoonful, then take it in.

Delicious.

Absolutely, surprisingly delicious.

"There's cinnamon in this," I say, going for a second bite. I eat a third before realizing he's just watching me. "I need this recipe. Does it say on the Crock-Pot who it's from?"

"This one's from me." He sees my expression. "Glad you like it, because you're the only one who did. You can take the whole Crock-Pot home."

"I will!" I am genuinely thrilled at the prospect. I just secured the next breakfast, lunch, and dinner for the next three days. It's so good I find myself squinting as I look at the line back inside. "I am not opposed to packing it up in my car now, actually. Nobody needs to expand their horizons tonight."

He laughs. "Tell you what. If anyone in there eats it—which I can guarantee you they will not—I'll make you more."

There's fire in his eyes, a genuine reflection of fire, and his pupils dance with the orange and yellow flames.

My own voice shifts at what he's saying.

The implication in all of this.

"Show me and it's a deal. So. You made vegan chili for a cook-off. With this crowd." I blink, my own lashes dancing. "You won't be winning any awards tonight for this."

"I'm not here to impress everyone."

I grin. Take another bite. The wind nips through my coat, and I reach in, pressing the button again. The fire is warm on my cheeks, but it's not close enough to do much against the bitter temperature otherwise.

So what are we doing here?

There's something in his eyes.

An intentionality as solid as the steed he rode on today.

Zaiah doesn't play games.

If he's not in this, he wouldn't pursue me for a moment, for a date, then ditch.

He knows this. I know this.

So what are we doing here?

I quietly turn the question off, along with the part of my brain trying to remind me that my life is in New York, not here.

"So." I tear a piece of cornbread off and dip it in the chili. "What was it you were going to tell me about your mom?"

"My mother is here."

"Oh." I don't know how or why that would've clicked with me, or why he should've expected it would. "Do I know her?"

"You share an office with her."

I halt, my hand halfway to my lips with cornbread. *"Peggy?* Your *mother . . .* is Peggy?"

"I thought you knew."

"And what would've been my clue? You guys are exact opposites!"

"Probably our last names."

"Smith is the most common surname in the United States," I counter. "If I went around assuming every Smith was related . . ."

"Or the fact that I go into the office every day. She's always kissing me on the cheek."

"She kisses everyone on the cheek," I retort. "I literally saw her kiss a tourist on the cheek. Your mother is an unusually affectionate person."

I laugh. Shake my head as I try to wrap my mind around this new reality. "So she moved out here then. When? Right after you?"

"No, it took a couple years of getting myself settled. Finding a halfway decent place that would work for us. Once I could afford it, I brought her out."

As he rises to adjust the logs on the fire, I find myself momentarily stunned.

It was clear from the little he said about his childhood that things were bad where he was. Where they were. I could just see him now coming back to the city at the ripe old age of twenty, determined to bring his mother somewhere better than where she had been. Spending all his time and money in those early years, saving up what little he was given to make sure she was in a better spot with him.

A good son.

"You get her the job too?"

He smiles. Shakes his head as he pokes the fire with a stick. "No. Once Mom makes up her mind to do something, she sticks with it till it's done. She met Terry and me for lunch one time and that was it. Next week I came to work and there she was. Secretary. It wasn't even a position back then."

"What, she just—"

"Just made it up. Convinced Terry he needed someone to answer the lines and bring him coffee."

I grin, thoughtfully dipping in another piece of cornbread as I imagine her in her first days, barreling through the office and insisting on a job. "Well, she is quite the coffee getter. The pot is always full no matter how many times everybody grabs a cup."

The couple across from us has begun kissing rather passionately, and I look down at my half-eaten bowl. "But seriously, Zaiah. That's really good of you. Taking care of her like that."

He sets the stick on the ground, returns to his spot on the log. "I'm her only child. I wouldn't have left if she hadn't been open to joining me."

He says it so matter-of-factly. As though of course he wouldn't have pursued his dreams. He would have given up everything entirely and stuck around in that crowded city, where the buildings touch the sky and . . . what had he said? *On my street the buildings were so tall I didn't see the sun until noon. Two hours later, it was gone.*

He would have opted to live there, to make the most of his life like a fish trying to breathe out of water, had Peggy not agreed to follow in his footsteps.

Who would Zaiah Smith be without his ranger uniform?

What sort of job would suit him in the city?

I run through all the options, coming up empty. And that leaves a foreboding feeling in my chest that I can't bring myself to consider. Time to think of something else. Talk of something else.

"So. Are you going to tell me what was going on at the coffee shop?" I throw out.

A shiver runs through me, both the fire and my jacket insufficient in meeting my needs. I put the bowl down on the ground. Cross my arms over my chest.

I didn't mean necessarily to jump back to *that* topic, but it's something we need to air out.

"Ah. The coffee shop."

"When I asked—"

"I know. I remember." He dips his chin as though trying to decide what all to say.

When he looks up again, I can tell that he's made a decision. "Two years ago I was seeing someone. Had been . . . for a while."

I frown slightly. It's none of my business, of course. More to the point, it's in the past. But still. I don't love the idea of him having dated someone *for a while*.

Something about the idea makes me . . . what? Jealous?

It is ridiculous. A ridiculous notion to be possibly jealous of someone who clearly isn't in his life anymore. Ridiculous to wish—is that what I'm actually doing here?—that I was the one in his life back then.

Ridiculous.

Truly. *Ridiculous*.

"Hannah was great."

Oh wonderful. Now she has a name.

"We met down at the coffee shop a number of years ago—"

A number of years?

Years?

"How many?" I ask suspiciously.

"About ten."

Were I still eating the cornbread, I would've choked. "Ten? You dated a girl for *ten* years?"

"We were friends for a long part of that time. She dated another friend of mine. When they broke up, we took a shot. And it worked. We worked."

We lapse into silence.

I smile. It's a little forced. "But . . ." I'll just have to nudge this along.

"But then she drove her car into two other people at the Honeypot and went to jail."

There's silence.

Even the other couple, who were so obliviously all over each other the moment prior, stop. Pull back from each other.

"What happened to the two other people?"

"One had minor scrapes. The other ended up in ICU."

The guy looks over at Zaiah as the girl rises. Glares as he follows, the moment lost.

"Oh my gosh." I squeeze my arms across my chest tighter. "That's awful. Did . . ." I hesitate to ask but want to know. "Did they make it?"

"We held our breath for forty-two days, but yes. Mark made it." He said this with a heavy calm, like he looked at his face in the mirror every single day and relived the memory.

Mark.

My heart sinks. "How did that happen?"

"Mark was out front at one of those little bistro tables when she hit the curb and drove right over them. Just going twenty-eight miles an hour."

I suck in a breath, the horror of it all too easily pictured in my mind.

"She was on her phone when she went through the stop sign and veered off the road."

"Oh no."

The words fall with a thud as everything connects.

The way he looks at me every time I use my phone. At every picture taken. Even the pictures for the sake of the park.

It all comes down to this.

The root of it all.

"Poor Mark."

So this was what happened to him. Sweet, energetic Mark who even tonight rolled around in a wheelchair equipped with what looked like off-roading mountain bike tires, looking like he hadn't a care in the world. "He seems to have handled it all so well. I can't imagine."

"Mark is a better man than me. A better man than us all. His"—there's significance in his pause—"willingness to forgive is astounding."

I frown. Something in his voice, in the way he averts his gaze, says that he is laying claim to some of that guilt.

Over *this*.

"You weren't the one driving."

"No." He shakes his head. "But I knew she had a problem for a couple of years. I never said anything."

He says it just like he would say she was addicted to drugs. As though he was supposed to call in an intervention. For what? Spending too much time on her phone?

"C'mon now, Zaiah. These aren't drugs we're talking about here."

"It's not?" He raises a brow. "You really don't think the dopamine hit your brain gets every time you get that like or comment or emoji is a problem? I've read all the articles about it. Hannah's lawyer defended her from that angle. Psychologically addicted, he said. Showed brain scans to the jury of social media addicts and drug users side by side. Explained in detail about how social media had changed the region of her brain that controlled emotions, attention, and decision making. Tell me this isn't about a drug-dependent person. Tell me I shouldn't have tried to help her."

My chest tightens as I hear these words. I've heard sprinkles of the same arguments over the years. Experienced them myself.

"What could you have done, Zaiah? I doubt she would've listened to you."

"Maybe. Maybe not. Regardless, I saw the problem and didn't say anything. I saw for a while I'd been losing her to all this, this"—he stares at the fire, searching for words—"*pretense* of significance, when in reality all she was doing was losing herself and her grip on reality."

He takes off his hat and sets it on the log. Rakes a hand through his hair.

I'm silent.

After all, what can I say?

"I know how I look to some people. I know my position on technology seems exaggerated and out of touch with reality."

I shake my head. "No. What's more real than what you just said?"

"I watched her lose herself. I saw it all start to finish. When she first talked about trying to do some posts on her life—*lifestyle* creator, she called it. Showing off outfits and recipes. All these videos of her life on a farm." He gives a humorless laugh. "*Slow living* is the term, I believe. Something about taking videos of all these sunrises and baking things and pouring tea from some kettle that she never used."

He shakes his head. "You know what? She didn't even drink hot tea. But she said nobody wanted to see her pour herself a Diet Dr Pepper, so she bought a bunch of tea off the internet and pretended. Always these inspirational words about taking it easy and living in the moment and making the most of each day. Making these eight-second clips that took her two hours and then spending the rest of the day with one hand glued to her phone, checking the post to see how many people liked it. She wanted to make it as a creator. Thought she had a special edge with how she lived in these mountains."

I am a terrible person in this moment, but a part of me can't help remarking silently, *Well, of course she did. These mountains. The hot springs. It's all so monetizable.*

"Was she successful?" I say.

He shrugs. "She had just cleared eight."

"Eight . . ."

"Thousand. Eight thousand followers right before the accident. She got a metallic balloon in the shape of an eight and made a big fuss giving away half her week's salary at Uncle Buck's to celebrate. I bought her a cake thinking she'd like it for her balloon video, but . . . she said that didn't work with the aesthetic. Something about how store-bought cakes don't resonate with a slow-living crowd. So she made one herself."

"Oh." I can't help pitying him, imagining him trying hard to make her happy, trying to do his best to understand her world, and seeing her brush it aside. I understood why she'd done it—she was right. Dr Pepper and store-bought cakes don't work for a slow-living niche. But still.

He deserved better.

"She was thrilled when a couple of businesses started to offer to send her things."

I raise a brow. "What kind of things?"

"One sent her a month's supply of dish soap. Another company gave her a discount on leggings and told her she could give a code to her fans and get some money if they made purchases."

Oh dear. The companies that scam new creators are a dime a dozen. "Let me guess. She bought the leggings she never wanted in the first place, made a post to promote them, and never made any money."

"I never asked. I'd learned early on not to probe too much."

"So what happened?"

"Eventually she got to where she couldn't go to the bathroom without her phone."

That's me. Shoot. That's everyone.

"Kept one eye on it through every conversation."

Check.

"Was a slave to that *ding*."

Check.

"Couldn't take a car ride with me without scrolling."

Check.

"I would see her sitting in the corner by herself looking miserable, turn the camera around and smile like she was having the time of her life, and then go right back to being miserable as she stared at the screen, trying to pick one."

Check. Of course.

"I tried to ignore it. I'm not immune to the way society works; I thought it was something I'd just have to get used to. And then, well. Then the accident happened."

Up until the last bit, he was explaining my life.

His observations of Hannah could've easily been of me.

Or Serena.

Or quite frankly, the population of the United States.

Back in the city the use of social media was a given. Half of the jobs relied on it in some form or another. The things he was saying she did were now so commonplace, people didn't even attempt to hide it. Answer your notifications? Sure. Scroll in the taxi? Of course. Take your phone to the bathroom and answer a few texts? Naturally. There are bathroom tissue holders that have resting spots for your phone.

His laugh is dark and deep. "You know what is so ironic about it all? She was posting a video about minimizing social media use to live without distraction. She was in the middle of writing those exact words when she hit Mark."

"Oh, that's awful."

It made me want to scream.

Cry out about the injustice of undeserved, freak horror.

"And I saw all of it," Zaiah says. "I watched her go from this happy, bright, intelligent woman who used to go cliff jumping off waterfalls for the thrill of it to someone who couldn't pick up her fork without trying to take a picture of it. So yes, I am guilty. Not of everything, of course, but of my part in all this. I'm guilty for not trusting my instincts and saying something. And that's why, long story short, I have a hard time going down to the Honeypot and looking Mark in the face."

"Even Mark has asked you to move on. It's clear he has."

Zaiah looks into my eyes. There's a subtle shake of his head as he tosses another twig in the fire.

I want to say that him carrying any guilt is crazy.

That she was responsible for her own choices.

But as easy as it would be to try to throw it all on her, this elusive woman I've never met, I can't. Even if simply because I know he wouldn't let me.

"She's still in jail?"

"No. Hannah went for a year. When she got out, she wanted nothing to do with me. Or this town. Or anything to do with the life she once had. I don't blame her."

I rub my face, trying to wrap my mind around this.

Trying to decide what to ask next.

Zaiah was seriously dating another woman. Things were going well. What does that mean exactly? Had the accident not occurred, would she still be in the picture? He had said years. Years is a long time.

This woman, Hannah, seriously injured Mark and another person because she was on her phone. The incident turned her life, and Zaiah's life, and Mark's, upside-down and she went to jail. Mark lost the use of his legs permanently. Zaiah feels guilt despite Mark's forgiveness and rather impressive ability to forgive and make the most of his life.

Zaiah is now single.

Zaiah is sharing all this with me.

Because, it would seem, he needs me to know. Why? Because it appears he's interested in me.

Zaiah, who from the sound of it has not so much as looked at another woman in two years, is opening up at last to the possibility of something more . . . with me.

The girl who is about to leave the second she gets her life back.

The girl who, for that matter, can't go one minute without her phone.

He's traumatized by a woman who sounds an awful lot like me.

I clench my jaw.

Not just sounds like me.

Is me.

The memory of checking Instagram that very first night on Main Street flashes through my mind. Me, checking as I did every few minutes to see how I was faring as I drove through the snow, in front of the Honeypot. *Right there in the same spot.*

I'm just as guilty as this woman in Zaiah's past. The only difference is I happened to get lucky.

The thought makes me sick to my stomach.

Makes my feet restless, forcing me to stand.

For someone who just one moment ago was willing to risk being freezing cold for the sake of keeping up conversation, I now find myself wanting to go inside. Wishing this conversation never happened.

Zaiah stands, concern on his face as he sees my arms wrapped around my chest. I didn't realize I was shaking until this moment.

"I needed you to know where I came from, Cat. I need you to know my hang-ups. This is why everything within me hates the apps you use for a living. Because everything within me hates what they do to the people who use them."

He is turning me down. All this, all the fireworks between us, and ultimately, he is turning me down.

"It's fine, Zaiah. It's your life. You don't owe me anything—"

"Why I promised myself I would never, ever, pursue a woman who used them—"

I raise a hand, a white flag, in the air. "Really, Zaiah. I understand."

"And then you came along."

My mouth is open, the words on my lips ready to beg him to let me go, to let me leave this conversation and this bonfire with the last shreds of my dignity. But then I gather what he's just said.

My tongue clicks on the roof of my mouth.

Halting.

"You and"—he pauses with a tiny lift of his lips—"your thousand suitcases."

I feel the shift in the conversation.

The wind changing.

I have a choice here, to leave or to stay.

I raise my chin.

"For the millionth time," I say, gathering my dignity, "it was a respectable six."

"And your vegan oat milk."

"Can you make fun of a person for lactose intolerance? It's an actual thing, Zaiah."

"And the way you can almost get yourself killed by taking a selfie with a moose."

He had me here.

I press my lips together.

The arrow hitting the heart. "I know, Zaiah. I know I have a problem."

"But then you go and ruin it all." He takes a tiny step toward me. "Then you go and make it your personal mission to help Mina get a business off the ground."

He slips his jacket off his shoulders. "Then you throw yourself into trying to help us keep our park alive."

He puts the jacket in one of his hands. "And then you risk that lovely neck of yours just to make Mina happy and keep the Kannery Park title."

"I need that saddle over my head," I say, raising a finger. "Without it, it would throw off the whole vibe."

"You took on a job and a project that I know wouldn't pay for a sandwich in the city, to please your uncle. You don't slap Jax in the face when he acts like an idiot—"

I laugh lightly. "That is worthy of an award, I'll grant."

His eyes flicker down. "You wear that necklace from your uncle around your neck, even with diamonds to choose from."

I feel the weight of his jacket as he slips it around my shoulders. The warmth is instant, his own body heat insulated inside as it transfers to my shivering torso.

"How long has your ridiculous coat been broken?"

His hands are still on the collar of the coat, around my neck. He's so close I can feel the welcome addition of his body heat as he stands inches away, looking down at me.

"About three hours, I think," I murmur.

His smile widens, his face just above mine. "You are stubborn to the core, Cat Cranwell. You know your mind. You are brave when you need to be. You've been through a lot in this life and still came out kind. You are gracious to your uncle. You are a good friend. And you, quite frankly, are stronger than anyone I know, given the way you've handled all you have going on right now."

A crease forms on my forehead. "I was starting to think nobody here knew about my problems. Or even who I am."

Zaiah gives a quiet laugh. "Everybody knows who you are, Cat. You are impossible to ignore. Your uncle just made very clear in no uncertain terms that nobody was to make note of it."

My brow rises.

"And you have a very intense friend who called before you came to tell me likewise. On my home phone. Which your friend somehow managed to find."

I laugh. Had I been told two months ago that essentially an entire town was sworn to pretend not to know who I was or direct attention to all my troubles splashed across the news for my mental health, I would've believed it impossible. But after tonight, seeing the way everybody in that barn talked to Uncle Terry, the way they treated him with such respect, such patience as he rambled on and on, I could believe it.

As for Serena, I could absolutely believe that too.

"You are impossible to ignore."

A breeze sweeps through and my teeth involuntarily chatter.

"Ready to go inside?" he says.

I clench my jaw, forcing them to stop. Forcing them to cease from spoiling this moment. "Almost."

There's a snap in the fire beside us, and I realize that somewhere in the past millisecond everything has shifted. The moment I've quietly waited for, hoped for, has come, and now I find I'm holding my breath. Waiting to see what will happen next.

Part of me wants to hold back, knowing that this situation is all wrong.

I am the weaknesses of his last girlfriend.

He doesn't realize the extent of my own dependence and struggles and anxieties and, yes, possibly depression linked to my life on the apps. He doesn't know just how fiercely I battle to overcome my own emotions and to uphold my own well-being and mental health when things go wrong, or even right. Or even superb.

The manic highs.

The devastating lows.

I believe every word he said about the lawyer's statistics.

I know them. I live them.

And that's scary.

And hearing what happened to Mark gives me the final push to realize I need to do something about it. I need to make a plan.

Not just for peace for myself, but for others.

I *will* do something about it.

I *will* find a way to start using social media as a tool, and not let social media use me.

I feel the determination in my bones as bold and sure as the night I left the hospital, and my home, at seventeen.

I'm aware of all this as I hold my gaze steady and the fire crackles besides us.

Aware of the work I have ahead of me to better myself, not just for Zaiah's sake because he deserves someone who looks him in the eye during dinner, but for me.

I want to be this person.

His hands slip down from the collar around my neck, to my elbows, as he takes a final step in.

I'm not the person he expected to fall for. He's the last person on earth I'd expect to fall for.

There's no promise of tomorrow, or an answer to how we can possibly make this work.

And yet.

There's now.

I lift my chin, and the silent conversation passes between us.

Do you want me to kiss you now?

Yes, very much, please.

And then he is. His hands drift back to the collar of the coat and tenderly, slowly, he lowers his face to mine.

One of his hands moves to my cheek. Cups my face. Slides softly to the back side of my neck, pulling what is left of the day's curls from inside his coat.

Everything feels gentle.

There's a timidness, even. Something I hadn't expected.

A controlled propriety, as if to say, "I want to be here in this moment, but want to make sure, absolutely sure, this is right, before giving away my whole heart."

So much communicated in such a kiss.

Part of me wishes for more, but another part of me, a wiser part, agrees.

When he steps back, it's only far enough to look down into my face. "I . . . like you."

"I . . . gathered that." I smile lightly.

"I'd like to take you out on a date."

"If this is you asking me out to that antique store that's half pawn-shop, half hot dog stand, I'm going to have to think about it."

His lips twitch, the smile beneath his beard rising. "Noted."

"And if your idea of a date is hiking ten miles in the snow, then I'll have to politely decline. Even if you are a three-time national skijoring champion."

At this his eyes twinkle. "I would expect nothing less than a handful of opinions from a fellow national skijoring champion. What did you have in mind?"

I press my lips together. "I'll accept any plan and place that is at least sixty degrees."

"Any other guidance here?"

I level my gaze. "Basically, I get excited when Kevin and Jax bring

Twizzlers from the gas station over for evening blitz games. I can assure you, as long as it's warm and not from an antique store, my bar has never been lower."

He smiles. "Would Friday work?"

"We work together. We basically live in a secluded forest together. The way I see it, we're the last two survivors on a deserted island. You bring me a coconut any night and you got yourself a date."

CHAPTER 16

The Date

9:25

Instagram ⌄

catcranwell ✓
Kennery National Park, Montana

1,200,455 likes

catcranwell I'd never thought I'd say it, but I could get used to this.

View all 96,232 comments

March 5

Serena's calling you again," Mina calls. "Want me to pick up?"

"I don't have time," I call back through the bathroom door.

I've been taking steps to distance myself from the phone. One rule being that I do not take it in the bathroom. Ever.

One would be surprised how infuriating that fact is to certain friends.

Like Serena.

"Now she's calling me," Mina calls.

"Really? How did she get your number?" The bathroom light flickers, the light on the curling iron shifting from red to black and red again. "You know what, never mind." I check my watch, racing the clock as I get the last bit of my hair in place.

My little comment about being on a deserted island with Zaiah is true.

It's the only thing that can account for the extreme, heart-pounding level of anticipation I have felt the past forty-eight hours.

I'm a grown woman.

I have my dignity; I sit in a folding chair at a desk, beneath a saddle made in China, where I see Zaiah Smith day in and day out.

I have probably been on no fewer than three hundred dates in my life. On each one, I have been cool and collected with rational perspective about the evening ahead.

But today?

I finally broke out all the suitcases. And just about everything inside them is currently strewn across the floor of my living room/bedroom. A fair bit, too, in Mina's.

Hastily I reach for one of the tubes of lipstick littering the vanity of the small bathroom with one hand, while the other hand holds a lock of hair in the barrel of the iron.

With my thumb I pop the cap off the lipstick. Use my thumb and forefinger to spin the silver tube until the rose-red color slides up.

At the front door, I hear a polite double knock.

A calm knock.

A sane knock.

I drop the curling iron onto the vanity. Manically tug at an overactive curl, running my fingers through it to calm it down.

"He's here!" Mina whispers excitedly, standing in the doorway. Her face is so bright and shiny you could go blind from staring at it too long. She clutches her phone in her hands, the camera facing me square on.

I look down at it, frowning. "What are you doing?"

Click.

Click.

Click.

"You're going to appreciate these one day," she says, as though she's a mother watching her daughter run off to prom.

"Ohhh, and look at *you*." She pulls the camera up higher. "Give me a spin."

I roll my eyes but take a steadying breath of confidence at her words as I do, indeed, give a slow spin. I hear a dozen *clicks* as I do so.

It's not like the man doesn't see me every single day of my life.

It's not like we didn't just stand side by side in front of the office kitchen's refrigerator four hours ago, sharing a bowl of carrots and hummus.

But still. There's something about having someone's undivided attention on a first official date. The declaration "Hey, we have mutually stated our interest and are willing to try on a night out for size."

It's all just an interview.

An interview thinly veiled with appetizers and drinks but at its core, just an interview.

You both like your salmon blackened with a lime wedge?

Lovely. One point.

You both have hilarious stories about friends who made fools of themselves at a Christmas party?

Even better. Two points.

But a deduction for every awkward pause and wrong answer stacks against you.

Get enough of them and you're done.

And here I am, for the first time on a date really, afraid to say the wrong things.

Every time we've seen each other before, that kind of stress was off the table. The clock was ticking.

But tonight.

Tonight is the real game.

My dress is a bitterroot pink, according to Kevin's lengthy lecture at its sighting today. The first flowers of spring, bravely facing the elements even before the snow has officially given up for the year.

My hair is half up, twisting and turning and secured by bobby pins at the back of my head as though I just tossed it up and it landed neatly that way (which it most certainly did not).

Lips meticulously covered and blotted with *So This Is Love* pink. (I used it for its pale-pink color that shimmers, oh-so-barely, and not as any sort of declaration.)

My eyes look extra-large, despite the fact that tonight I decided to play it safe and go for the triple application of mascara, opting to leave the falsies at home.

A double spritz from a bottle I found in France four years ago and only take out for special occasions.

And yes, some would call it unlucky given the first and only time I put them on was on that horrible birthday night, but the golden crystal shoes on my feet were too beautiful and sang to me too much with their siren song from their velvet lining inside the suitcase.

Besides, a tiny part of me wants to see his reaction too.

This is a part of me.

I'm not going to instantly turn into a Carhartt-wearing rodeo girl just because he asked me out. I will always like my lipstick and my curls. Yes, even on days when nobody sees them.

Overall, I couldn't have put more effort into tonight than I have. I'm pretty sure I put more effort into getting ready tonight than people going to the Grammys.

Mina prods me out of the bathroom and I grab my white coat. My heels dig into the floor as I turn, taking in the living room. Gone is the stack of board games that had built up on the coffee table. In its place is a flickering single candle. The place is spotless—*Is that scent Pine-Sol?*—and on the countertop in the kitchen bubbles a full pot of coffee with three mugs.

Three.

"Actually . . ." Mina steps in front of me at the last second, motions for me to go back to the bedroom like this is the protocol. When I don't move, she sighs and opens the door a few inches.

"Oh, hello, Zaiah," she says, one hand firmly on the door. "Cat is just finishing up."

From the open sliver of the door, he catches my eye.

I shrug.

"Do"—she looks over at me, giving one more shooing motion before giving up—"come in."

We look like we live in a gingerbread house as he all but ducks inside. He's wearing that same plaid shirt I complimented him on at the coffee shop. His beard looks freshly trimmed from this afternoon. He's wearing a new pair of leather boots I've never seen before. And in his hands is a bouquet of winter-red holly paired with twigs covered in pine cones, tied up in a simple red bow.

He looks quite . . . I take in a small breath. Force the adrenaline back down in my stomach. Nice. He looks quite nice.

"Aw. And he brought you a bouquet. Couldn't have splurged on roses, I see"—she tsks, giving him a look—"but how nice. Care for a cup of coffee before your evening begins?" Mina steps backward toward the kitchen.

She's taken on an accent. A motherly, slightly British, 1950s accent.

Zaiah's mouth pops open in surprise. He glances over to the mugs on the counter. "That's very thoughtful—"

"No, we probably ought to get going," I say hastily, refraining from adding *Mom* on the end.

She presses her lips together. Nods as though this is unfortunate, but she understands. Expects it, even. "Just a few pictures it is."

Twenty shots of us posing awkwardly together in front of the couch later, and we finally head to the truck.

"I feel bad," Zaiah says under his breath, although the quickness of his steps says not quite enough to turn around. "Should we . . . stay for a minute?"

"Don't." I match his stride and then some. "This is what happens in every movie storyline. Frankly, if we hadn't said no, she wouldn't have known her next lines. And now we turn and wave."

Together we stop at the passenger side of the truck and turn around.

Sure enough, she's standing on the porch, hand clutched to her chest. Waving back.

That's it. Enough movies. I have got to get her out more.

He opens the door for me and then moves to the driver's side, and as the truck rumbles and he lifts his foot off the brake, he says, "What's next?"

"Oh." I give one last wave as the truck begins to move. "I think this is the part where she's going to go inside, drink the whole pot of coffee herself, and reminisce on how her baby is growing up too fast. I think tonight I've somehow moved from roomie status to child. I should probably call Kevin and Jax to save her."

I reach in my pocket and then stop.

He looks over as he drives, waiting. "What?"

"Oh, nothing. I just didn't bring my phone." I say it casually, and it probably means nothing to him, but to me, to me this is everything. I can't think of a single memory in the past decade where I haven't had my phone at my side. It's unnerving, but another little rule I added to my growing list in this quest for healing.

If I can't trust myself to give the person I've decided to spend time with my full attention, then I will leave it and make it easy. No brain cells spinning in the background of our conversation hunting for picture opportunities. No thoughts in the back of my mind of whether someone might have called or texted or posted or messaged, wanting my attention.

I could wait to hear about who Serena ran into at Don Pierre's.

I could even wait a few hours to hear from my lawyer, if he emailed.

I would live fully in the moment.

"Oh." There's surprise in his voice. He seems to grasp that this really means something. "Oh, no problem, take mine."

I smile as I take the silver flip phone in my hands and open the screen. I have absolutely no idea what to do from here.

"His number's 834-228-0912." He looks over as the truck rumbles over the gravel spotlit in the otherwise black forest. "Then the green button."

I laugh out loud. "You have Kevin's phone number memorized."

He raises a brow. "I have everyone's number I need to know memorized. If it's not, I don't need to call them. How many numbers do you have memorized?"

"Me?" I think. "No one. Not a single person."

He shakes his head as he turns the wheel. "I can't believe that."

"Serena's starts with a 646."

"All Manhattan area codes start with a 646." He glances over, lips twitching.

"Fine." I press the green button and put the phone to my ear as it rings. "What's my number?"

"It's 646-228-5464," he says, as quick and automatic as if I'd asked him the number for 911.

Kevin and Jax hear me out about Mina, and aside from Jax calling out totally inappropriate comments about the date—I try to keep Zaiah from hearing by muffling the phone while pretending to fuss with my hair—they take up the torch to bring Mina into town.

We take more turns than I anticipated through the gravelly woods, turning at brown road signs every now and again until even they end. We keep going.

"You know, I forgot to worry about if you were going to murder me," I say, watching us turn onto a single path. "I've been out here too long. I'm completely losing my street skills."

"I find it much more exhilarating to worry about the stray anaconda."

"There are *anacondas?*" I say, my breath hitching. "Tell me you're kidding, Zaiah. I know you're kidding."

He stares straight ahead.

"I need to hear these words. I need to audibly hear them in this space."

He pauses. "There are no anacondas in Montana." He takes my hand and gives it a squeeze. After my exhale he adds, "Just cougars, mountain lions, wolves, grizzlies, rattlesnakes, and the stray poison."

I open my mouth to retort, but I'm distracted by the way his hand is covering mine. He rubs my skin with his index finger in an automatic way, as though comforted by the soothing feel of my skin.

As though he's done this a thousand times with me.

As though this is our normal.

I blink as I glance out the window nonchalantly, finding myself holding my breath for fear he'll stop. "Fine. Cougars, mountain lions, wolves, grizzlies, rattlesnakes, and stray poisons. But after that, I'm putting my foot down."

"Noted. As senior ranger I will be sure to tell all other dangerous animals we are full and to try Canada."

He holds my hand until we reach his cabin, and when we do, I can't help but feel my lips part in surprise.

"*This* is your cabin? *This*? I've been living like a girl in the house on the prairie, and you've been living in *this*?"

Zaiah smiles as he pops open the door. "You ask Terry if you can build out your own cabin. I'm sure he'd let you too."

"Wait," I say, just as he shuts his door. "You built your own cabin?"

The cabin shines like a beacon in the surrounding canopy of black forest. There is an opening between the trees directly above it, and the sky is so bright it almost looks unbelievable, like someone has taken the sky and photoshopped it with an additional hundred thousand twinkling stars to give it such magnificence. I have never seen so many stars.

Lights shine from the two-story cabin, standing tall and secure, welcoming us in.

I follow him onto the wraparound porch.

He opens the door.

"So what *exactly* about this was the original part of the 'precious historic' build?" I say as I move onto the kitchen barstool twenty minutes later, still marveling after insisting upon a tour. "Was it the coat closet on the first floor? It was the coat closet on the first floor."

His lips twitch mischievously as he opens a stainless-steel refrigerator. Returns with a bottle of wine. "Close. Chicken coop in the back. But don't tell your uncle."

I laugh and take a glass from him.

The cabin isn't quite the level of the A-frame chalet I visited last Christmas, but compared to what I've been living in and what I'd expected, it may as well have been a retreat for the president. The cabin is clean and thoughtfully decorated. Deep-seated couches, simple but matching wooden tables, and cozy-looking blankets fill the living room, all facing a wood fire that is crackling away happily. A couple bedrooms upstairs, one for him, another for a guest. A small area with a small array of workout equipment and computer tucked into one corner. And, of course, the kitchen.

The cabin is warm, all wood and black, red, and yellow patterned blankets. Essentially the opposite in every way of my penthouse back in the city. But charming. Perfectly suited to its own setting.

And, best of all, warm.

Warm enough, I tug off my coat and move toward the thermostat to read it. "Seventy-three degrees," I say in astonishment, turning to face him. "*You* keep the thermostat at seventy-three degrees."

"No." He slices a long loaf of bread. "But you said you wanted warm. I'm giving you warm."

I laugh, touched by his thoughtfulness, but also well aware of how he pulled up his sleeves the second we stepped inside. "I'm actually quite warm. Want me to turn it down a few degrees?"

His words say, "Sure, if you want," but there's a tinge in his throat that also says a desperate, *"Please!"*

I drop the temperature down to sixty-eight (still *at least* a good ten degrees higher than our cabin) and turn my attention to the picture in the frame on the table by his keys.

Sure enough, there is a much younger version of Zaiah standing beside a much younger version of Peggy. She has a full head of permed brown hair, earrings adorning her in their large, dangling variety.

"Where's your mom live? Surely you haven't left her to fend for herself in one of those cabins while you're up here living the high life."

"No, she opted for her own place in town a while ago." He scoops something into two bowls and brings them over. "She has a loft over one of the buildings in the city."

"The city?" I raise a brow as he sets the bowl before me.

"Her words, not mine."

We sit at the kitchen island as we eat. The dining table is set in the other room, but somehow we never make it there. It is cozier here, leaning over bowls of korma curry. I discover as we eat how similar our tastes are, barring the whole vegan situation, and realize I shouldn't have been surprised. He grew up in the city, with the same access to the world of options and ethnic tastes that I have had the last decade. With Zaiah's mom working a lot, takeout was easy, and of course in the city, the options endless. Evidently a kindly babysitter neighbor who took care of him in his earlier years was Indian, and as a consequence, he learned quite a few cooking skills.

By the time we finish up the sticky rice covered in peanut shavings and mango slices, quite literally my favorite dessert *in the world,* I'm feeling quite cozy, the jitters of a few hours earlier gone. My heels are discarded at the foot of the barstool. My bare foot bounces happily as I scoop another bit of rice into my mouth, taste buds in heaven.

He sits back, admiring me. "You are without question the best person to cook for."

"I haven't had someone cook for me in weeks. I would have been happy with box spaghetti. This," I say, pointing my fork to the plate, "I would have given you my heels for *this.*"

"I have had my eye on them too." He glances down at the toppled-over pair.

As I excuse myself and slip into the bathroom after dinner, I look into the mirror and take stock of how the date has gone. My bare toes rub against the soft bath rug, and I smile a little at myself in the mirror. My eyes are sparkling. Cheeks rosy hued, and not just from the blush I applied earlier in the day.

I pull out my travel-sized lipstick tube from my pocket. My reserve tube. Funnily enough, I realize I can go without my phone, but I draw the line at lipstick.

When I move back to my chair, there's an amiable silence. Quiet but for the flickering of the fireplace across the room.

"So," he says at last. "For the next part of the date."

I lower my fork, all but raising a brow. "Yeah?"

"I have made a decision."

My fork drops even farther. "Is that so? Do tell."

"I have decided you pass stage one. Congratulations. You have earned your way into stage two."

I laugh. "You do realize that if *anyone* other than you were saying this right now, I'd be clicking my bracelet for security backup."

"Nothing like that." He reaches for my bowl, which is empty save a few lonely pieces of rice. I jab at his hand with my fork all the same. He laughs, pulling his hand back. "You're also a feisty eater, you know that? You remind me a little of a starved animal."

"You're really nailing this date stuff, Zaiah." My fork scrapes the bowl as it resumes pulling the rice together for a final bite. "Giving me a test score *during* the date. Comparing me to wild animals. Really top-notch."

"Well, I couldn't let you into the second part of the date just like that. It's not something I could let you in on and then change my mind on later. It's not something I can take back."

I pause, fork halfway to my mouth. "Are we referring to marriage now? Is that where you're going with this?"

He grins. "No. But it's something we take very nearly as seriously. I'm letting you in on the best-kept secret in town."

\|(/

Poker night.

This incredible, best-kept secret in town is a senior citizen poker night.

I laugh as I throw down my cards.

It was a heavy battle, full of blood, sweat, and so many hours new logs had to be thrown on multiple times, but I finally have to throw in the towel. "Congratulations, Peggy. You win."

Peggy gleefully pulls in my towers of red, white, and blue chips, her own dangling earrings quite literally replicas of the chips she's gathering in her hands. "You played a good game, honey. For a first-timer, you held yourself well."

Zaiah, the only one besides me under forty in the group, pours coffee into the raised mugs of the group circled around the poker table. I cover my mug with my hand to decline when the carafe nears mine. With my other hand I stifle a yawn.

How Peggy, Uncle Terry, and the half dozen other senior members of the circle can look at the clock hovering in single digits like it's not five hours past reasonable bedtime is beyond me. And to find out they do this on a *weekly* basis . . .

"I think your beau is getting sleepy," Peggy announces, pushing up her glasses as she slides the first card toward herself.

"She's not his beau," Terry grumbles, slapping cards out on the table as he deals. "She's just a nice young lady who happened to come by."

I'm on a first date with my uncle.

And my coworker.

And half a senior citizen group.

This has actually happened.

This was actually Zaiah's plan.

And yet. It worked.

This may have actually been my favorite date ever.

Zaiah, who finally gave up on his flannel two hours ago, throws his cards down after one look at me. He runs a hand down his beard, then pushes his chips to the center of the table, despite the fact that he is far and away the strongest player. "I'm out. You all carry on. I'm going to take Cat home."

He's reduced to just a base layer T-shirt. Just a plain white V-neck that cuts into his biceps.

I'd complain, but I'm at that point where when I blink, I'm starting to see double.

"C'mon, blinky," Zaiah says, helping me out of my chair and into my coat. "Let's get you to bed."

"You all know you have work in four hours," I call back, watching as Peggy and Uncle Terry stare at their cards, pensive and undeterred.

So this is why they're always dragging on Wednesdays.

"That was . . ."

We're standing beneath the glowing porch light of my cabin. He's straddling the hole in the porch we all take for granted now. Me opposite. It's freezing (when is it ever not?), and like a moth attracted to the flaming heat, I find I'm standing closer to him than the average person would were they not kissing.

Which is what we're not doing.

Kissing.

Which, quite frankly, is the only thing wrong with the moment.

"I'd invite you in for a nightcap, but given you've plied me with coffee the past six hours and I have to be up in four . . ."

I'm whispering. The inside lights are out, and given Mina's performance when we left on our date, I have little doubt she has some theatrics planned for our return.

"That's probably a good call." His voice is husky as he whispers back. "I hear your boss is a real stickler for timeliness."

We both grin at each other. Me, because I can still picture Uncle Terry up at the cabin, surrounded by his hoard of chips. Him? Well, I suppose he's just grinning at me.

Which he's done just about all evening.

"Thank you for inviting me into your super-secret club," I whisper.

"Super-secret society," he counters. "Club just sounds juvenile. And you're welcome. I hope you realize you've been inducted into a lifelong membership. Hope you don't carry commitment issues."

I whisper-laugh, which sounds a little more like a horse neighing than I would've liked. All the same, he takes a tiny step forward, closing the gap between us. Our breath mingles and hovers in the air, drifting toward the porch light. Somewhere in the distance an owl gives a weary hoot, its shift nearly done for the night.

I realize the moment has finally come, and I am more than ready.

My fingers tingle, not because they want to draw near to a phone (which, admittedly, they sort of do, just to call Serena and unleash an eruption of words about this evening), and not just because they are halfway frozen (which they are, but I've come to the point where that's a given), but because they are hoping, waiting, inching forward to grab hold of his jacket and pull him toward me.

Oh, the things I'll be telling Serena about this night.

The things I can't wait to say.

And then, there is Serena.

In an enormously oversized truck roaring up the driveway and spewing gravel as she comes to a hasty stop.

There she is, throwing open the door of the poorly parked vehicle still halfway in the road, wedging herself out of the truck in a massive puffy coat twice her size. Only her petite, heart-shaped face is visible around the marshmallow puff encompassing her body. That, and her heels.

"Oh good, Cat," she says, stumbling out of the mammoth truck. "You're up."

CHAPTER 17

The Best Friend

Serena?" I step toward her in a daze.

This isn't because I've missed her calls today?

Surely . . . surely that's not possible.

She wouldn't . . . couldn't.

But that would be crazy.

I give her marshmallow-white coat a hug, never actually feeling anything besides the insulation around her, and step back.

She waves a hand, seeing my obvious state of shock. "I know. You should've answered your phone."

"I don't answer once and so you fly across the country to check on me?"

"I told you not to ignore me." She gives a shrill laugh. Then, seeing my expression, she adds, "I'm kidding." I don't laugh, because I'm still not so sure. "*Obviously.* But it was six. Six times you didn't answer your phone, for the record. I was beginning to think you were dead. Shall we?"

I open the door and she makes as though to breeze past me, but her coat gets stuck between the doorframe. The polyester scrapes across the jamb as she moves. We follow her into the living room, clicking on lights behind her.

She makes four strides into the room and turns. Pinches the bridge of her nose. "I have two things to tell you, Cat. But I just went through nine of the worst hours of my life beside a woman who sold Mary Kay. First give me all the aspirin and coffee you've got."

I'm never going to sleep.

I'm going to drink coffee until I die.

I move to the kitchen. To both my disbelief and absolute expectation Mina has left a pot of coffee on in the corner, along with a Post-it note saying: *For the inevitable nightcap. XOXO.*

That's it. She seriously is the best roommate ever.

Serena waits until she's finished her first cup (which takes about ten seconds—nobody can down a cup of coffee like Serena) to speak. Meanwhile, I stand over her, tapping my foot impatiently. Zaiah sits on the couch.

Other than the snoring coming from Mina's room, the air in the room is saturated in serious anticipation.

"What's your news?" I take her cup the millisecond she's finished and fill it again.

This has to be about the lawsuit. She often hears things one step ahead of me.

That has to be why she's come.

Good news.

Here to be the first to celebrate with me.

That has to be it.

Unless it's bad news.

So bad that she decided she had to come and tell me herself. Be a shoulder to cry on.

I hold my breath as I watch her pop the aspirin in her mouth.

Searching for clues.

Is this an "I'm so sorry to tell you this, but your life is over" way to down an aspirin? Or a "We are about to celebrate bigger than that New Year's Eve party back in 2022" aspirin throwdown?

"They found Bobby."

I nearly drop the coffee cup. "Where was he?" I say, images of men in official jackets leading him in handcuffs through Caribbean airports.

"The idiot ran out of money and was squatting in his own apartment. Some Realtor was bringing in a couple to see it when she found him watching Netflix on his phone in the bathroom."

I sink down onto a chair.

"And while he doesn't have a cell in his brain, he does seem to have a fleck of decency, because he confessed that you had nothing to do with all of this."

My shoulders drop forward. I exhale until my forehead rests on the kitchen island.

I can't believe it.

Bobby confessed.

He *confessed*.

"Murphy says with everything they've got on record, you'll be exonerated. You're free. News of his confession is starting to leak out. People are going nuts."

I blink back tears as I feel the cold counter of the kitchen island on my forehead.

I will be publicly proven innocent.

Everyone knows the truth: I wasn't trying to extort them.

The hundreds, *thousands* of people who betrayed me, who turned their backs on me, who threw me hate mail and public accusation. All of them. Publicly wrong.

My career, my life back.

My home.

Everything back the way it was—or no, even better than the way it was, no doubt.

The only thing better than being a successful content creator is this: being a recently wronged one.

The flood of support will be overwhelming.

At this level?

Tsunami.

My fingers itch desperately for my phone.

"Which brings me to the second reason I'm here."

I sit up to see Serena has pulled a folder out of her coat.

She slides it over the table.

There's a hexagon logo with long, thin script inside: "Whitman Agency."

"What's this?" I open the folder. Inside, clear script at the top reads: "Agency Agreement between Serena Whitman and Catherine Cranwell."

I scan the page quickly, the words "partnership" and "15 percent" and "termination when one or both parties decide to cease their contractual relationship."

I hold the page up. "What is this? You want to go into partnership together? What brand—?"

"I don't want to partner with you as an influencer. I want to be your agent."

"What?" I give a half laugh. "You don't need the job. Why would you want to be an agent?"

She takes a deep breath, preparing her speech as if she expected this. "I've done a lot of thinking the past few months, all that time taking care of your sorry, pathetic self moping around the streets of New York."

My cheeks flush as my eyes flicker to Zaiah sitting on the couch.

"I wouldn't exactly say it was that bad—"

"You know, reminding you to eat—"

"Now that's not entirely—"

"Getting you to take showers again."

I squeeze my eyes shut.

"Shipping you off here before you imploded your entire image. And I realized something. I *like* organizing other people's lives."

She counts on her fingers with her glossy *My Life in Red* nails.

"I like encouraging them when they need an emotional lift. I like finding and negotiating brand deals. You wouldn't believe some of the parties I went to, to get you things. I even like doing damage control. Gabby, for the record, is really pulling back together. I *like* being a manager."

She drops her hands. "Now, take as long as you need. We all know you've learned to get a lawyer to read a contract over, but I hope you—"

I slap the paper on the table. "Serena. You didn't need to pull all this together to convince me. You're hired. Pick your percentage. I'm in."

She halts. Whatever she was about to say in this grand pitch of hers stalled. "Good," she says after a minute, picks up the folder, and slips it back into her coat. I understand why she might've gone to such lengths as to fly out here to ask. I know what this means for her; the standard 15 percent commission on all deals plus the portfolio of attaching herself to my name, well . . . she's starting her career out on top.

But then, I can't think of anyone better suited to the job.

She slips her coat back on. "Murphy wants to see you as soon as possible to go over everything. I picked up our flight tickets already and brought three dresses from Lucy Liu, *dying* for you to wear them off the plane. They want exclusivity, but I have the Kate Spade team wanting to throw in a handbag that would be perfect, so we'll see if we can get them to give. And Prada wants to see if you could make an appearance for their spring show on Thursday. First, though, I want to wake Mina up and ask about her cozies. I have a *fantastic* opportunity with Elle Décor she's going to die over."

"I . . ." I hesitate, my eyes flickering toward Zaiah. "I'm not sure. Murphy needs me there as soon as possible?"

"As soon as possible. Then—" She hesitates, her brow furrowing as she glances to Zaiah, then back to me as if to say, "We're not serious here, right, Cat? This whole mountain man date thing was just for fun?" When I don't respond right away she finishes, "I suppose . . . you can come back after to tie up your loose ends."

"Yeah," I breathe, saying the word but feeling a million miles away. My thoughts are flying in a thousand directions. Jobs. People. Lawsuits. Apartments. Careers.

Zaiah.

As Serena moves off to terrorize Mina, hovering over her bed with promises of fortune and fame, I turn to Zaiah, my mouth agape at the whirlwind of news in the past ten minutes. It's hard to grasp. My body can't even keep up. It's shivering.

Zaiah looks at my trembling fingers as they still clasp Serena's mug. He comes over and takes the mug out of my hands. Sets it down. Returns to hold them, still them, in his own.

"Well." He exhales, looking deep into my eyes. "Congratulations, Cat. You must be so relieved."

"I am," I say, nodding. Nod again. "Yes. I am."

There's a monumental pause between us.

No sound but the scream of Mina waking up to Serena in her room.

"It's going to take me a while to process this," I say. Then I laugh a little, a bit of adrenaline that's pent up inside me seeking a way out.

"Of course." He hesitates. "I'm sure."

"It's not that I necessarily want to go yet, but she's already bought the tickets. And I'm sure there will be lots of paperwork—"

He squeezes my hands. Strong. Reassuring. "You don't need to explain anything to me, Cat. I understand. I'm . . . happy for you."

There's a sadness in his eyes as he holds on to my hands for a few more seconds. Then slowly relinquishes them. Steps away toward the kitchen. "You have a long night, and day, ahead. I'll get you some more coffee."

And I should've said no then.

I should've said, "I don't need any more coffee. I'm going to stay right here in this job in a folding chair in the corner, writing newsletters about frog season and watching Peggy and Uncle Terry complain about the rising cost of gas at Uncle Buck's."

But I don't.

I can't.

Because staying here, in *this* life, doing that job, just isn't what I want for myself.

I love the people. I like the mountains. But I also very much want to get back a part of my life that was perfectly sculpted for me. That is . . . also . . . me.

And honestly, what can a pair of golden suede and crystal heels do here? Really?

So I let him make me that cup.

I let him help me into my coat and even drive me to the airport.

I let him kiss me beside the airport bench where he first laid eyes on me and my line of suitcases, one last memory to pocket away.

Never shutting down officially the hope of something more between us. Never saying officially, "Well, that's it."

But we knew it all the same. Knew our time had come.

Because I am Cat Cranwell.

He is Zaiah Smith.

And all the way across the country, in the glittering city that never sleeps, I was famous for a living.

CHAPTER 18

The Bench

There's a green bench on the corner of Eighth Street that faces a particular cherry blossom tree. In spring the pink blooms that cover the tree are so beautiful it is rumored Italian designer Giuseppe Russo was so inspired, he plucked one for inspiration and kept it by his side as he sketched a dress so desirable women fought for the honor of paying thirteen thousand dollars for one of the limited editions.

These blooms cover the tree like frosting, and for a few magical days when the cross breeze hits during a break in traffic, they fall like snow, skating along the sidewalk as people pass, keeping up with their pace.

This is one of those afternoons.

I try these days to slip outside as much as I can. When I came back to the city I was changed a little. Hyperaware of how much time I spent indoors. Finding myself stretching out my hand to touch the bark of the delicate trees as I passed them on the sidewalk. Finding myself looking up as I walked between buildings reaching to the sky, searching for the sun.

Montana ruined me.

I frown as I flip through a few options on the editing app, sliding my finger over the temperature gauge to see the picture through different filters.

Me in a flair dress covered in tangerines, midstride across Bowery Street in a strappy pair of orange heels. The rattan tote is spilling over with pink tulips and yellow daffodils. My smile is there, but something about it looks forced, despite how many pictures I take these days. I'm not certain if anyone else can see it. The follower count certainly doesn't suggest they do, but still. It's there.

The sponsored brand is the rattan tote, and I'm working to warm the picture without changing the natural color of the rattan.

That, and erase several unsavory objects in the background.

I slide my finger over several objects and tap to erase the offenders.

A crumpled cup lying beside a drain hole.

A slumped-over bag of trash propped beside a trash can.

A rusted-out car from the seventies with two busted-out windows covered in cardboard.

All erased with a tap of a finger. Add ten degrees for an even warmer, sunnier feel. Get a bit of gold glinting off those flowers.

Make the world look . . . perfect.

Glossy. And, of course, not reality at all.

Yes, there was a certain thrill stepping off that plane with Serena and getting my life back like it used to be—in some ways, even better.

People flocked to me, everybody wanting to comfort the girl who had been wrongfully scorned.

Brands came by the dozens trying to get me to clutch their water bottles, picnic baskets, and vacuums while talking about finally getting justice in an unjust world.

Serena took so many calls I half wondered if she'd want to quit on me. But of course she stayed. Haggled with the cunning of a fox and ferocity of a lion. Bias of friendship aside, she truly is the best agent out there, and those in the influencer community agree.

Happy with the last round of edits, I screenshot it and send it off to Serena with the caption. By tomorrow night, she'll have taken a look, made sure my caption meets the legal requirements (and answer the question: *Should I pull the contrast up a few degrees?*), and sent it off to the brand for final review.

There's a new email from Mina and I take a minute to slip back onto the page for Kannery Park and check on its progress: 220,000 followers strong.

A startlingly healthy rise of 16 percent since this time last week, and the engagement rate nearly doubling in the past two days. The latest shot is a picture of Brody on top of Cades Peak, standing in a squirrel suit with a group of others.

No he didn't.

He told me he had something special planned, but surely he didn't mean *this*.

He didn't jump off that mountain in a squirrel suit.

It's a carousel post and sure enough, as the next eight pictures show in terrifying detail, he did.

I smile to myself as I tap a heart on the picture and then share it on my personal feed. One of the best things to have happened the past six weeks is finally being able to use any pull I have to draw people into the park, and into the park they've come.

Eleven of a dozen influencers I bargained with in the beginning made the trek down to the park. All show pictures of themselves standing beside the big brown sign, wandering along walking trails lined with fairy slippers and glacier lilies, and, if they were brave enough, camping out in those peak-top cabins at the end of their hiking journeys.

Sure enough, Zaiah was right about those cabins. As influencers posted about their experiences, the idea caught on about roughing it, and people began to race to the reservations pages, trying to get their "in" on the schedule so they, too, could make the 14.2-mile hike up the mountain and spend a night in the unheated, salt-of-the-earth cabins in the sky. Pictures are making their way around the internet of grinning groups trading false lashes for flashlights, lofty captions full of the beauty of slowing down, and often the poem, occasionally correctly attributed to the author, from above the door. Followed the next day with a pose in a bright-pink crop top beside a Ferrari with the caption, *Miami, here I come.* But I digress.

Between the efforts of those initial influencers and the continuous plug I made for the park in my own feed and stories, change was happening. More and more people were beginning to visit the park. More and more moms out there saw pictures on Instagram of the beautiful waterfalls and jaw-dropping mountains, more of them went on Pinterest only to hear about how Kannery Park was "one of the nation's best-kept secrets" and "the best place to vacation with young children," and sure enough, when it came time to decide on a family vacation, the words that popped out of their mouths were, "You know, I saw this gorgeous little park out in Montana . . ."

And that is how a trend was born.

That is how, for good or bad in this bizarre little world of screens in the twenty-first century, a culture was created.

And with such power came great responsibility.

I bought the cabins new heaters.

Mina told me one day an HVAC crew pulled up to the office, hauling split-system heat pumps and telling Terry to "Sign here."

And along with a monetary donation covering a few other odds and ends (like new desk chairs, for one thing), the park got both an allegorical and literal fresh coat of paint. With this, stats showing the rising number of visitors, and the bizarre but very real number of people purchasing Kannery Park official propaganda online (including, unbelievably enough, the terrible trash can T-shirts with their terrible taglines), the decision was made not to assimilate the park into Glacier after all.

I'm not certain—I only have my suspicions—but there's also a very real chance Serena called somebody in the government threatening to pull my support if they pulled the plug on the people I loved.

And I do love them.

I think about them every single day.

I smile wistfully as I scroll through the latest pictures from the park's page. With a little instruction Mina took over the page, and her eager personality and excitement to share all about the beauty of wildlife shines through. The pictures are not always the most professional, but they're improving. She's learning.

I skim past the ones of mountains, trails, and birds and pause at a recent group photo of the staff members. Mina, the first, has been promoted. She proudly holds her new badge, "Mina Marsero, Junior Park Ranger."

An alarm sounds from my purse, crisp and clear in its *ding*.

Ding.

Ding.

I ignore it for a moment to make a congratulatory comment, then run my finger to the side button. Power it down.

I slide the work phone into my bag.

Reach for my personal phone inside. Turn the alarm off.

My neck is taut from looking down so long, and I stretch it to one side, then the other, reminding myself to really make a habit to follow my chiropractor's instructions and raise the phone more to ease the neck pain.

I take a moment to check for any calls from Serena on my personal phone—not work Serena but friend Serena.

Work Serena makes her calls (read: prodding demands that are ultimately genius) during work hours.

Friend Serena makes her calls (read: what are we eating for dinner and a list of Chevy's latest errors) during off-hours.

Sure enough, there's a text.

I'm canceling on dinner. What are you wearing?

I raise my brow and reply. *S. Just because I had some dark days* (yes, technically at my lowest, there was an incident involving braving the elements in a spaghetti-stained bathrobe for a paper) *doesn't mean you have to keep up on me forever. And why? What's up?*

Are you wearing lipstick?

I frown slightly. I am, in fact, wearing lipstick. A lighter pink shade out of respect for the tree I sit under. My fingers are poised to reply, when I see him in my periphery.

Make no mistake, I have seen him before.

On the corner beside a newspaper stand.

Striding into a bookstore.

Getting into a taxi and slipping out of view.

Zaiah Smith the last six weeks has been everywhere and nowhere.

The first days were the hardest, hoping he'd come. Hoping he'd show up on my doorstep, declaring our love could make it work, that somehow we'd defy the fact we lived and worked on opposite sides of the county.

But, of course, he is much too practical for all that.

When a man owns a flip phone, the idea of a successful long-distance relationship is a stretch for even the most optimistic of hopefuls.

We keep up a bit. He texts me on occasion with blurry pictures of soups he makes and the rare bear sighting; I text back pictures of whatever I'm eating at whatever restaurant and get his opinion on which bouquet of half a dozen I should get from the flower market. Friendly conversation, and when it gets too friendly, a bit wistful. Nothing further.

I do look for his likes on every one of my posts, and sure enough, he's there, quietly giving it a thumbs-up. He's become the one I make my posts for, the one I write my captions for, the one I write poignant things to and not-so-poignant things to. The one I talk to when I make stories of myself doing something a little silly. Every content creator has their "person" who represents their ideal audience they think of when creating. And somehow in the past few weeks, despite how impractical it is, the role has shifted to him.

Because sure, my demographic of females ages thirty and above totally resonates with a mountain man in Montana.

I ignore the familiar-looking boots standing six feet off through my lashes, blink, and resume.

But then he speaks. "You know, I know of a little place down the street from here that has the best curry."

I look up, and in that moment a breeze sweeps by, plucking a hundred cherry blossoms off and showering them down. They fall around me, landing on my pale-pink dress, onto my lightly curled hair, as I lower my phone and smile at Zaiah Smith.

Smile because sure enough, it's really him.

He looks a little weather-beaten, with a bulging canvas backpack over one shoulder with airport tags flapping in the breeze, but his eyes are bright. His smile warm.

My breath catches in my throat. "Don't bother. I've had the best curry in a little place out west. Nothing here can tempt me."

He walks toward me, and after setting the phone down, I rise.

"But you're in luck," I add. "My dinner date just bailed."

I catch his foot slowing, the hiccup in his confidence. "I saw you might be dating someone."

I shake my head at his misunderstanding. No doubt he's referencing the pictures floating around of a tennis player I met at a party a couple weeks ago. We shook hands. Smiled like normal human beings. The media went wild. "Don't you know, Zaiah? You can't believe what you read on the internet."

If I'm not mistaken, I catch a little exhale from his lips.

"My dinner date was Serena. Although now that you're here, I'm beginning to piece together why she may have dropped out." I level my gaze. Lower my voice. "What did she do?"

He looks a little skittish as he sets his backpack on the ground. "It's not important."

I raise my brow. Wait.

"There's a slight chance she called me up."

"What exactly did she say?"

"Well. To be entirely honest, she said you had lost your glow and she tried everything in the book to get it back but nothing was working and so it was of vital importance that I come here and ask you out to dinner."

I hesitate.

A rebuttal is on my lips, but the fact is, I'm too happy to see him to be embarrassed by her intervention, or to attempt to deny the fact that I haven't been myself since I left Kannery.

My chest is fluttering madly as I look at his weather-beaten but bright eyes.

So he didn't just want me to leave and get on with life. Here he stands, the mountain man trekking thousands of miles for me after all.

"Apparently, I have been propositioned to recharge you," he says.

"You know, you could've just told her no. I know she is small and terrifying, but you've got a whole country between you—"

"She knows where I live. And the more I learn of her, the more I'm convinced she would find me no matter what, anywhere I went. Besides, I did say no."

My brows shoot up.

As they do, I see the smallest shadow of a smile on his face.

"Did you now?" I say. "No interest in dinner."

"Yup. I'm here because I took what you said to heart and decided it was time to do some of those things I've never tried before. I'm on my way to see those big mountains you spoke of in Switzerland. See if they really can compare, though I doubt it, to mine. And I was hoping"—he pauses, pulls a couple tickets from his backpack—"I was hoping you might be able to spare the time to be my plus one."

I look down at the airline tickets in his hand.

Sure enough, there is one in my name: Catherine Cranwell, printed in typewriter font across the front. Leaving today.

My stomach seizes.

I barely have breath left in me when I look back in his eyes. "You're serious?"

"If you want to."

He blinks as I slowly take the ticket from his hand, processing. As the seconds tick by, his confidence starts to crack.

"I won't take it personally if you don't, Cat. I—I know who I am. I know what I have to offer, and it's not much compared to all of this. It's just, when Serena called me and told me how you were feeling lately, I hoped that—"

"I'll go." I pull the ticket to my chest, looking up at his face. "I don't know how this could work," I say, referencing him and me, "but I'm willing to try."

His beard breaks apart and his temples crease, revealing the widest smile I've seen yet.

I raise a finger. "But on one condition. You have to be the one to tell Serena to reschedule everything I've got for the next"—I look down—"two weeks."

But even as I say the words, I know what he's going to say.

"She already has, hasn't she?" I say just as he says, "Done."

I laugh a little, and he continues. "I've already been tasked with picking up a ski jacket for you from Stöckli. She also wants to know if you'd be opposed to a swimsuit skiing shot."

"Yes," I reply automatically.

"She also asked me if I've ever considered creating an account. Apparently I have a very nice beard that deodorant companies would be all over. How beards can possibly be related to deodorant . . ."

I laugh. Put my hand on his scratchy beard. "It is quite nice."

He takes a small step toward me, just as another breeze slips by.

Petals fall around us as his nose dips down, meeting mine. Touching, oh-so-briefly, before drawing forward, the prickle of his beard on my cheek. His lips on mine.

The air smells of blossoms and pine, the scent of my morning perfume mixed with a touch of airport coffee on his breath. A mix of us, mountains and city. Soft and hard.

I pull back, realizing something. "You know what? I don't think you've ever called me pretty. Do you think I'm pretty, Zaiah Smith?"

"I think you're a lot of things, Cat Cranwell, all of them beautiful."

A warmth spreads from my chest. I've spent half my life with the number on the tag of my dress and the glow of my skin being the starting and stopping point of every conversation. Beauty equaling power. Power equaling money. Money equaling stability. And frankly, watching myself start the process of losing those first petals of my youth had been daunting. Terrifying.

Until I met Zaiah.

And Jax. And Mina. And Kevin. And Peggy.

And went to live in a place where people were just too busy living life with the ones they love to worry about such a small thing as skin.

"I appreciate the hard work you've put in to get my glow back." I wrap my arms around his waist. "You know? I believe it's already starting to work."

"Anything for Serena," he murmurs softly, grinning as he cups my chin and draws me back in.

EPILOGUE

The Business

Family
December 12

TWENTY MONTHS LATER

*Y*ou know what turns out to be better than following the life of Cat Cranwell in the glittering city? Following the life of Cat Cranwell in the great wide world.

It was on the Swiss trip that this fact became apparent.

More specifically, it was while showing off the Matterhorn in the distance (which Zaiah begrudgingly admitted may be just a tiny bit more impressive than those in Kannery) and, yes, admittedly having written a caption about slowing life down and enjoying the beauty of nature that the idea formed.

Serena was skeptical at first, because of course to her, what could possibly be more appealing than a thousand glowing windows of a hundred towering buildings stretching toward the evening sky?

But as I began to share more and more of the natural world around me on our trip, and less and less of the perfectly polished life I'd pretended to have, we found it worked. A dash of my life in New York or some other city here or there, yes, but a solid amount spent in the tiny, but healthily growing, town of Kannery.

Yes, my demographics slowly shifted, shaken like dyed sand in an hourglass. The male demographic dropped off, and the female demographic of women in their thirties and beyond rose. And frankly, that was just fine by me.

Montana life resonated with my following.

People appreciated me showing off the dirty kitchen sink on

occasion. Hauling feed out to what turned out to be rather unruly chickens.

Even as the world around me shifted, even as I shifted, people followed along.

I even started to let pictures go public without me blurring out every unhandsome line. Even let my eyes go public without a triple application of mascara.

I wasn't seventeen anymore. I was aging, albeit gracefully, and I was learning to accept it. And for those people who couldn't, who would leave if I couldn't meet their impossible standards, then so be it.

"Your uncle couldn't have worked at the Grand Canyon." Serena drags her suitcase through the snow in her marshmallow puff jacket. And heels.

Zaiah moves to retrieve her bags.

Meanwhile, I flip on the coffee.

Serena makes use of our guest bedroom at least once a month. And every single visit declares this time, *this time*, will be her last.

I also heard from Mark that she's looking at condos. They've started . . . well . . . I'm not sure what to call it. Maybe aggressively dating.

"C'mon. The game's started," I say.

"Fine, but if I win, you're flying back with me to give Gabby *the talk*. She's fallen off the bandwagon again. One chat with you and she'll snap out of it."

From the very conception of the Whitman Agency, Serena did something groundbreaking in the industry—she folded mentorship and counseling into the partnership. She's not only offering nego-tiating services and filling our slates with top-notch deals, but also giving holistic support for influencers' financial, creative, emotional, *and* mental needs. Through several conversations I even worked with her to develop the rule sheet and the plan.

She helps us ride the beast without getting trampled underfoot.

Rejoices with us in the benefits of social media as a career, but also keeps a keen eye out for any psychological or mental problems that arise.

The mentorship so far has been a tremendous success—most significantly, I think, because Serena is the best at giving accountability and support and making us feel like we're not doing it alone.

The living room is crowded as we move into it, even more so with the Christmas tree Zaiah cut down glowing in the corner—its branches drooping with the overflow of stitched ornaments Peggy made for us for our first Christmas in our home last year.

The fireplace crackles below the stockings lining the mantel, a number of glinting, wrapped presents covering the hardwood floor. The scent of leftover chili wafts through the room, mingling with the balsam fir needles and over-perfume of at least a hundred fragrant diaper boxes covering the dining room table (brand deal gone awry).

I nudge Kevin over on the couch to make room for the pair of us. Jax glances up from his chair as Serena begins dumping several wrapped presents beneath the tree. Just as he reaches for one, she points at him with beady eyes and a silent, *Don't you dare. You wait for the elephant gift exchange.*

Uncle Terry is leaning forward, rubbing his mustache as he stares at the cards in his hands. He's got a pile of chips in front of him. His gaze shifts to the jack, six, and nine of clubs on the table. "All in."

As he pushes his pile of chips, there's a unanimous roar of "Noooo" around the room.

Mark puts his head in his hands, trying to explain for the zillionth time. "Terry. You can't just go all in the first time *every time.*"

It's a fair point. During the last six poker nights, he has ended up going all in the first shot he can and losing all his money fifteen minutes in.

"You can if you've got what I've got," he replies, his mustache twitching. "Bet me."

"You know, this wouldn't be an issue if we just played our game," Mina says, holding her cards to her chest. "It's going to be a big deal soon. Right, Serena? How's the copyright coming?"

"Oh, terrific," Serena lies, taking a swig of coffee and averting her eyes.

Serena took Mina on as one of her clients for cozies over a year ago, and unsurprisingly, the brand has continued to grow and evolve. Then Mina, Jax, and Kevin decided two months ago that Snowball Cornhole Risk Blitz had the magnetism it took to make it in the gaming world, right up there on the store shelves beside Monopoly. They absolutely *would* be sued by Risk if they tried to do it, given you literally play the Risk game and then run outside for a variety of cornhole stunts, but Mina was so positively overboard about the idea, Serena decided to hedge the topic and wait until the right time to tell the truth.

Which may be forever.

"I'll take that wager." Peggy slaps a jack and nine on the table.

Terry crumbles at the two pair with his three and nine, and everyone groans. "Too bad," he says. "I get the baby." His bushy mustache twitches as he reaches over and takes the sleeping newborn from my chest.

He holds little Everleigh May Smith up to his face, then settles back into his seat.

I raise a brow.

"If I didn't know better, I'd think you lose on purpose to hold her."

"Nonsense," he says, as the little blue-eyed girl's eyes flutter in her sleep. "She just coos for Grandpa Terry."

The moment I showed him that first ultrasound picture, he began referring to himself as Grandpa Terry. I never corrected him, and by the time Father's Day rolled around, he was getting a *Best Grandpa Ever* coffee mug in his gift bag.

"You know, Grandpa, she calls for you at four in the morning too." Coffee in hand, Zaiah takes his seat on the ledge of the couch beside me. "Why don't you stick around if you want to hold her then?"

I laugh.

Someone takes a picture.

Later that evening, in the quiet as I nurse baby girl, I look at it.

I'm surrounded by people as I'm laughing, sleep deprived as I hold baby girl on my chest, makeup far removed from my face. The oversized T-shirt I'm wearing is one of Zaiah's, plus red-and-white-checkered pajama bottoms. My hair is pulled back, twisted up in a knot. The angle is horrible, showing a clear double chin.

Two years ago this picture would've been burned before it could ever show its face on social media.

And perhaps, maybe, I'll tuck it away somewhere special just for me.

But not because I don't care for it. No.

Because it's so precious, such a beautiful depiction of my life—my real life—among friends, among family, among those I love most, that it's too valuable to show on the internet for just anyone to see and scroll by.

This is my life.

I am Cat Cranwell Smith.

And my life, just as it is, I love living.

Do I Have a Problem? Quiz

Developed with and taken by Cat Cranwell personally

1. Do I feel unusually anxious when I'm separated from my phone?

2. Would I be embarrassed to admit my screen time statistics per week to others?

3. Have I checked my phone in dangerous or socially inappropriate situations (i.e., while driving or at a wedding or funeral)?

4. Do I find myself tempted to check my phone while having conversations with others in person?

5. Do I find myself happy during the days when my latest posts are doing well, and sad or moody during days my posts tank? Are my moods directly affected by my analytics?

6. Do I check my phone the second I get up and check it the last thing before bed?

7. Do I have anxiety about staying relevant or with the trends?

8. Do I sometimes find myself "hearing" the *ding* of my notifications only to find it was in my head?

9. Do I open apps that I've closed just one minute prior, just to "check" again?

10. Do I scroll through my phone anytime I have a minute of waiting with "nothing to do"?

11. When I post something, do I feel anxious and stressed as I refresh and watch for likes/comments/shares/follows?

Influencer Support

SOCIAL MEDIA USAGE GUIDELINES

Created with and used by Cat Cranwell personally

1. I will have two phones in my possession. Work phone (A) will be for all things work related during predetermined work hours. After hours, work phone will be turned off and I will use my personal phone (B) as desired.

2. I will have my phone(s) silenced and not in view while operating a vehicle.

3. I will not check my social media analytics and/or statistics more than once per day.

4. I will be present with whomever I'm in physical company with and not use my phone while we are in conversation.

5. For brain health, I will let myself be "bored" sometimes when waiting somewhere and in that "boredom" allow for creative thought, spontaneous conversations with others, and/or reading physical copies of books.

6. If I am feeling depressed or sad or anxious, I will put my phone down and, hopefully, get perspective. If this doesn't work and after forty-eight hours I'm still feeling anxious or blue, I will tell Serena about my emotions and we will work together to form a plan.

7. I will talk with Serena once a week about how I'm feeling and support her efforts at accountability for my mental health.

8. I will not respond with hate on social media, as this ultimately doesn't help my image or my personal well-being, but remember to pity those who bully me, for they must be hurting themselves.

9. I will remember that social media doesn't define my self-worth, either the highs or the lows.

10. I will take a break from my work phone at least one full day, once a week, and rest.

Discussion Questions

1. Cat Cranwell didn't realize the extent of her addiction to social media until she found herself surrounded by those with different lifestyles. How about you? How did you fare on the quiz?

2. What is the range of emotions and thoughts you've had when you've used social media? Have you ever identified with Cat and her struggles, and if so, how?

3. There are some interesting and wonderful uses of social media, but just like a match, it can be used to warm your toes by the fireplace or to torch a forest. It is a tool, but for some people, it is a self-destructive weapon. How has social media contributed to your quality of life? What is your overall opinion of social media?

4. Where would you rather live: the biggest city in the United States or in a tiny town within a national park in Montana? Why?

5. Do you think you would enjoy Cat's career? Why or why not?

6. Sometimes what seems so normal in your own friend and family group, job, or culture is far from normal to others. Cat found her lifestyle challenged when she left her life in the city. Have you ever been in a situation where something seemed normal to you until you found yourself dropped into a different circle of people? What was it and how did the experience affect you?

7. Which character's weaknesses did you identify with most? Why?

8. Which character's strengths did you identify with most? Why?

9. What does Cat learn throughout her time in Kannery National Park that changes her? How?

10. Who is your favorite character and why?

11. In the end, Cat decides to put in place a set of self-regulated rules to help her deal with her addiction to social media while continuing her career. She could've, however, stepped away from her career entirely. She chose not to. Do you think this was the right call?

12. Cat was the victim of a lot of judgment, particularly from strangers across the globe. How quick are you to judge others? How often do you yourself feel unduly judged? How do you handle the criticism in a healthy manner?

13. What is your favorite scene and/or quote and why? *(Side note: I'd love to hear your answer to this! Please don't hesitate to message me on Instagram or tag me with your answer at @ our_friendly_farmhouse. —Melissa)*

From the Publisher

GREAT BOOKS

ARE EVEN BETTER WHEN THEY'RE SHARED!

Help other readers find this one:

- Post a review at your favorite online bookseller

- Post a picture on a social media account and share why you enjoyed it

- Send a note to a friend who would also love it—or better yet, give them a copy

Thanks for reading!

Enjoy this excerpt from
Melissa Ferguson's

Meet Me in the Margins

THOMAS NELSON
Since 1798

Prologue

From: Claire Donovan
Received: 9:17 AM
To: Savannah Cade
Subject: Manuscript?

Savannah,

Have you made any more progress on that book idea you
brought up to me at conference last year? I was just sitting
in an editorial meeting, and your story came to mind.
Would love to take a look.

Best wishes,
Claire Donovan
Chief Editor, Romance
Baird Books Publishing

Draft
From: Savannah Cade
Saved: 9:21 AM
To: Claire Donovan
Subject: Re: Manuscript?

| Dear Mrs. Donovan

Draft
From: Savannah Cade
Saved: 9:22 AM
To: Claire Donovan
Subject: Re: Manuscript?

| Dear Claire Donovan

Draft
From: Savannah Cade
Saved: 9:24 AM
To: Claire Donovan
Subject: Re: Manuscript?

Dear Claire,

Thank you so much for your email! I'm so, so sorry I didn't
get to it right after conference as I said. I promise I'm not

one of those aspiring writers who unloads a thousand details of the story in their heads on every stranger they land upon at conferences but then can't follow through when an editor actually requests to see the manuscript. Truly.

It was just that I realized after talking with you that the final scene was missing the big bang at the end, and Cecilia's character really wasn't all that likable after all, and then when I finally managed to amend those issues my manuscript was twelve thousand words over. So then I spent the next month agonizing over where to cut (you know, King's whole "kill your darlings" thing is really true from the writer's side—here I'd been casually telling my own authors to slash their manuscripts for two years and never really understood how truly GUT WRENCHING it is. I killed off a whole character and am still weepy for him).

But I am in edits now and just need to go over it a couple more times. So sorry again to have had you waiting on it. I'll be sure to have it to you in ~~two weeks~~ ~~three weeks~~ one month, tops

* *

Delivered
From: Savannah Cade
Sent: 9:26 AM
To: Claire Donovan
Subject: Re: Manuscript?

Dear Claire,

How thoughtful of you to reach out. I plan to have the manuscript to you by the end of the day.

Warmest regards,
Savannah Cade
Assistant Acquisitions Editor, Pennington Pen

Enjoy Melissa Ferguson's debut novel,

The Dating Charade

AVAILABLE IN PRINT, E-BOOK, AND AUDIO

THOMAS NELSON
Since 1798

Melissa Ferguson's charming rom-com proves that good fences make good neighbors— and that sometimes love and hate share a backyard.

THOMAS NELSON
Since 1798

About the Author

Taylor Meo Photography

Melissa Ferguson is the bestselling author of titles including *Meet Me in the Margins*, *The Dating Charade*, and *The Cul-de-Sac War*. She lives in Tennessee with her husband and children in their growing farmhouse lifestyle and writes heartwarming romantic comedies that have been featured in such places as *The Hollywood Reporter*, *Travel + Leisure*, *Woman's World*, and BuzzFeed.

She'd love for you to join her at www.melissaferguson.com
Instagram: @our_friendly_farmhouse
TikTok: @ourfriendlyfarmhouse
Facebook: @AuthorMelissaFerguson